L J MORRIS

Legacy of Hate

A Logan Palmer Thriller

To all my readers. Thank you.

Chapter 1

The air in the maximum-security prison's private visiting room was stale and warm. There were no windows or air conditioning, and there was an overriding stench of sweat. Despite the searing heat of a typical Texan summer and the lack of ventilation, George H. Carver wore a suit and tie. It was uncomfortable and the collar of his shirt rubbed at his neck, but he had to maintain his image. Some people expected a man running for governor to be well turned out all the time, but that wasn't the only reason he dressed the way he did. The long sleeves and fastened collar helped to hide the myriad of tattoos that adorned his body. Although being inked didn't have the stigma that it had in the past, his body art was made up of swastikas, Nazi slogans, and various other white power symbols, a Definite turn-off for your average voter.

Once he was alone in the room, Carver took off his jacket and hung it on the hook on the back of the door. A bead of sweat ran between his shoulder blades and left a damp patch on his shirt as he loosened his tie and undid his top button. He retrieved a handkerchief from the inside pocket of his jacket, wiped the moisture from his face and neck and sat down. The metal chair and matching table were the only pieces of furniture in the room, and both had been bolted to the floor. He looked at his watch, what was keeping them? He had places to be.

With a metallic clunk, the door, opposite the one Carver had come through, opened. Brandon Carver was led in and handcuffed to an identical steel table on the other side of the plexiglass screen that bisected the upper half of the room. He was the spitting image of his father but instead of wearing an expensive suit, he was wearing a standard, prison issue, baggy, white t-shirt with orange overalls pulled down and tied at the waist. His short cropped brown hair had greyed at the temples and matched the stubble that covered his chin. His skin was pale and lined, his eyes sunken. Fifteen years in prison had aged him beyond his forty-five years.

George Carver lifted the black, plastic telephone receiver from its cradle and held it to his ear, but his son didn't respond, he just stared back with a blank, uninterested expression. It wasn't any less than he had expected. To say that he and his son weren't on the best of terms would be a massive understatement. He replaced the handset in its cradle and took out a notebook and pen. With a sigh, he scribbled a note and held it up to the glass.

It's about your wife and daughter.

The note had the desired effect. Brandon's expression dropped when he read it, fear flashing across his eyes. The old man knew this was a scenario his son would have played through his mind every day of his sentence. What would he do if something happened to his family?

Brandon snatched at the telephone handset and shouted into it.

George watched his son's rant in silence, seeming to enjoy

the panic, before slowly lifting the telephone back to his own ear. 'Calm down, Brandon. Panicking won't get us anywhere. Now, take a deep breath and start again.'

'What have you done to them, you bastard? I told you to stay away from us. Mom killed herself because of your shit. I don't want you and your hate infecting my daughter.'

George Carver cleared his throat. 'It's bad news I'm afraid, they've been kidnapped.'

Brandon's eyes widened. 'Who by... what do they want?'

'We don't know who they are yet, but they've demanded a ransom of twenty million dollars. They've probably seen my campaign ads on TV and assumed I'm rich.'

'You've had nothing to do with them for years. I moved them away. They're using different names. How did they know they were related to you?'

George Carver shrugged. 'Who knows? It's impossible to keep secrets in prison, you always confide in someone sooner or later. Wasn't your cellmate murdered a couple of months ago? Maybe he knew something.'

Brandon Carver stared at the table, shaking his head, mumbling to himself. It was obvious that he was trying to work things out. Whether he had given something away, even in his sleep? He looked up. Tears in his eyes. 'What am I going to do?'

'Well. I'd love to help, but I don't have that amount of money. Even if we got them to come down to ten, or five even. All my cash is tied up in my election campaign.' George paused as if wracking his brains. 'There is another way.'

'I should have known. Did you plan this? Or are you just low enough to jump on it and take advantage?'

'It's nothing to do with me son, I'm just trying to help. Look, when you left our… organisation…'

'You mean gang.'

George Carver ran his fingers around his collar. 'Call it what you like. When you left, you took all our money. All I'm saying is that it would be more than enough to pay the ransom, that's all.'

'And the fact that I also took some incriminating evidence that would bury you and all your white power buddies doesn't come into it.'

George Carver forced a smile. 'Look, all that information won't bring anyone down now. It's fifteen years old. Hell, some of the people you're trying to threaten are dead. I'm just trying to help you get your family back. For that, I need to know where the money is.'

'That money is the main reason I'm still alive. I wouldn't have lasted in here without some protection, you provided that. My family are safe because I have that money. I told you you'd get it back when I get out and my family have a new life. If I hand it to you now, what's to stop you from having us killed?'

'It's your choice, of course, and I'll abide by whatever decision you make, but I'm not sure these kidnappers will wait another eight months until you're a free man.'

'Are the police involved, the FBI?'

George shook his head. 'The FBI will just tell us not to pay the ransom. It's their standard operating procedure. We won't involve them until it's necessary. The question is, do you want your family back or not?'

'What's in this for you? Why do you suddenly care after all this time?'

'At some point, this story will become public. If I walk away,

I'll be seen as the man who let an innocent girl and her mother die. That won't do my election chances any good at all. On the other hand, with your wife and daughter being,' he searched for the correct word. 'Mixed race, helping them won't do me any harm with a certain section of voters. I'll be seen as a man of the people, all the people.'

Brandon closed his eyes. 'You don't know where Simone and Zahrah are, they could still be at home. How do you know the kidnap is genuine?'

George reached into his pocket and removed a box the size of a cigarette packet. He removed the lid and held it up to the plexiglass. 'Because they sent me your wife's finger. It still has her wedding ring on. That is her ring, right?'

Brandon Carver gagged and held his hand up to his mouth. He focussed on the bloodstained finger in the box, taking deep breaths, swallowing hard to stop the vomit. 'I'll give you the details, the location of the money is with my family. Save them, and you'll get what you want.'

George Carver clicked his pen and started to take notes as Brandon told him where he could find the information that would lead him to his missing millions. This wasn't going to be as easy as he was hoping though. Brandon was clever. He had made sure that his father couldn't just take the money and walk away. The only way the money could be recovered was by rescuing his wife and daughter.

When the prison guard unlocked Brandon Carver's handcuffs, he was still trembling. The shock of what he had been told had hit him hard. George knew it would. Fifteen years of keeping them safe, fifteen years of staying alive, and now, at the end, Brandon knew he had failed.

George Carver walked back out into the Texan heat; his

jacket slung over his shoulder. He watched through the chain link fence as the other inmates poured out of the cell block and into the exercise yard. This was a dangerous, violent, place where gangs ruled, and scores were often settled. At the corner of the fence, a group of inmates sat on a collection of concrete benches, surveying their territory. This was their corner of the yard, and they would defend it, violently if necessary.

Carver crouched down behind the group as if to tie his shoelace. The man who turned to look at him was as big as a bear. A very scary, heavily tattooed, white power bear. Even Carver felt a little threatened. He was sure this man could rip his way through the double razor-wired fence if he wanted to. Carver stood up, nodded to the man once then carried on along the path to his car.

The bear ran his fingers through his beard and turned back around to his brothers. Their instructions were clear. Today would be a busy day for the guards.

Chapter 2

Logan Palmer sat on the deck of the dive boat. A torn, canvas tarpaulin that he'd rigged up as a sun shield flapped in the breeze above his head. His wet suit and oxygen tanks hung in the cabin. They were bone dry from lack of use. He hadn't been in the water for two days. A combination of no students and no money for fuel, along with his dwindling motivation, meant he spent most days just sitting on the deck, lost in his thoughts.

His friendship with Jerry Scarlett, the owner of the dive school, was as strong as ever. Old military buddies were like that, their relationships remained strong no matter what. Jerry's wife, on the other hand, was another matter. Palmer got the impression that Subha would be happier if he wasn't around. He didn't blame her. She just didn't want to be constantly reminded of the past. Especially when that past involved her husband almost being killed.

Coming to work in Indonesia was supposed to be a new start for Palmer, a life in paradise away from the rat race. It hadn't turned out as he'd expected. Then again, for him, it never did. Visitor numbers had never really recovered from the impact of the pandemic on global travel. People deciding to stay at home and avoid the extra cost and hassle of international holidays had hit the business hard. The school was already struggling when he arrived, but they were all optimistic about the future. Optimism doesn't pay the bills though. No money meant no new equipment and no advertising. No advertising meant no visitors, and no visitors meant no money. It was a downward spiral they had no way out of. Jerry and Subha were barely able to support themselves, they certainly couldn't afford to pay him to sit idle.

Palmer took a deep breath and blew out his cheeks. The sun was beating down. Even under the shade of his torn tarpaulin, it was stifling. He reached into his cool box and pulled out a fresh bottle of beer, pulling off the lid with the opener that hung from a string around his neck. It was a family heirloom, the only one he had. Some families had houses and land passed from father to son. Some had jewellery and art that filled their grand houses generation after generation. He had his Granddad's bottle opener. He took a long drink and then ran the bottle around his face in a pointless attempt to cool down. It didn't help. He closed his eyes, rested his head against the back of his worn deckchair, and dozed off.

Palmer's eyes flicked open at the sound of a voice shouting his name. He didn't know how long he had been asleep. It felt like he had just closed his eyes, but his beer bottle was now warm so it must have been twenty minutes, at least. He lifted his head and watched as a figure, blurred by the heat, gradually came into focus.

A tall, casually dressed man was making his way along the wooden jetty towards the boat. He wore cream, linen trousers and brown boating shoes. The short sleeves of his thin shirt strained around his muscular arms, and the sun glinted off his mirrored sunglasses. He had the gait of a man who had spent years in the armed forces and still sported a military issue haircut. Palmer was willing to bet that this guy was ex US Marines.

The man stopped at the end of the jetty and shielded his eyes against the sun. 'Logan Palmer?'

'Yep.'

'Cool, mind if I come aboard?'

Palmer drained the rest of his warm beer and gestured towards another worn deck chair that was folded up and resting against the wheelhouse bulkhead. 'Have a seat.'

The man stepped down onto the deck. 'Thanks, man.' He held out his hand. 'My name's Cody Wickes.'

Palmer shook his hand then reached into the cool box and took out two fresh beers. He removed the tops with his family heirloom and passed one across. 'What can I do for you, Cody Wickes, you looking to go out for a dive?'

Wickes drank half of his beer in one gulp then wiped his forehead with the back of his hand. 'Maybe another time. I'm here to offer you a job.'

'I've got a job.'

Wickes looked around at the unused wet suits and oxygen tanks that lined the jetty. It looked more like a deserted shipyard than a thriving tourist hotspot. 'Looks quiet.'

Palmer shrugged. 'Yeah, we have busier days.'

'Maybe we could help each other out. You get some extra money; I build my business.'

Palmer sat up. 'What business would that be Cody? From the looks of you, I'm guessing you're an ex-marine, so probably some kind of close protection or private security?'

Wickes grinned. 'Is it that obvious?'

Palmer shrugged. 'Once a marine, sempre fi and all that.'

'You're right about the Marine Corps. I was a Gunnery Sargent, Eighteen years' service.'

'And what about the job?'

'Yeah, you're close. I represent a company of kidnap and ransom consultants. We've got a potentially lucrative contract we'd like you to help us with.'

'I haven't been in the K and R business for years. Why come to me?'

Wickes took a sip of beer then looked down at his feet. 'I want to be honest from the start, so I'll just lay it out.' He looked up at Palmer. 'The company is a consultancy on paper. In reality, it's just me. I'm just starting out and this is the biggest contract I've ever had.'

'Fair enough, you've got to start somewhere, but I'll ask again. Why me?'

Wickes smiled. 'I knew it wouldn't be as easy as just offering you a job.' He let out a short laugh then paused. 'Okay. I'll get to the point. The big K and R consultancies have enough work from the insurance companies to keep them going for years. They can pay experienced consultants, like you, big money to make sure they don't go and work for someone else. You have a great reputation in the business, and you're available. I've had my eye on you for a while, this just brought things forward.'

Palmer sat forward in his chair. There had to be more to it. 'What's wrong with the job? No offence, but why aren't they using one of the big firms?'

'My client doesn't have K and R insurance, and the big firms won't work with him.'

Palmer raised an eyebrow. 'Who's your client.'

'George H. Carver.'

Palmer's head dropped. 'The white supremacist piece of shit that's trying to get elected?'

'Yeah, that's him.'

'I know you're just starting out, but why would you work with someone like that?'

Wickes pointed back to the dive school's main building. 'I've left some paperwork in reception. It'll give you the full story, but, when it comes down to it, this is about a young girl and her mother. It isn't about George Carver. Just read the file and if you aren't interested after that, I'll leave you alone.'

'Okay, I'll take a look, but I'm not promising anything.'

'That's all I ask. I can pay you a hundred grand if you're interested. I'll need you stateside within the week.'

Palmer pulled two more beers out of the cooler and handed one to Wickes. 'I'll be in touch as soon as I can. Like I said, I'm not promising anything. Have another beer before you go.'

Wickes took the offered bottle and clinked it against Palmer's. 'Thanks, man. I'm sure we'll be working together soon.'

Chapter 3

Palmer sat in his beach hut. The fierceness of the day's heat had eased, and a cool sea breeze now wafted through the net curtains that hung at his always open windows. The leftovers of a meal he had hastily cobbled together sat on the table in front of him along with a large jug of water and ice. He was drinking too much beer these days. He didn't want to become dependent on it again.

He took a drink of water from a glass then flicked through the paperwork that Wickes had left him. Whoever had put the file together had been meticulous in their research. Photographs, copies of court documents, and prison records were now spread out across the table. It was a story of hate and discrimination, of violence and betrayal, but, overall, it was a story of love and hope. Love that crossed boundaries and hope for the future.

Brandon Carver was the accountant for the Aryan Alliance. A loosely bound group of white supremacist militias and outlaw biker gangs based in Texas. He tracked their finances, moved money around so the FBI wouldn't find it, and made payments to corrupt officials. His Father, George H. Carver, was the Alliances de facto leader and Brandon was seen as a potential heir. That was until he broke one of their cardinal rules. He met, and fell in love with, a strong, woman of colour. Although, that's not how they described her.

Simone Kalu was half Nigerian. Her father was from Lagos, her mother, an American, from Chicago. Simone was an activist in the civil rights movement and met Brandon during a debate at his university. Despite their obvious differences, they hit it off straight away. He loved her passion. He had never met a woman like her before. She educated him. She explained why everything he believed, everything he had been brought up with, was wrong. She changed his life, and it almost cost them their lives.

It took the Aryan Alliance six months to find out about their relationship. Brandon was beaten so badly that he spent a month in a coma and needed significant physiotherapy that put him out of action for the best part of a year. Simone's house, the one thing that her parents had been able to leave her when they died, was burned to the ground and she went into hiding. It was during that time that a plan formed in their minds. Brandon knew he needed leverage to keep them and their newborn baby safe, so he emptied the Alliance's bank accounts. He took incriminating evidence of the group's activities and walked away. But, as Shakespeare put it, "The course of true love never did run smooth." Their plan soon came apart.

Within a year, Brandon Carver was arrested by the FBI for fraud and money laundering. They had been watching him since he started university and judged that now was the time to bring him in. They were hoping that, after the way he had been treated, he would turn on his old associates and clear up a whole bag full of crimes in one clean sweep. When Brandon refused to accept the plea deal and inform on his father, he was sentenced to fifteen to twenty years in federal prison, an example to others. His daughter would be a young woman by the time he got out.

Palmer turned the page. Stapled to the back of the report was an email dated two weeks ago. It was from the prison governor to George H. Carver. It read,

We regret to inform you that your son, Brandon Carver, was involved in a violent altercation with members of a prison gang in the exercise yard. He suffered several stab wounds and was pronounced dead on arrival at the prison's medical facility at 07:30 this morning.

Palmer shook his head. How much worse could this shit have got. The guy's family were going to be devastated by this, if they survived. Palmer couldn't help thinking the two events were somehow connected.

The rest of the file was full of details about the kidnapping. Time, date, and location of the last place they were seen, a copy of the crudely written ransom demand, and, worst of all, a photograph of Simone Kalu's finger in a box of cotton wool.

The whole file had been put together to play on his emotions, and it worked. His thoughts strayed to images of his own son. The mistakes that led to his brutal murder and Palmer's inability to protect him. The tears that were never far away during his tortured nights began to well up. Palmer closed the file and rested his head in his hands, rocking slowly in his seat as the grief overwhelmed him again.

Chapter 4

Palmer stepped out of the air-conditioned concourse of George Bush Intercontinental Airport and into the dry heat of a Houston summer. It had taken him more than a day to get here from Jakarta and the time difference had his body thinking it was the middle of the night. All he wanted was a shower, some decent food, and a lot of sleep, but there wasn't time for that. He had to meet with Cody Wickes as soon as possible and go over the plans. They couldn't afford any more delays. This kidnapping had gone on long enough.

He walked over to the line of yellow taxis that were parked in front of arrivals and handed a piece of paper to the driver. 'You know how to get there?'

The taxi driver looked at Palmer as if he was speaking a different language. He slipped off the bonnet of his car and pointed at his dashboard. 'I've got satnav.'

Palmer's brain wasn't working at a hundred per cent. 'Of course.' He opened the door, threw his holdall on the back seat, and climbed in. 'Take me straight there. I'll give you a tip if you don't take the scenic route.'

The driver started the engine. 'Welcome to Houston, sit back and enjoy the ride.'

Palmer was tempted to snatch some sleep, but it was just

over a half-hour drive to Downtown Houston. The last thing
he wanted was to wake up feeling worse than he did now
and with a crease across his forehead from resting against the
window. That wasn't the first impression he was aiming for.

The driver pulled onto John F Kennedy Boulevard and
headed south. Palmer looked out at their surroundings. The
area they were driving through wasn't the urban sprawl
he expected from America's fourth largest city. No huge
office buildings or depressing blocks of flats. The area
was surprisingly green. They drove past low-level wooden
buildings that looked like they had been there since the Civil
War. There were neon signposts directing traffic to the strip
malls that serviced North Houston's suburbs, and, here and
there, fast food outlets and gas stations tried to entice people
off the freeway.

After twenty minutes, Palmer began to see the first skyscrap-
ers. Massive, monuments to the wealth created by the oil
industry, they reflected the sun and shimmered in the heat,
like a mirage that beckoned weary travellers. As the road
barged its way through the scenery towards the billion-dollar
skyline, the taxi turned onto a service road and stopped at
a set of traffic lights. Sitting at the side of the road, under a
ripped golf umbrella, was a man holding a cardboard sign that
said, *Will work for food.*

The curls of the man's hair, long since turned silver by age,
stood out in contrast to his weather worn skin. He wore an
old US Army jacket and had the haunted look of someone
whose head was full of memories he didn't want. Palmer
realised that this was the no-man's land between the middle-
class suburbs of the north and the capitalist cathedrals of
Downtown Houston. This was the stark reality of living in

a large city. Poverty and homelessness were just as much a problem here as anywhere else in the world.

Palmer rolled down his window and beckoned the man over, handing him a one-hundred-dollar bill, it was the smallest note he had. The man tried to hand it back, his pride not allowing him to accept such a large handout. Palmer shook his head, his sense of guilt not allowing him to sit in the car and do nothing. The man stepped back and nodded, putting the note into the pocket of his worn jeans. Palmer felt disgusted and embarrassed. People like this man were invisible. If the taxi hadn't stopped at the lights, Palmer probably wouldn't have noticed him either. He rolled his window back up, sat back in his seat and sighed. The world could be a shit place sometimes.

Ten minutes later, the taxi stopped outside one of the mirrored towers. An imposing structure that loomed over its surroundings and reached for the azure sky that seemed to go on forever. Palmer handed the driver a hundred. He could tell by the look on his face that the man was hoping to keep the change. Palmer waved his hand. 'Thank you, my friend. You have a nice day.' He needed to get some smaller notes.

The driver accepted the note with a broad smile. 'Gracias, amigo.' He sounded his horn and drove off looking happy.

Cody Wickes jumped up from his seat when he saw Palmer exit the revolving door into the office's reception hall. 'Logan.' He held out his hand. 'I can't tell you how pleased I am that you decided to take the job.'

Palmer took Wickes's huge hand. 'I suspect that you created that file specifically to tug at my heartstrings. You knew I'd agree to come.'

'I hoped you would. Your history suggested you were a man

17

with a conscience.'

'Yeah, and it sometimes gets me into trouble.'

Wickes smiled. 'We aren't expecting any trouble on this one. All the negotiating has been done. We need proof of life then deliver the ransom and recover the hostages.'

Palmer admired the man's optimism but had seen situations like this go wrong too many times to match it. 'If you weren't expecting any trouble, I wouldn't be here.'

'Well, you can never be too careful.'

Palmer gestured upwards with his head. 'What's the plan when we go up and see this guy? Does he need to be managed?'

'He knows we, well... you, are the expert. He just wants to meet you before the op. He's trusting us with his family's lives.'

Palmer hated this part of the job. A lot of families asked him to promise that everything would be okay. He could never do that. He had a feeling that it wouldn't be a problem in this case. 'Not unexpected. When do we go up?'

Wickes's phone buzzed. He picked it up and swiped the screen. 'It's from the man himself, you ready?'

'Let's get on with it, then I can get some sleep.'

Chapter 5

The glass tower they were in wasn't cheap real estate in which to have an office. The people in this building were some of the richest in America. The higher up the tower your office was, the greater the prestige and, as always in big business, the more it cost. The tenants at the top of the tower were worth billions and paid for their view across Houston. Carver's office was just one floor above reception. His view was of the road outside, but the rent was cheaper. It was obvious that he was trying to create an impression of wealth, of power. He had money, but he wasn't a member of the elite.

Palmer and Wickes exited the lift and followed the polished chrome signs to Carver's campaign office. The old man smiled from a large photograph that was fastened to the door. Smaller pictures were set out underneath that showed him shaking hands with voters and kissing babies. Across the middle of the poster, a blood-red slogan shouted out George H. Carver's election message. *Your Governor, Not Theirs.*

The room on the other side of the door was cramped and crowded. Six people sat two to a desk sharing a phone and a laptop. Two of them folded letters and slid them into envelopes while a third licked and sealed them. It didn't strike

Palmer as the campaign hub of a politician who was a serious contender. It looked more like the headquarters of a small university newspaper. Either the campaign had no funds, or Carver was keeping the money for himself. Palmer had already decided which one he thought was the case.

A second door, on the opposite wall to the one they had used, opened and a man who looked like a big toe beckoned them over.

The second room was the same size as the first, but not as crowded. It housed a single desk, a couple of filing cabinets, and a handful of soft chairs. The Big Toe welcomed them in and invited them to take a seat.

Sitting behind the desk, in front of a large window, was Carver. The smile he gave them wasn't as friendly or polished as the one he gave in photographs. This smile was more of a grimace, a sign of disdain from someone who considered himself superior. He didn't stand up, there was no offered hand or warm welcome. He simply nodded and got down to business.

'How do I know I can trust you?'

Palmer and Wickes exchanged a glance. It was Palmer who answered. 'My name is Logan Palmer, this is my colleague Cody Wickes, and you two are...?'

The Big Toe stepped forward. 'This is George H. Carver, the next governor of the great state of Texas, and the man who is paying your wages. Show some respect.'

Palmer raised an eyebrow. 'I've got no interest in your political ambitions, they mean nothing to me. As for my wages, if I was doing this for the money, you'd be paying me a lot more. I'm here because your family need help. I want them safe. I assume that's what you want too.'

Carver sat back in his chair. His arrogance oozed out of every pore. 'Let me tell you how this is going to happen. The ransom has already been agreed, so no need for you to do anything there. You will go to the arranged meeting and check that my family are still alive. I want pictures of them, timestamped.'

Palmer pointed at himself and Wickes. 'You don't trust us at all, do you?'

Carver carried on as if Palmer hadn't spoken. 'The meet is for two people. You,' he pointed at Palmer. 'Will go along with Buttermill.'

'Who's Buttermill?'

The Big Toe raised his hand. 'That would be me, Nate Buttermill.'

Palmer shook his head. 'That won't work. If I'm going in to get proof of life, I need Cody to be there with me. If it goes wrong, I need someone watching my back.'

'Well, I need someone to watch my money. You might agree to anything, maybe add a little on top for yourself.'

Palmer stood up. 'I don't need this shit. I'm out of here.'

Wickes held up both hands. 'Let's just calm down. We all want the same thing. We all want Simone and Zahrah Kalu returned unharmed, right?'

They all nodded.

'Okay, that's good. So, Logan and Buttermill meet with the kidnappers to get proof of life. I'll stay here and coordinate things. When Mr Carver gets the pictures, he'll release the money into the kidnappers' account. Logan brings the hostages back home. We all get what we want. Are we agreed?'

Carver nodded. 'I'm not releasing any money until I know I'm not being scammed.'

Palmer tilted his head. 'And that your family are okay.'

'What?'

'You want to know that your family are alive and unharmed.'

Carver shrugged. 'Of course.'

Palmer let out a deep sigh then took a step towards Buttermill. 'If anything happens, you're on your own. My priority is the hostages.'

Buttermill puffed out his chest. 'I can take care of myself.'

The tension was broken by Wickes. 'Okay, the exchange is taking place the day after tomorrow. I suggest we all take that time to make sure everything is in place. Logan and I will firm up the operational details, Buttermill does exactly what Logan says. Agreed?'

Carver nodded, Buttermill grunted, and Palmer shrugged.

Wickes stood up. 'Wonderful, I love it when a team bonds. We'll be in touch.' He opened the door and stepped out.

Palmer stared at Carver in silence for a few seconds. 'As much as I've enjoyed our little get together, it's been a long day and my underwear won't change itself.' He turned his gaze to Buttermill. 'See you in a couple of days, Buttercup.' He turned towards the door and walked out.

Nate Buttermill slammed the door. 'I don't like him, Boss. He's an asshole.'

'He serves our purposes. That's all we need.'

'It's a dangerous game we're playing here, with some hardcore outlaws. If things go wrong...'

Carver shook his head. 'Look at the big picture. We get them back, I'm the man who paid twenty million for his mixed-race family. All the racist accusations start to fade away. If they die, we'll have a big funeral. I'll cry my heart out. Either way, we win.'

'And the money?'

'Let me worry about the money. You just make sure Palmer doesn't do anything to mess up our plan.'

Chapter 6

P almer spent the rest of day one crashed out in his hotel room trying to convince his body that it wasn't 3 o'clock in the morning just yet. He was surprised at how quickly he had slotted back into his old life of work and travel. It didn't matter what country he was in after a while. The routine and the surroundings were the same. This room was no different to every other one he had stayed in over the years. Plain, neutral walls and carpet with a double bed, desk in the corner, and a door that led to the small bathroom. It was what he called a Goldilocks hotel. Budget hotels weren't secure, expensive ones were overpriced, but this one was just right.

He never fully unpacked his bag. Just took out the toiletries he needed and some clothes for the next day. Why unpack things that you weren't going to use? He had a shower, washed his socks and underwear, an old military habit, and climbed into bed.

After eight hours of restless sleep and another shower, his head no longer felt like it was full of cotton wool, now it felt like it was full of spiders. Big, hairy, pissed off spiders that were having a party. His eyes felt like they were full of grit and his throat was dry. He drained the dregs of his second cup of coffee and checked the time, it wasn't even five o'clock. He had slept as long as he could, but his body clock thought it was late afternoon. He needed some air and to stretch his legs. He made his way down to reception and asked for directions to the nearest internet café.

Out on the street, it was as if he was the only person awake. That wasn't just because it was early. He had noticed when he arrived that the large crowds you would expect in a city of this size just weren't there. Nobody walked anywhere here, everyone drove. To the supermarket, to bars and restaurants, to the mall. Well, when in Rome. He flagged down a passing taxi and gave the driver the address.

The building the taxi delivered him to was more of a gaming café. Even at this time in the morning, it was half filled with teenage gamers who spent their lives inhabiting fantasy worlds online. Had they been here since last night or had they arrived early? Why weren't they Asleep? Maybe they had jetlag too.

Palmer grabbed a large latte, his third of the morning, from the counter and made his way to the side of the café where a handful of non-gaming internet PCs were installed. He picked the chair farthest away from everybody else. It wasn't that he was trying to hide anything or that he was expecting trouble, it was just habit. Never sit with your back to a crowd. If something happens, you'll want to see it coming.

Something else he learned over his years in security was that you can never do too much research. He wanted to know everything about George H. Carver, his family, and his whole operation.

After three hours he had all the information he needed. George H. Carver had no redeeming qualities whatsoever. He had a long history of crime and violence, although no criminal record. That meant one of two things. Either he had a very good lawyer, or he had powerful friends. He was, without doubt, a shot caller. A man who made the decisions, instigated the violence, but never got his hands dirty. It meant he was untouchable. It also meant he was able to run for public office.

Palmer was no expert in tracking down information, but even he was able to find Carver's alleged links to white supremacists, outlaw biker gangs, drugs, human trafficking, money laundering, the list went on and on. Old newspaper stories and court reports gave the full details. There was no attempt to hide any of it. But here he was, trying to act like none of it had happened, that he was respectable and was a candidate for governor. Palmer found apparent links to big business, but none of them would admit it. There was a leaked list of supporters in local and federal government and law enforcement, although several court cases had sought to wipe the list out. With no evidence to support the allegations, it never went far. Carver had even managed to sue a couple of newspapers for libel.

Palmer scrolled through page after page, scribbling notes in his book, but something was missing. Even with the orgy of information that was easily available, Palmer couldn't find anything that showed how Carver would be able to raise the ransom.

There was no doubt that he had, legally or otherwise, amassed a good amount of money, but it wasn't real money. He didn't have a fortune big enough to raise twenty million for a ransom without impacting his own lifestyle. Carver didn't strike Palmer as someone who would be willing to do that, it didn't make any sense.

Palmer emailed the details to his friend, Anna Riley, and asked her for a favour. He knew he couldn't call on MI6's official help on this job, but he and Riley had history, and he was sure she would help. What was taking him hours, she could do in twenty minutes.

He looked up at the oversized digital clocks that were attached to the opposite wall. Each one told the time in a different part of the world. Palmer wasn't sure why gamers needed to know the time in Munich, but, then again, he didn't really understand the online world. Maybe the internet had its own time zones. The clock in the middle told him that, in Houston time, it was eight thirty. Time to sort out a hire car and pick up a few things before his meeting with Cody. He closed his browser windows, cleared the computer's cache and search history, and logged out.

Chapter 7

P almer walked through the Galleria shopping mall towards the diner where he had agreed to meet Wickes. There were plenty of people about by this time. Shop workers, shoppers and mall rats mixed with families who were out for the day. Palmer watched pensioners taking lessons on the ground floor ice rink while others, more proficient on skates, zoomed around the perimeter spinning and turning in time to the music coming out of their headphones. It was a good place to be anonymous.

Palmer had suggested meeting here because Wickes didn't have an office in Houston, and Palmer needed something to eat. He had spent the morning shopping for clothes. One of the reasons why he travelled light was that he didn't know exactly what he needed until he was in country and had the details of the job. He was now the proud owner of a rugged backpack which held ex-military issue boots and combat trousers. He had bought several plain, dark-coloured t-shirts, underwear, socks, a compass, and a multi-tool. The kind of things any self-respecting hiker might carry. All he needed now was a plate full of cooked breakfast and he was good to go. He pushed open the door to the diner and stepped through.

Although it was located on a busy section of the Galleria,

the diner was quiet. It wasn't like back at home where people wanted to get into town early to get a parking space before the crowds got too big. The Galleria was huge. Parking wasn't a problem and the locals in Houston didn't come to the mall until later in the morning. There was no breakfast crowd, and it wasn't quite lunchtime yet, so most people were still shopping or sliding around the ice.

Cody Wickes sat in a booth at the far end to the right of the door. He almost had the place to himself. The only other customers were an elderly couple sitting by the counter, well out of earshot. Palmer walked over to Wickes's table, planted his backpack on the seat and sat down next to it. 'Morning, Cody.'

Wickes looked up from the folder full of papers he had been scribbling notes on. 'Mornin', Logan. You get some sleep?'

'Yeah, feeling okay now. Well, better than I was.'

The server walked over to the table, pencil and notepad at the ready. 'What can I get ya?'

Palmer looked at the menu that was under the Perspex tabletop. 'I'll have bacon, scrambled egg, hash browns and a large coffee, please.'

The server jotted it all down with a smile. 'No problem. Be right back.' He put his pencil back behind his ear and hurried away.

Wickes placed a smartphone, still in its box, onto the table and slid it across to Palmer. 'That's brand new, local sim card. It's all set up and ready to use. The single number in the contact list is mine. I didn't want you using your own.'

'I don't have one, I always pick one up when I arrive. It was next on my shopping list.'

Wickes cast an eye over Palmer's bag. 'Looks like you've

been on a bit of a spree.'

'Just the essentials. Can't do this job in shorts and flip-flops.' Palmer pointed at the folder. 'Is there a problem with the plan?'

Wickes raised his eyebrows and let out a sigh. 'The plan is okay, it's the rest of it that has holes in.'

'Like what.'

'What would you expect the ransom to be for a kidnapping like this.'

Palmer shrugged. 'In South America or Somalia, they would ask for something like ten million then negotiate down to less than one. Here, I would expect one or two.'

'Exactly. These guys asked for twenty. That means they are probably first-timers. They don't know how much hostages are worth. Either that, or they think they've got their hands on someone special for some reason. That makes them dangerous. They have expectations that don't match reality. Unless they know something that we don't.'

Palmer pointed to one of the sheets of paper. 'The gang asked for twenty and that's what we're paying. Yet Carver said the negotiations had been done. Either the negotiators were on a percentage of the ransom, or we've got amateurs on both sides.'

'You ever see anything like this before?'

Palmer shook his head. 'I usually work for companies who take over the whole thing from day one. Ransom demand, proof of life, hostage recovery. Bringing us in at the end and paying the full amount...? Smacks of desperation.'

Wickes closed the folder. 'That's the way I see it too. Are you still happy to run with this, Logan? I mean, I'd understand if you weren't. I don't want to be responsible for you getting hurt.'

'I should be on a plane right now, winging my way back to my Indonesian dive boat.'

'But you're not.'

Palmer smiled. 'Cody, when it comes down to it, I just keep thinking about Zahrah Kalu. She's sixteen, she's been kidnapped by a group of arseholes who are doing God knows what to her. Her dad is dead, and to cap it all off, her white supremacist grandad, who hasn't had anything to do with her life up to this point, because she's mixed race, is using her as a pawn to score votes. Did I miss anything?'

The server came back with Palmer's breakfast and coffee. 'Sorry, buddy. Don't want to interrupt.' He placed the plate and mug down on the table.

Palmer sat back. 'That's okay,' he looked at his name badge. 'Lou. We were just getting to the end of our business.'

Lou smiled, spun on his heels, and headed back to the counter.

Wickes put his folder into his briefcase. 'Like I said, are you still happy with this?'

Palmer picked up his knife and fork. 'I'm a big boy now, I can look after myself. Besides, no one ever accused me of being too smart.'

'I'd be happier if I was going in as your backup.'

'Yeah, me too. Buttermill is just a thug, used to threatening weaker people. If it hits the fan, I expect him to shit in his pants.'

'You just make sure you use him as a human shield, okay?'

Palmer nodded. 'We've got until tomorrow night, I'll drive there today, it'll take about four hours. I'll check out the handover location and let you know if we're going ahead.

If you find anything out, pull the plug and we'll walk away. We can arrange our own handover, our way.'

Wickes stood up and held out his hand. 'Good luck, Logan. I'll make sure everything at this end goes smoothly.'

Palmer took the offered hand. 'Watch your back, Cody. I don't trust Carver at all.'

Chapter 8

Palmer was a big believer in the value of good recon. There was no such thing as too much intel. The more familiar you are with an area, the more likely you are to get away if you need to. It was the main reason why the police struggled to catch criminals who operated in their own neighbourhoods. They know all the ins and outs. The last thing you want if you are being chased is to be running blind in unfamiliar surroundings.

Obvious routes to and from the meeting and the less obvious escape routes for emergencies had to be checked. Palmer needed to know if there were any natural hazards that would block his progress or force him along a specific route to an ambush point. Lack of local knowledge affected tactical awareness and could bring an escape and evasion to an end before it even got going. Especially with hostages in tow.

The exchange was taking place in the Hill Country northwest of Austin. The location they had been given was between the Balcones Canyonland Wildlife Refuge and the Colorado River. It was a rugged, rural area of trees and limestone canyons, but also popular with tourists, retirees, and professionals who worked from home. This meant there was a growing number of suburban neighbourhoods and affluent retirement communities mixed in with holiday homes and marinas. There was a big enough transient population, and enough houses and cabins to make it easy to hide hostages, but it also had remote areas where an exchange could be carried out away from prying eyes.

Palmer had checked into a cheap hotel on the opposite side of the river. It wasn't somewhere he would normally have considered. It didn't meet his Goldilocks rule. He picked this hotel because, from the map that he had, it looked like it would give him an almost uninterrupted line of sight to the meeting point and the road that accessed it. If these kidnappers were anything other than complete amateurs, they would be keeping an eye on the area to check for any police stakeout. While they watched for police, Palmer would be watching them.

When he checked in, Palmer asked if they had a room with a view over the water. He said he was a keen birdwatcher and was hoping to see a golden-cheeked warbler, or maybe a black-capped vireo. He held up his binoculars to show he was serious. The receptionist knew it was unlikely Palmer would see anything from the hotel, but he was happy to pretend otherwise and take the extra money that was on offer. He handed Palmer the key to room twenty-seven and wished him a happy stay.

Room twenty-seven, the Rodeo Room, sounded like it should be in a brothel. It was at the back of the hotel, up a flight of stone steps, and was separate from the main building. It sat on top of a rocky outcrop which meant it was level with the second floor of the hotel. Unlike the rooms Palmer normally stayed in, the décor in the Rodeo Room was anything but plain. The wallpaper had a covered wagon motif running through it, and the lampshades looked like Texan flags. A print of The Alamo adorned one wall and opposite was a framed, black and white photograph of a cactus. The bed's headboard looked like an old wagon wheel and a small, silver statue of a rodeo cowboy on the back of a bucking horse sat on one corner of the desk. The label attached to the horse's leg said it was available to buy from reception. Everything was a cliché, reinforcing the view that outsiders had of Texas. It was a low budget attempt to create an atmosphere for the tourists.

Palmer closed the door and threw his bags on the bed. He had a little over five hours until the light started to fade. The room's window faced east so he didn't have to worry about the sun blinding him at this time of day. He dragged the small desk over to the window, threw the silver rodeo rider onto the bed, and closed the curtains until they were eight inches apart. His birdwatcher cover story would be enough to explain his behaviour to any curious onlookers but there was no need to advertise what he was doing. He attached his binoculars to a small tripod he had bought in Houston and positioned them on the desk next to two bottles of water the hotel had kindly provided. With his pen at the ready to write down any details, he focused the binoculars and prepared for a long afternoon.

For the next few hours, Palmer sat and watched the other side of the river. The opposite bank was higher up than he was, so he couldn't see the exchange location clearly, but what he could see was the road that led up to it. It started low to his right, then rose steeply to the plateau where the clearing was. It was too far away to reliably identify the drivers of any vehicles, and he couldn't read the licence plates, but he could make out the colour, type of car and any distinguishing marks. Most vehicles drove the road in one direction, they were just passing through, but one had caught his eye. An old grey panel van had driven the road in both directions, twice. That didn't mean it was mixed up in anything, it just made it stand out. As the sun began to dip below the hills that rose in front of the hotel, it was time to have a closer look at the terrain. Palmer grabbed his backpack and headed for his car.

The four-wheel drive he had hired wasn't anything flashy. He had made sure it looked beaten up enough to be a working vehicle, something that a forest ranger might use. He made his way through the newly built suburban area next to the hotel and followed the course of the river downstream. House lights were beginning to come on as residents settled in for the night to watch overpaid celebrities on oversized flat-screen TVs. It didn't strike Palmer as the sort of place where people did a lot of socialising in bars and clubs. It seemed like more of an affluent middle-class community. Expensive cars were parked in front of even more expensive looking houses. Children's toys and swing sets were nowhere to be seen and, here and there, the Stars and Stripes fluttered from flagpoles in the corners of manicured lawns. It was like the Disney version of small-town America.

At the point where the white painted houses and spotless gardens began to thin out, but before the nearest town was fully in view, Palmer took the fork in the road that curved towards the river. There was a change in road noise as his wheels hit the deck of the metal bridge and he left the lights of Stepford behind.

Chapter 9

The road up to the plateau was narrow and rough. In the absolute darkness that enveloped the car outside of the reach of his headlights, it would have been easy to drive right off the edge. The luminous paint on the marker posts was too infrequent to signal some of the sharper bends before it was too late. Any drivers who didn't keep their wits about them on this track could come unstuck very fast.

Palmer crept along the road, avoiding the multitude of potholes while shining a torch into the trees on his left. After half a mile, he found what he was looking for. A group of trees had either been cut down or had fallen in a storm. The logs had been cut into equal lengths and piled up in a layby just off the road ready for collection. Palmer pulled in and parked the car out of sight behind the wood pile.

The first spots of rain began to fall as Palmer climbed out of the car and slung his backpack over his shoulders. There was no need for a lot of kit. This wasn't going to be an all-nighter. The area of the handover was small and only had a couple of potential access and escape routes. He was liking this job less and less the more he found out about it. He turned up his collar and pulled his beanie hat down as far as he could over his ears. It wasn't as good as wearing cam cream, but it would do.

Suddenly, the sweep of a vehicle's headlights lit up the layby and Palmer dropped to the ground. From a prone position, he looked underneath his car and watched the grey panel van heading up the slope on another trip up the hill. He checked his watch. The van was making the same journey every four hours. Exactly what would happen if there was a team up there working shifts. He waited for the van's tail lights to fade then set off through the trees.

The clearing was over a mile further up the road. Palmer took a more direct route up the slope to the edge of the plateau and got there as the van was reversing down the dirt access track. The vehicle's back doors were thrown open and two men, dressed like they were off to fight in a jungle war, jumped out and rolled into the undergrowth. Two other men, dressed more for desert combat, skirted around the edge of the trees and dived into the back of the van. The doors closed and its wheels spun as the driver gunned the engine and powered back towards the road.

Palmer watched the changing of the guard through his binoculars. He now knew that he was dealing with amateurs. He was sure that these men thought they were being professional, but it was obvious they had learned their tactics from some survivalist on YouTube. It was a good idea to monitor the area where the exchange would take place, to make sure the police weren't staking it out, but not like this. Real professionals would have tabbed up to the clearing on foot, as he had. If a vehicle had to be used, the brake lights would have been disabled, the headlights switched off, and, most of all, real professionals wouldn't have used the same vehicle every time.

Palmer crouched behind a tree stump and rested his binoculars on its freshly cut top. The opposite line of trees, and the two men, were clearly visible through his night vision that bathed the area in a stark, green light and made it look like a CCTV image. The men had tried to cover themselves in foliage, picked up from the recent tree felling, but it didn't help. They hadn't covered their heads and one of them was on his smartphone. He shielded the screen with a gloved hand but, in an environment this dark, even a pinpoint of light was visible a hundred meters away.

Thirty minutes into his vigil, it started to rain, heavily. Palmer decided it was time to get a closer look at his two adversaries. They hadn't moved at all and weren't using any kind of scope or night vision. The rain would cover any noise Palmer made as he slithered through the long grass at the edge of the clearing, and visibility was low. He put his binoculars into his pack and crawled out from the trees.

Palmer looked down to his left, the long grass ran around the edge of the plateau. If he veered off course a few feet, there was a ten-foot drop onto rocks followed by a steep slope to the cliff edge that dropped to the river. Going over that in the dark would be a surefire way to end up swimming back to the hotel.

After ten minutes of dragging himself through the grass, Palmer reached the opposite line of trees. His initial opinion of the two men proved to be correct, they weren't watching at all. Number one was still engrossed by the screen of his phone. If nothing else, it would destroy his ability to see any movement in the dark. Even if the rain wasn't masking Palmer's progress, he doubted if this idiot would have noticed him anyway. He was a young, white, man with a scruffy goatee beard and wore a camouflaged bandana, like a character from a bad Vietnam War film. Number two, a middle-aged man with a belly like he was smuggling a pumpkin under his shirt, was asleep. Whoever was paying these two wasn't getting their money's worth. Palmer crawled to within ten feet of them and could have killed them both.

It was time to head back to the hotel, there was nothing more to see here. Palmer crawled through the trees, giving the men a bit more clearance this time, and emerged back into the long grass. The rain was hammering down and turning the ground into a sea of mud as the water ran across the plateau and over the edge to the river. The slither back to his car wouldn't be easy. His hands were starting to go numb. The cold water running over them, as he tried to gain purchase in the mud, had found its way inside his gloves. He would have to move further up the clearing and crawl through the shorter scrub where the mud didn't seem too bad. As he reached out his arm and turned to crawl up the slope, he heard a sound. One that stopped him in his tracks.

A man was standing no more than three feet away from Palmer, behind a large oak tree. He whispered into a small radio. 'Are you two idiots still awake? Get your assess out here, I heard something.'

Palmer hadn't seen this guy at all. He must have crawled behind him. The man was dressed head to toe in black. Trousers, jacket, gloves, the works. His face was smeared with cam cream, and he looked like he could handle himself. He didn't come here in the van; he must have been here already or arrived on foot. Palmer had been lucky not to get caught. It was the noise of the rain that had saved him from detection. The other two watchers might be weekend warriors, but this guy was a professional, he was the boss.

Palmer laid flat on his chest and smothered mud across his face. He hadn't been spotted yet, but it was just a matter of time before one of them tripped over him. The other two men had broken cover and made their way across the clearing to the edge of the plateau. One of them was sure to spot him. Palmer pushed himself, inch by inch away from the man in black, aware that he was dangerously close to the edge and the ten-foot drop.

The two goons squelched their way towards their boss. Goatee beard arrived first. 'What's goin' on?'

'I heard a noise, back there in the trees. The only way out is through us. You stay here, I'll flush them towards you.'

The pumpkin smuggler plodded up behind them. He was wheezing like an asthmatic bull. 'What's happenin'?'

The Pro turned and looked at him. 'How did you end up in this job...? Never mind, just search the area.' He watched as the two men splashed around like kids looking for crabs at the beach. He shook his head, turned, and melted into the darkness.

Goatee and pumpkin started to search the grass. Palmer hadn't noticed before but they both carried AR-15s with which they were now prodding the undergrowth.

Palmer edged further away, his right hand slipped over the edge of the drop and his whole body flexed as he tried to stop himself from following it down. His fingers dug into the mud, trying to get some grip, but it was too wet. He was sliding towards the edge.

Goatee and pumpkin carried on with their search, each second bringing their prodding closer to Palmer's position. He thought he could take them, but they were too far apart and their AR-15s ready to fire off panicked shots as soon as he stood up. The Pro was nowhere in sight, but he wouldn't be gone for long. Once he was back, Palmer was trapped. He took a deep breath and slid his legs over the edge of the drop.

He had gone over drops of this height countless times in training. Ten feet wasn't far to fall if you landed correctly. Palmer didn't. He hit the rocks at the bottom of the cliff like a broken mannequin. He gritted his teeth against the pain and forced himself to stand up. His ribs screamed, his lungs tried to suck in air, and his legs trembled as he stood with his back flat against the cliff face.

The Pro re-appeared, shouting at the others. 'There was something back there, there are tracks. No sign of whatever it was now though.'

The pumpkin smuggler was still out of breath. 'It's this rain, Boss... it's causing landslides... There's mud everywhere.'

The Pro took one last look around the clearing. 'Get back to your positions, and this time stay alert.'

Palmer crouched down. His whole body ached. The rain and mud that cascaded off the top of the cliff poured onto his back. His breathing was harsh, that was a close one, but at least he knew he was dealing with at least one person who meant business. He wouldn't be so lax next time.

Chapter 10

The bruises on Palmer's back and left side were beginning to show. He stood under the shower in his hotel room and ran his hand around his ribs, nothing felt broken, but they were going to hurt for a few days. His hands and forearms were a mass of cuts and scrapes, but he couldn't worry about that now. The exchange was at 9 pm, a little over twelve hours from now. He had to be ready. There was no time to make any changes to the plan to allow for the involvement of a professional. If he had any sense, he would have called it off and gone home, but he couldn't stop thinking about Zahrah and Simone Kalu. He would just have to deal with whatever came up. He turned off the shower, grabbed his towel and stepped out.

Palmer wiped condensation from the mirror and stared at himself. He looked rough, but no more than usual. He hadn't had a shave in a while and still wasn't over his jet lag, but at least he had no damage to his face. If he turned up to the meeting with obvious cuts and bruises, it might give away the previous night's excursion. If the kidnappers put two and two together, the plan would start to fall apart and that could cause all kinds of problems he didn't need. With a headache starting to build behind his eyes, he dried himself off and got dressed.

Palmer popped two paracetamols out of a foil strip and washed them down with a glass of water. The first thing he needed to do was get something to eat, it was going to be a very long day. He had noticed a roadside diner on his drive in from Houston and was looking forward to the biggest fried breakfast they could fit on a plate. He picked up his cash and the phone that Wickes had given him. He swiped the screen and logged into his encrypted email, there was one message. He knew who it was from, even though it looked anonymous.

The email address he used couldn't be traced to him. It had been set up by Anna Riley, one of his few real friends. She was a genius when it came to technology and the online world, much more than he was. It was why MI6 valued her so much. She had told him never to use an email account that wasn't as secure as possible. Riley had set up anonymous addresses for them both which gave them end-to-end encryption of all their messages. Nothing was guaranteed to be completely secure. All they could do was make it as difficult as possible for anyone who wanted to try to hack their accounts. All the encryption in the world soon fell apart if operational security wasn't followed though. Always keep your password safe, and never write it down. No use of real names, and, most of all, never mention your location. If she needed to know where he was, she could find him.

Palmer opened his inbox and read the message. True to form, Riley had kept it simple and stuck to their rules. All it said was, *Call me*. That could mean good news or bad news, you could never be sure with Anna. It was after midnight in the UK. If she had something to tell him, he couldn't wait until a more sociable time. He would have to wake her up. Using the smartphone to call her wasn't a good idea, he couldn't risk her being linked to this job. The diner he was heading to for breakfast was bound to have a landline, two birds with one stone. He picked up his car keys and left the room.

The diner was a single-story, rectangular building with a front wall made up almost entirely of windows. Beside the road was a large, neon sign that flashed in red and green as it announced, *All day breakfast.* Perfect.

The paint on the diner's exterior was bright and the car park was freshly tarmacked with no potholes. It looked like it hadn't been up very long. With the population growing and the speed of development in this area, it wasn't surprising that new businesses were appearing. Palmer's main worry was, would a building this new have a public telephone in it? It was more likely to have Wi-Fi and internet access. Still, he needed something to eat no matter what. He parked the car, walked up to the front of the diner, and opened the door.

The inside of the building was decorated in a nineteen fifties style, the golden era of the diner. Directly in front of the door, the counter was painted cream with a red top and had chrome foot and handrails around the front. A row of bar stools mirrored the counter's colour scheme as did the four-seater booths that ran around the outside walls. The pale blue painted walls were decorated with old licence plates and hub caps interspersed with photographs of Elvis, Buddy Holly, James Dean and Marilyn Monroe. It had been designed with retirees in mind. Maybe they wanted to revisit their youth. That's why the diner did all-day breakfasts, pensioners had all day to do what they had to do.

Each booth had red and white faux leather seats, a cream and chrome tabletop, and its own little jukebox. It was pleasant enough, but it wasn't authentic. Palmer wasn't around in the fifties, but he was willing to bet that this was the sanitized, nostalgic version. A bit like an Irish themed pub. He picked a booth which had a good view of the door and took a seat.

The server that came over was an older woman with a broad smile that deepened her laugh lines and wrinkled the corner of her eyes. 'Good mornin' and welcome to Buddy's Diner, what can I get you?'

'Can I please have the biggest fried breakfast you have and a large cup of black coffee.'

She scribbled on her order pad. 'Sure can, Hun. Anything else?'

'Yeah, do you have a phone I can use?'

She pointed to an old phone booth that sat in the corner opposite the toilet door. Palmer had assumed it was just there for show. 'There's one in the booth, Hun.'

He felt a little foolish. 'That's perfect, thank you.'

'You're welcome.' She smiled and hurried off to the kitchen hatch.

Palmer unwrapped a roll of quarters and fed them into the phone's money slot. He dialled Riley's number and waited for it to connect. While the international connection went through, Palmer checked to make sure no one could overhear his conversation, but he needn't have worried. The other customers were sitting at the far end of the diner and not interested in what he was doing.

The phone rang once, and Riley picked it up. She didn't sound tired or like he had just woken her up, she must have been waiting for his call. 'Yes?'

'It's me.'

'Good. I've looked into your person of interest and none of

it makes sense.'

Palmer wasn't surprised. 'He doesn't have the funds, does he?'

'His personal worth is around twelve million. Three million in various bank accounts and another ten tied up in property. His campaign fund is up to four million from various donors, but he can't access that without setting off alarm bells. There's no way of knowing if he has money elsewhere though. He could have billions hidden away in another name for all we know, but it's unlikely.'

'That's what I thought, it doesn't add up. Thanks for your help, I owe you one.'

Riley laughed. 'You mean another one. You aren't in danger, are you?'

'Not at all, just a routine job. Nothing to worry about. I'll be finished by tonight, might have a trip home.'

But Riley was worried, she could tell when Palmer was lying. 'Where are you?'

'No locations, remember? Look, you can trace this call. I have a brand-new mobile with me. I'm sure you can put the two together.'

Riley sighed. 'Promise me you'll be careful.'

'I promise. I'll speak to you soon.' Palmer hung up and got back to his seat just as his breakfast was arriving. Bacon, pancakes, eggs, hash browns, toast, orange juice, and a steaming hot cup of coffee. He was looking forward to this.

'If you need anything else, Hun, just let me know.'

'Thank you.' Palmer took a long drink of his orange juice then picked up his knife and fork, and dug in.

Chapter 11

With his breakfast finished and, if he was honest, feeling like he had overdone it a bit, Palmer walked back to his car. The call to Wickes could be done on the mobile, it belonged to him anyway, no need to hide it. He dialled the number and waited.

Wickes was expecting the call and answered after a couple of rings. 'Logan, how you doin'?'

'I'm good, Cody. Are we still on for tonight?'

'Yes, we had a confirmation from the kidnappers this morning. They are happy with the arrangements and good to go. I've made sure the old man hasn't got cold feet. Did you manage to check out the location?'

'You could say that. I almost ran into them. They've got people up there watching the clearing already.'

Wickes scoffed. 'Why would they waste time doing that? We're paying them the money tonight. We aren't trying to double cross them.'

Palmer knew that he and Wickes weren't planning a double cross, but he wasn't one hundred per cent sure about Carver. 'I imagine they're just being careful, making sure the police don't turn up and catch them unawares.'

'I guess so. What's the location like?'

'There's only one way in and out by car, and they will be in control of it. I would expect them to have spotters along the road checking everyone.'

'I don't like the sound of one way out, especially if the kidnappers are first-timers. If they wanted to, they could block off the access and kill everyone. Did they look like professionals? I mean, do we have to worry about the Colombians setting up a kidnap for profit operation up here, or is it amateur hour?'

Palmer chuckled. 'The first two looked like a pair of sur-vivalists. Weekend warriors who spend their time prepping for the downfall of civilization. The sort of people who fantasised about being in a plucky band of survivors in a post-apocalyptic wasteland, but, when an actual pandemic hit, couldn't last more than a month without a haircut and a bucket of chicken.'

Wickes laughed. 'I know the kind you mean, man. Ready for the end of the world, not ready for the end of fast food and toilet paper. Amateurs then?'

'Amateurs, but heavily armed. If they get spooked, the shit will most definitely hit the fan.'

Wickes sounded concerned. 'You said first two?'

'Yeah. There was a third guy there, a professional, maybe ex-police or special forces. He must be the guy they've brought in to advise them on security. It was obvious that he was in charge of the other two.'

'Are you okay with just having Buttermill with you?'

Palmer paused. 'It's too late to back out now. The kidnap-pers know they're getting their money, why would they cause a problem for us now? As long as Buttermill does as he's told, things will be okay. We hand over the money and free the hostages. How is it at your end?'

'The old man has set up a cryptocurrency wallet with twenty million in coins in it. I've no idea how that works, but they've agreed to it. As soon as you confirm that the hostages are alive, he'll give them the password.'

'Sounds simple. Whatever happened to a sack full of used notes in the trunk of a car?'

Wickes laughed. 'Welcome to the modern world, my friend. Easier to carry and untraceable. Cryptocurrency is the future.'

'Do you know where this money is coming from? I've looked into Carver, and he doesn't have twenty million to drop on a ransom.'

Wickes cleared his throat. 'To be honest, I don't know. He could be borrowing it from any number of organised crime sources. It could be illegal gains from his various enterprises.'

'If he's borrowed it, how the hell is he planning to pay it back?'

'When he becomes governor, he'll have a lot to offer. Maybe he's selling future influence. But, if we get the hostages back, I don't care what happens to him. If the people he owes money to decide to beat it out of him, I won't lose any sleep.'

Palmer scoffed. 'There's no way he's becoming governor. People in Texas aren't voting for a white supremacist, but, if the Mob or a cartel are involved, they don't take prisoners.'

'You need to watch your back, Logan. Let's get out of this clean. You got the business card I gave you?'

'Yeah, what time should I expect Buttermill to get here?'

'He should be there about... seven o'clock.'

'Okay, plenty of time. I want to be at the exchange by eight, before it's totally dark. I'll call you later with an update.'

Palmer started the car. He had a few things he needed to

do before Buttermill turned up and tried to take over. Palmer wanted some insurance before he put his neck on the block.

Chapter 12

P almer drove the hour back to Austin. He could buy most of the things he needed within a few miles of the hotel, but not everything. Some things required a specialist supplier. He stopped the car in front of a flat roofed, squat looking building that was set back ten meters from the road. It reminded him of Moe's Tavern. The neon sign that flickered above the door announced to passers-by that this was Ernie's Sports Bar, the finest selection of imported beers in Austin. Palmer doubted that very much. He expected that the choice in beer was drink it or leave. Judging by the posters in the grimy window, it would be most busy on game days, but Palmer didn't imagine it got that busy at any time. He pulled on the scarred wooden door and went in.

The inside of the bar was dark, made worse by coming in out of the sunlight. Palmer stood at the entrance for a few seconds, waiting for his vision to adjust. He could only see two other people inside. The bartender, who sat on a stool reading a newspaper, and a middle-aged man who looked like he had passed out. Palmer let the door close and walked up to the bar.

The bartender looked up from his newspaper. 'What can I get ya, buddy?'

Palmer threw ten dollars on the bar. 'Beer. Keep the change.'

The bartender took the ten dollars and replaced it with a freshly opened bottle. 'Thanks.'

Palmer nodded. 'You know a guy named Asher?'

'Who's askin'?'

Palmer held up Cody Wickes's business card then turned it to show the handwritten note on the back.

The bartender reached out to take the card, but Palmer withdrew it and slipped it back into his pocket. 'Asher?'

'He's over there.'

In the far corner of the bar, in an area Palmer hadn't noticed when he first walked in, a man sat on one of two leather bench seats which stood on either side of a rectangular table. He was looking through a bundle of papers and making notes. Palmer checked the rest of the bar. The drunk was still asleep by the door and the bartender had gone back to his newspaper. Palmer picked up his bottle and walked over.

Asher was a muscular man. Not sculpted like a bodybuilder, but toned and lean. The hardened physique that came from years of military training. His grey hair was cropped short, and he had a scar that ran from the corner of his eye to his hairline.

Palmer stopped short of the corner seat. 'You're expecting me.'

Asher shuffled his papers and placed them in his jacket. 'Take a seat.'

'Thanks. So, is Asher your first name or your last?'

'Neither. I like my privacy.'

Palmer smiled. 'Fair enough.' He looked around at their surroundings. 'This your normal office, or am I getting the VIP treatment?'

'It's dark, quiet, and has no CCTV inside or out. People coming and going doesn't look unusual. What more could you want?'

'And no one minds you doing your business here?'

Asher shook his head. 'There's no one to mind, I own the place. Let's go to my office.'

As Palmer followed him through a door behind the bar, Asher called out to the drunk by the door. 'Keep watch.'

The drunk sat up. 'Sure thing, Boss.'

Asher closed the door behind them. 'I keep my clientele very selective. Professionals, people I know won't fuck up. I work by recommendation, and I can be a good friend. If you bring any heat down on me or bring the cops to my door, I'll put a contract out on you so big you won't even make it to your car. You good with that?'

Palmer nodded, considering what Asher had said. 'Selective… cops… won't make it to the car… yeah, I got it. Seems reasonable.'

'Everyone who comes here gets that speech, once. There are no second chances in my world.'

'Maybe I should have asked Cody to recommend a strip joint instead. I don't think their entrance requirements are as tough.'

Asher smirked. 'Cody Wickes tells me you're one of us. A limey, but a marine all the same. That's a good enough recommendation for me. Now we've got the pleasantries out of the way, what do you need?'

'I'm going into some shit where I might be searched. I need something small and light, easy to conceal inside a bag. Obviously, I'm a visitor to your fine country, so I'll be wanting to avoid any unnecessary paperwork and waiting periods.'

Asher picked up his mobile and opened an app. When he pressed his thumb to the fingerprint reader, there was a buzz and one of the wall panels clicked open. 'I only keep a selection here, if you don't see what you want, I can get it for you.' He opened the door all the way to reveal an alcove the size of a double-door fridge freezer. A metal rack held examples of Pump action shotguns, assault weapons, and a bolt action rifle. Underneath the rack were two steel fronted drawers, he opened the first one. 'Help yourself. Glock 19 would be my choice, but you'll know that.'

Palmer lifted one of the handguns out of the drawer. It was vacuum packed in clear plastic and had two magazines with it. 'This'll be fine for what I need. Are they clean?'

'They aren't traceable back to me if that's what you mean. There are no serial numbers, but if they manage to uncover them with acid, they'll show up as stolen in various home robberies. They're wiped clean of prints then sealed.'

'That's excellent. I wouldn't want to accidentally drop anyone in it. You have ammo?'

Asher pulled two boxes out of the second drawer. 'That's two hundred rounds. I'll throw in a couple of extra magazines. If that's not enough, you should probably have something bigger, and some backup. All in, let's call it two grand.'

Palmer handed over two thousand dollars and put everything in his jacket. 'Thanks, man. It's been a pleasure doing business.'

Asher held out a matchbook with *Ernie's Sports Bar* printed on the front and a phone number. 'If you need anything, give me a call.'

'Thanks.'

'And say hello to Cody for me.'

Palmer nodded. 'I will.' He emptied his beer and walked back through the bar, nodding to the drunk by the door as he left.

He made his way back to the hotel via a few extra stops. He bought water, energy drinks, protein bars, and a sizeable first aid kit along with painkillers and antiseptic. There was no way of knowing what condition the hostages were in physically and mentally, or what these people had done to them. They already knew that Simone Kalu was missing a finger. The removal won't have been carried out by a doctor in clinical conditions. Palmer had seen hostages mutilated before and the wounds were always infected. Their first stop after the handover would be the nearest hospital. If everything went to plan.

Back in his room, he sat at the desk and, in between stints of watching the other side of the river, loaded the Glock and taped it in the bottom of the first aid kit. The bandages, plasters, and creams were then packed around and on top of it so that any casual check wouldn't spot it. He hid the two extra magazines in emptied out protein bar wrappers and put them in the bottom of his backpack with one of the hotel's hand towels. The water and energy drink went on top, then he tied up the bag and closed the Velcro fastening on the flap.

His next job was something he did whenever he was working. He wrapped his passport and cash in clingfilm and put it all inside a waterproof bag. It was a bit over the top, but it was an old habit and it had saved his life at least once. If everything went wrong, he had the means to get out of the country.

He had prepared as much as he could. There was little chance of being able to shoot his way out with the hostages, but he might be able to hold the kidnappers off until help arrived. With any luck, it would be a simple exchange, and everyone would leave happy. He checked his watch. He had thirty minutes to get to his arranged rendezvous with Buttermill. Time to go to work.

Chapter 13

Palmer walked to the far end of the bridge and stood at the side of the road. He had parked the car at a shopping mall and left the keys on top of the front tyre. He could have arranged to meet Buttermill closer to the exchange, but something was nagging at him. There were too many questions he couldn't answer. Not just where Carver was getting twenty million from, and who the pro was keeping an eye on the weekend warriors' stakeout, but why would a bunch of redneck survivalists kidnap Carver's family anyway? If they asked him nicely, Carver would probably have given them money. Palmer's head was spinning trying to make sense of it all. He needed to focus. It was too late to figure it out now. That would be for another time.

He checked his watch, Buttermill was late. Palmer hated that. Like most people who had spent time in the military, he had a deep-seated anxiety about being late for anything. In combat, being late could cost lives. He knew Buttermill couldn't be trusted. None of them could. It started to rain again, perfect.

Palmer fastened his jacket and turned up the collar. It looked like they were in for another downpour the same as the previous night. That could make things interesting. It would be dark, and visibility would be poor. People can get jittery when they aren't sure what is going on. At least he wouldn't be crawling through the grass this time. He checked his watch again, come on.

A set of headlights rounded the bend, sparkling in the raindrops and throwing shadows across the grass verge. A red saloon pulled in at the side of the road, splashing Palmer's legs in the process. The driver's window rolled down a couple of inches and Nate Buttermill peered out. 'You lookin' for a lift, sweetheart.'

Palmer shook his head. 'Prick.' He walked round to the passenger side and climbed in, staring at Buttermill as he slammed the door. 'You're late, numb nuts.'

'Yeah, well, I got held up on something.'

'Don't tell me, there was a queue at the Ku Klux Klan cookout.'

'Fuck you.'

Palmer enjoyed baiting Buttermill, but they had to get a move on. 'Just drive, Buttercup.'

'It's Buttermill. Nate Buttermill.'

'Yeah, whatever.' Palmer pointed ahead of them. 'It's that way.'

Buttermill floored the accelerator and spun the wheels as he pulled back onto the road. He shook his head and muttered to himself.

Palmer took his phone out of his damp jacket pocket and wiped the moisture off it. He pulled a waterproof bag out of his backpack, slipped the phone in, and put it back into his top pocket.

Buttermill watched him. 'What's the idea behind that? Some secret agent trick to stop you being tracked.'

'No, it's a secret agent trick to stop it getting wet in the rain, dickhead. Look, I don't like people like you, and you don't like me, so why don't we cut the small talk until we get to the exchange site, okay?'

They drove the rest of the journey in silence. Palmer closed his eyes and went through everything in his head over and over. The clearing, the access road, escape routes, it had been a few years since he had done this, and the hostages' lives depended on him getting it right. He didn't want to put them at any more risk than they already were.

The car bounced as Buttermill pulled off the road and into the clearing. 'Here we are, what now?'

Palmer opened his eyes. 'We wait until we get our instructions. The kidnappers control what happens, they hold all the cards. Remember, you are the money man, I'm just a medic that the family brought in to confirm the hostages are alive and healthy.'

'Why do we need a story?'

Palmer didn't believe the guy was this dim. 'Because if they think I'm just a medic, they might not watch me as closely as they would if they knew who I really am. If I'm the medic, they'll have to let me see the hostages so they can get their money.'

The realisation dawned on Buttermill's face. 'Right, got it.'

'Just do your job and watch my back.'

Two sets of headlights appeared at the entrance to the clearing. One vehicle, a dark coloured pickup, looped around and parked twenty feet away. The men who got out weren't the two from the other night or the pro. These two were smartly dressed in suits and raincoats. They wore silver tipped cowboy boots and had slicked back hair. They each carried a small umbrella and walked around to stand in front of the vehicle.

The second vehicle, a large SUV, parked behind the pickup and switched off its lights. The six men who got out were the muscle. They were dressed for the weather, but not in combats. They were armed with submachine guns, not AR-15s. These men were nothing like the weekend warriors. Palmer was getting a bad feeling about this. Who were these guys and where were the rednecks? Where was the pro?

One of the men from the pickup gestured for Buttermill and Palmer to get out of the car. Buttermill switched off the wipers and took out the keys. 'You ready?'

Palmer turned to look at him. 'Remember our story. Keep your eyes on the two suits. Nothing will happen until they give the go ahead. Follow the plan, and we might just get out of this alive.'

For the first time, Buttermill grasped what was at stake. 'You really think this could go bad?'

'How much do you trust Carver? I'm sure it'll be fine. Just don't do anything stupid to spook these guys.'

Buttermill's mouth hung open. He looked worried.

'Are you up for this, Nate?'

He nodded.

'Good. Let's get it done.'

Chapter 14

The rain was bouncing off the roof when they opened the doors and got out. Palmer wished he had brought an umbrella. He looked over at Buttermill. He must be wishing he had brought anything other than the flimsy jacket he had on. Water ran in rivulets across the ground, bubbled over their feet like they were standing in a stream, and pooled in the tracks left by the pickup's tyres. The men from the SUV didn't look happy, Buttermill looked like a drowned rat. Palmer didn't care, he had a job to do. He slung his backpack over his shoulders, picked up the plastic first aid kit, and squelched his way towards the two men.

It was only when they got close to the pickup that the nagging doubts in Palmer's head went into overdrive and set off Big Ben sized alarm bells. All the men, the suits, the muscle, looked South American. The way they looked, the way they were dressed, Palmer would say these guys were trigger men for a gang. They might not be a southern cartel, but it was a good bet that they were affiliated with one. It didn't matter who it was, each was as brutal as the next. One thing they wouldn't do was use rednecks as muscle or hire a pro to look after security, they did their own. The kidnapping was starting to make more sense now. Cartels had been using kidnap and ransom as a source of income for decades.

Palmer looked at Buttermill and gestured towards the two suited men. 'Tell them who we are.'

Buttermill cleared his throat. 'I am a representative of George H. Carver.' He pointed at Palmer. 'This man is a medic brought in to confirm the health of the hostages before the handover.' He sounded like he was auditioning for the school play.

Suit number one called over the muscle. One of them patted down Buttermill then turned his attention to Palmer. He patted him down then checked the backpack.

'All good, just drinks and protein bars.'

The muscle pointed at the first aid kit. 'Open it.'

Palmer looked at the two suits. 'It's medical equipment. Bandages, medicine. I don't want to get it wet.'

'Open it.'

Palmer made a big fuss of cracking open the lid while he shielded the contents from the rain. The muscle shone a torch into the kit, had a cursory poke at some of the bandages then shrugged.

Suit number one nodded, Palmer had got away with it. His heart started to beat a little slower. Suit number two lifted a phone and made a call. Almost immediately, a third vehicle arrived at the clearing. It was another black SUV. As it drove in, two more guards took up position on the access road, blocking it off. No one was getting in or out until this was over.

The third vehicle drove down the slope, passed all the other cars and stopped ten feet from the edge of the plateau. It was an obvious tactic and one that Palmer had fully expected. They were splitting Buttermill and him up in case they tried anything. Palmer nodded to Buttermill then set off across the clearing.

Palmer's main instructions were simple. Carver wanted to know that his family were alive, and he wanted pictures to prove it. He stopped short of the SUV and waited for the driver to move out of the way. He must have been told to join his buddies while the exchange was taking place. They were getting their money, there was no need to make things any shittier for Simone and Zahrah Kalu. Palmer was encouraged by that. These kidnappers didn't look like they were planning to screw them over. Palmer put his Bluetooth headset into his ear. They were all joining the same group call. No one could hide anything. Everyone would know exactly what was going on step by step. He made sure his phone had connected and moved up to the car.

Simone Kalu was laid out across the back seat of the SUV. She was in a bad way. Her left hand was wrapped in a makeshift bandage, and she looked like she had a fever. Zahrah Kalu sat in the front passenger seat. She was shaking. Maybe from the cold but more likely because she was terrified.

Palmer handed her an energy drink and put his hand on her arm. 'I'm a medic. I'm here to help you, okay?'

The girl nodded but looked like she wasn't taking any of it in. Her eyes were glazed, and tears ran down her face.

'I'm just going to look at your mum first, okay?'

Again, the girl nodded but with the same vacant stare.

Palmer opened the back door and knelt beside Simone. 'How are you doing, Simone?'

She grabbed Palmer's arm and tried to sit up. 'Make sure my daughter is safe.'

'It's okay, I'm here to help. I'll make sure you both get home.'

She gripped Palmer's arm harder. 'Promise me, you'll keep my daughter safe.'

'I do, I promise. We're all going to get out of here and get you to a hospital.' He opened the first aid kit and gave Simone two painkillers and something to help with the fever. He unwrapped the dressing from her hand and examined the wound. It was ragged and still seeping. Whatever they had cut her finger off with wasn't surgically sharp. Palmer washed it with anti-septic then applied a clean bandage. He checked her pulse and took her temperature. She needed to be seen by a doctor, quickly. As Palmer put the first aid kit away, he took out the Glock and tucked it into his waistband.

'Show me pictures.'

The voice in Palmer's ear belonged to Carver. He didn't ask how Simone and Zahrah Kalu were or try to comfort them in any way. He just wanted to see pictures. Maybe it was the stress, it had a strange effect on some people. Maybe seeing the pictures would calm Carver down. Palmer was still giving him the benefit of the doubt, but he was skating on thin ice.

'You can wait until I've treated them and made sure everything is okay.'

He gave Simone a bottle of water then moved back to talk to Zahrah. 'I want you to take some deep breaths and try to stay calm. I'm going to get you out of here.'

This time Zahrah Kalu smiled and nodded. She looked a little more aware of where she was.

'Can you tell me your name?'

'It… it's Zahrah.'

'That's good Zahrah. Now, whatever happens in the next few minutes, I don't want you to panic, everything will be okay. I need you to stay calm and follow instructions. Can you do that for me?'

Zahrah nodded again.

Palmer rubbed her shoulder. 'Good girl.'

Nate Buttermill had his phone on hands free so the suits could hear what Carver was saying. 'The memory stick you have been given allows access to an account which has twenty million dollars in it. All you need is the password to get the money. Before you think of beating it out of my man, he doesn't know what it is. As soon as I know that my family are alive and well, I'll tell you what it is. Over to you Mr Palmer.'

If Palmer could have reached down the phone and beaten Carver to a bloody tattooed pulp, he would have. Never, never use actual names. For fuck's sake, it gave the kidnappers someone to look for if it went wrong. He pulled his phone out of its plastic bag and switched on the camera.

Palmer started with Simone Kalu. He zoomed in on her face and got her to say her name and the date.

Carver sounded uncaring. 'What about the girl?'

Palmer was going to punch him square in the face if he ever saw him again. He moved around to the driver's side and filmed Zahrah as she also said her name and the date.'

'Get her to sit square on to the camera. I want to see it's her.'

Palmer moved his position rather than get Zahrah to pose to order.

'That's it. Now, zoom in a little.'

Christ, what was he doing? Palmer had had enough. 'That's it. Do the exchange. I have patients who need hospital treatment.' He put his phone back in its bag and put it into his pocket. He spoke to Zahrah Kalu calmly. 'I'm just going over there to make sure everything is okay. I'll be right back and then we'll go home.'

'Thank you.' Zahrah was starting to look more normal, less terrified.

Palmer walked back up the slope, listening to the call. Carver was still talking about pictures, going over them again and again. Palmer butted in. 'They're alive, pay the ransom.'

Suit One had handed the memory stick to a young man who was sitting in the pickup. He had it plugged in and had brought up the account's login screen. The suit spoke for the first time. 'Your man is correct Señor Carver. Pay the ransom.'

His accent was Latin American. Palmer was right, these weren't rednecks. Who the hell were the weekend warriors he'd bumped into? They can't have just been out for a little exercise. He looked up to where Nate Buttermill was standing with the other suit, and something caught his eye. A red flash over to the right-hand side.

Suit One was getting agitated. 'Give us the password now, Carver, or they all die.'

He waved at the group of muscle that stood by the other SUV. One of them turned and started to walk towards Palmer. It was going wrong. Palmer knew he shouldn't have got mixed up in this. He stepped towards Simone and Zahrah. There it was again, a red flash over on the right. 'Give them the password, Carver.'

Carver shouted into his phone. 'Valkyrie.'

Chapter 15

P almer had seen a lot of action in Afghanistan and always got the same feeling just before the shooting started. Whether it was fear, excitement, or simply a fight or flight response, he wasn't sure, but when he saw the tell-tale red line of a laser sight picked out by the raindrops at the edge of the clearing, he knew what was coming.

The red dot settled on the back of Suit One's head, and he fell to the ground. Suit Two pulled out the most blinged-out, gold-plated Colt 45 Palmer had ever seen and shot Nate Buttermill in the centre of his forehead. At almost the same time, a second shot from the laser sighted sniper brought Suit Two's bad day to an even worse end.

Palmer ran back to the SUV. 'Stay down.'

The Cartel's men were all crouched behind their car firing blindly into the trees at assailants they couldn't see. A hail of machine gun fire returned from whoever was in the woods, shredding the vehicle's tyres and shattering the windows. From the number of rounds that were being fired, Palmer knew there must be at least ten heavily armed men up there.

The man who had been walking towards Palmer dropped to one knee and opened up with his sub-machine gun, raking the SUV with a stream of bullets. A single shot from Palmer was enough to stop the man, but the damage was done. Simone Kalu had taken two bullets to the chest, her unseeing eyes staring back at Palmer as he looked through the shattered window.

Carver was screaming. 'Buttermill, what's going on? Buttermill?'

Palmer pulled the headset out of his ear. He didn't need to hear any more. He had been set up. He looked back up the slope as the mystery assailants broke cover and came out of the trees. Ten or twelve men, all wearing combats and carrying AR-15s were emptying their magazines into the Cartel's SUV. At the back of the group was the pumpkin smuggler, trying to keep up as usual. These were Carver's men. The old bastard had set up an ambush and dropped Palmer and Buttermill right in the middle of it.

Palmer ran to the SUV. There were no keys in the ignition. There was no time to frisk the driver. Palmer released the hand brake. 'Get your head down.'

He pushed as hard as he could, his feet slipping in the mud as he tried to get the car to move. 'COME ON!'

Behind him, the Pro came out of the trees and levelled his rifle.

Palmer saw the red dot reflect in the window and ducked. The high-velocity bullet smashed into the side of the car and destroyed the wing mirror. Palmer pushed harder. If he could use the car as a shield, he might get them to the trees.

The car started to move inch by inch then gravity caught it. Palmer jumped into the driver's seat and ducked down. The car built up speed as another bullet came in through the rear window, went over Palmer's head, and shattered the windscreen on the way out. Palmer tried to steer, but without

69

the keys in the ignition, the steering lock stopped him.

Behind them, the muscle were holding their own. They had driven the rednecks back into the trees and the pro had taken cover. It wouldn't last though. The rednecks had more people and more ammunition, it was just a matter of time before they prevailed.

Palmer looked over the dashboard, they were no longer heading for the trees. The car was skidding sideways in the mud towards the edge of the plateau. If he had been on his own, he would have rolled out of the door and taken his chances. He grabbed Zahrah Kalu's arm. 'Put your seat belt on, NOW!'

The SUV was a solidly built car, it could take a ten-foot drop. Its crumple zones were designed to absorb impact in a collision. This would be no different, just more vertical. It might hurt, but they would be out of sight. As they reached the edge, the front wheels dug in, and the car started to turn. The back wheels went off the plateau first and the car hung, for what seemed like an age, before it tipped over and went down backwards.

Palmer braced himself. 'HOLD ON!'

Zahrah Kalu screamed and pushed herself back in her seat, her head against the rest.

The impact was harder than Palmer was expecting. The windows that weren't already broken, shattered. The body-work crumpled and one of the back doors sprung open. They came to rest for a couple of seconds then, with the sound of metal scraping over rocks, the car tipped onto its roof. It slid a few feet further down the slope and rolled onto its side then, with a clunk, it came to rest at the foot of a large tree.

Back on the plateau, the Cartel's soldiers were done, and

the shooting had stopped. Palmer didn't know if any of them had escaped but, if they had, their bosses would know what had happened. They had lost men. They had lost money. George H. Carver had double crossed them, and they would be looking for retribution.

Chapter 16

I nside the car, the only sound was the rain hitting the bodywork. Palmer shook his head. He checked his arms and legs, nothing felt broken. He had added a few more bruises and his painkillers would be taking a hit in the morning, but the adrenaline was masking the pain for now.

He looked on the back seat, Simone Kalu had gone. She had been thrown clear as they tipped over the cliff. Palmer hoped she wasn't lying just outside the car. He had to get Zahrah out and safe. He couldn't afford any hold ups.

He undid his seatbelt and checked on her. She had a trickle of blood on her head but, otherwise, looked okay. 'Can you move?'

Zahrah nodded. 'I think so. Where's Mom?'

'You can't help her now, Zahrah. We have to get you out of here.'

'No, NO! MOM!'

Palmer put his finger to his lips. 'Shhh. I know it hurts, but, right now, your life is in danger. Your mom made me promise to look after you, yes?'

Zahrah nodded.

'Good. Now, unfasten your seatbelt and follow me out the window.'

They climbed out of the wrecked body of the car, through the broken glass, and took shelter behind it. Palmer checked his pockets; his gun was still in the car. 'Shit.'

'What is it?'

'Don't move, I'll be right back.' Palmer kicked out the shattered windscreen and crawled back inside the SUV. His backpack was right in front of him, all he wanted was the ammunition. He took out the magazines and zipped them into his jacket. His weapon had been in his hand when he jumped in the car, but there was no sign of it. He checked the footwells, the dashboard, and under the seats, nothing.

Above them, the pro was barking instructions. 'Find the other SUV. If they're dead, I want the bodies. No one does anything without me... Go.'

Palmer crawled over to the back. He ran his hands around the seat cushions and under the mats, still nothing. If the gun had been thrown out of the window, he would never find it. There was one place left to look. He removed the headrest from the back seat, to give himself more room, and squeezed through to the back.

Palmer knelt on the broken glass that used to be the side window and looked at Simone Kalu's broken body. She was lying half in and half out of the car. Her legs sticking out of the side window, her torso crushed by the weight of the SUV. Palmer brushed the glass from her face and closed her eyes. 'I'll look after her, I swear.' He lifted Simone's arm, picked up the Glock from where it had fallen and tucked it into his belt.

The Pro shouted, 'Palmer... Palmer. We're here to help.'

Palmer squeezed his way back through to the front of the SUV and out of the windscreen. Zahrah sat with her back against the roof of the car and her knees pulled up to her chest, exactly where he had left her.

'Palmer… We just want to take the girl home. You've done a good job, you'll get paid.'

The pro was trying to get them to give it up. He wanted the easy option. Carver wanted the girl alive. Palmer knew that he was dead the minute he broke cover. They didn't need him. 'What the fuck are you doing? Why are you trying to kill us?'

'It was a mistake, Palmer. Things got pretty hectic there for a minute. Fog of war, you know how it goes.'

Palmer shook his head. The pro had deliberately targeted them. There was nothing panicked or accidental about it. 'Fuck you.'

Bullets began to ping off the underside of the car. Zahrah hugged her knees tighter and began to cry.

Palmer took out his weapon and fired two aimed shots, taking down one of the rednecks. 'That should keep their heads down.'

He was right, all of them hit the deck and crawled back from the edge. All except the Pro. He looked at the cowering men with disgust. 'Amateurs. Palmer… If you walk away, I'll let you live. I just want the girl and her mother. Carver just wants them at home and safe. He's told me to do whatever it takes. I'll give you a couple of minutes to think about it.'

Palmer looked all around them. It was at least a hundred feet to any real tree cover, left and right. There was no going back up to the plateau and in front of them was a drop to the river. 'Can you swim?'

'What?'

'Can you swim? That's our exit. We run as fast as we can straight in front and jump into the river.'

Zahrah sat up and tried to see down to the water. 'Are you

crazy? How far is it?'

'It's only a few feet. Like jumping off the diving board at a swimming pool. You've done that before, haven't you?'

'Yes, but… I can't. What about Mom.'

Palmer turned and held Zahrah's hand. He looked into her eyes. 'There's nothing we can do for your mom. Do you want to go with them, do you want to be with your grandfather?'

Zahrah shook her head.

'What would your mom tell you to do?'

Zahrah took a deep breath. 'She'd tell me to jump.'

'Damn right she would. Okay, when I shout go, you run. Don't stop, don't hesitate, and do not wait for me. Run as fast as you can and jump into the river. You got it?'

Zahrah nodded.

The Pro was back at the edge. 'Palmer… Times up. I haven't got all night. What's your answer?'

Palmer looked at Zahrah. 'After three… One… Two… THREE!'

Zahrah sprang to her feet and ran. Palmer stood up, emptied his magazine in the direction of the rednecks, and ran after her.

The Pro got off his knees and shouted, 'Kill them both, NOW!'

The rednecks opened fire, but it was too late. Palmer and Zahrah had already reached the drop. Without slowing down, without hesitating or breaking stride, they threw themselves into the void and fell towards the river.

* * *

Carver jumped out of his chair, knocking it over, and slammed his fist into the desk. 'How can they have got away?'

The Pro spoke calmly. 'Just what I said, Palmer and the girl threw themselves off the cliff edge and into the river. What do you expect me to do, follow them?'

'Get down there, they have to come out somewhere. You can pick them up.'

'Unless they're dead.'

'Then get a boat, use divers if you have to, I don't care how you do it. Find the girl. What about the mother?'

The pro paused. 'She's dead. She took a couple of bullets in the fire-fight.'

'I want her body and all of her belongings back here.'

'I'll arrange that. By the way, your man, Buttermill, is dead.'

Carver let out a sigh then spoke through gritted teeth. 'I'm sure someone will be upset by that, just find the girl. That's what I'm paying you for.' He hung up and threw the phone across the room.

Cody Wickes kicked the door open. 'What the hell are you doing? It was all set up, all you had to do was pay the ransom.'

Carver smiled. 'Twenty million… that's a great deal of money.'

'You never had it, did you? You sent Palmer in there as a distraction, you had no intention of paying them the money. You set him up.'

Carver pointed an accusatory finger at Wickes. 'All your man had to do was take pictures then stay out of the way.'

Wickes stepped forward, threatening. 'Do you care about them at all? Do you realise what you've done?'

Carver pulled a nine-millimetre from a holster under his jacket and pointed it at Wickes. 'I'm just getting started. I am going to find them, and you're going to help me.'

Chapter 17

Palmer hit the water hard but, thankfully, he didn't hit the bottom. There was no way of knowing how deep the water was before they jumped. He and Zahrah could have been seriously injured or even killed but staying where they were would have been a worse choice.

He broke the surface without making a sound. Years of Royal Marine training had given him the confidence to operate in open water without panicking. He looked around, it was pitch dark and there was no sign of Zahrah. The only sound was that of the running water that was dragging him downstream. He ducked back under, but visibility was non-existent, he could barely see five feet. Back on the surface, he took a deep breath, ready to go down again, when Zahrah popped up twenty feet from him.

She was breathing in gasps, desperately trying to gulp down air. She thrashed her arms as she tried to stay on the surface. He could see that she was struggling. It wasn't that she couldn't swim, it was that she was panicking. Sudden immersion in cold water can trigger a shock response that causes involuntary inhalation. When someone who hasn't been trained for this starts to take in water, that's when panic sets in. Palmer swam towards her as fast as he could but before he could grab her, she disappeared below the water again.

He dived, angling down to where he had calculated she would be and reached out in front, blindly grasping the water, until his fingers brushed against something. Whatever it was, he grabbed it, he knew this was the only chance he would have. He kicked his legs and pushed for the surface until he appeared above the water, dragging Zahrah coughing and spluttering into the night air behind him.

Palmer supported Zahrah as they floated along in the current giving her time to recover and take in air. He knew they were safe for now and that the river was putting distance between them and the pro, but it wouldn't last long. He didn't know why they wanted Zahrah so badly that they would risk killing her, but they wouldn't give up easily. No one puts that much firepower into something and then simply walks away. He had to get them somewhere safe so he could think and plan their next move. He started using his right arm to steer them in the direction of the bank and out of the fast-flowing centre of the river. If he could get them out of the water and back to his car, he could put hundreds of miles between them and Carver.

As they rounded a bend, the bridge that he had used to get from the hotel to the exchange came into view. It looked like it was still a mile further along, but he could clearly make it out in the darkness. The bridge was lit up by the headlights of several vehicles.

'Zahrah, are you okay?'

Her breathing was quieter, and she had stopped fighting to stay afloat. 'I'm good. I just got a shock when I hit the water, breathed a load of it in and started to cough. I couldn't swim like that.'

'I need you to swim with me now. We have to get to the bank and hide until we can find a way out. Can you do that?'

'I'd like to get out. I've had enough of water for now.'

With Palmer still holding on to her hoodie, they both paddled towards the bank. Palmer kept an eye on how close they were getting to the bridge but didn't tell her he was worried. He thought she had been scared enough.

After ten minutes of fighting their way across the current, Palmer's feet touched the bottom. They both stood and climbed their way up the slippery bank into the tangled undergrowth that ran along the river. With arms and legs aching, and water pouring out of their sodden clothes, they collapsed, both breathing heavily.

Palmer was the first to recover and sit up. He crawled back to the river's edge and looked at the bridge. They had made it to the bank with four hundred meters to spare. Any closer and they might have been visible in the water. Although the vehicles on the bridge were just a series of silhouettes, Palmer was sure that one of them was the grey panel van that the weekend warriors had used. On top of that, the man that was leaning on the handrail scanning the surface of the river, looked like The Pro. Or was Palmer just being paranoid? The most worrying thing that Palmer saw was the two vehicles with blue flashing lights.

Palmer should have been able to go to the police and feel safe. He should have been able to walk into any station and know that they would be taken care of. In fact, that was his first escape plan. If Carver had contacts in local law enforcement, which wouldn't have been out of the question, Palmer didn't know who he could trust. White supremacists existed in almost all walks of life. It was a sad reflection on how the world was, and Carver was relying on it to get him elected.

Palmer calculated that they were around two miles from where he had parked the car. It would be a hard slog in the rain, keeping out of sight, but at least they were on the right side of the river.

'We have to go. We need to get back to my car and get away from here. We'll change cars once we're clear. Are you ready?'

'I can do it. Just show me where we need to go.'

Palmer helped her to her feet. 'Keep your head low and follow me. One foot in front of the other and keep going.'

'Wait.'

Palmer turned back round, checking the bridge to make sure they hadn't alerted anyone. 'What is it?'

Zahrah was feeling around her neck and looking at the ground. 'My necklace, where's my necklace?'

'Leave it, it doesn't matter.'

'No, my dad gave me that, it's all I have of him.' She was on her hands and knees, frantically running her fingers through the mud.

Palmer should have grabbed her arm and dragged her off, but he could see how much it meant to her. She had lost everything that had meaning in her life, the necklace was all she had left. He joined her on the floor, retracing their path out of the river, looking for a cheap necklace that, right now, was the most valuable thing in the world.

They searched for several minutes, but it was taking too long, they had to leave. Palmer looked at the bridge again, there was movement and one of the vehicles left. 'We can't do this, Zahrah. Let's go.' He grabbed her arm, but she pulled free.

'NO!'

The shout was loud enough to be heard downstream. This could get out of Palmer's control fast. He had to do something. He grabbed the back of Zahrah's hoodie and dragged her away from the riverbank. She twisted and swung her arm at him. Palmer held tight and pulled harder. As he did, the necklace fell out of Zahrah's hood.

She grabbed it, squeezing her hand tight. 'That's it. I told you I wouldn't lose it, Dad.'

Palmer put his hands on her shoulders. 'Put it somewhere safe and let's get out of here.'

Zahrah smiled. 'Okay, I'm ready now.'

They crawled up to the top of the bank and away from the river.

* * *

On the bridge, the pro watched the water that flowed down the river on its way to the Gulf of Mexico. He played the column of light from his torch across the surface looking for any sign of Palmer. Carver wanted him dead, and the girl picked up. He didn't know why, and he didn't care.

He knew Palmer wasn't just an ex-Royal Marine. He was ex-special forces and wouldn't be stupid enough to get caught like this, but the pro had to make it look like he was doing everything he could to find them. None of this made any sense. If Carver had the local sheriff in his pocket, why was he even here? Why didn't Carver just use his police contacts from the start? What was the old man hiding?

The pro knew that searching the river was a waste of time, if they spotted them in the dark, it would be pure luck. If they waited until daylight, it would be too late. They were more likely to find Palmer well away from here in a few days, once he had relaxed and assumed he and the girl were safe. Until then, the pro would go through this pantomime so that the amateurs could report back to their boss, then he would get on with the job he had been brought here for.

Chapter 18

Anna Riley knocked on Victoria Thomson's office door and went in. Thomson was, unofficially, number two at MI6. Her boss, Edward Lancaster, trusted her implicitly. She was party to some information that others weren't. Lancaster saw her as a confidante, and that made her unpopular in some circles, but she didn't care. The Service was her life.

Riley knew that Thomson participated in all aspects of the Service's operations and anyone who wanted to speak to the boss, had to speak to her first. That meant that if Palmer was involved in anything for MI6, official or otherwise, she would know.

Thomson looked up from her laptop and gave a broad smile. 'Anna. Please, come in. It feels like I haven't seen you for ages. Have a seat.'

Riley closed the office door and sat in a soft chair off to one side of the desk. 'Thanks.'

Thomson sat in the soft chair beside Riley. 'How've you been? Is everything okay?'

'Yes, thank you. I've been taking some time off in between visits to Yardley Manor. My therapist says I'm well on the way to... Well, on the way to not being as messed up as I was.

I'm still on a little medication though.'

Thomson placed her hand on Riley's arm. 'You've been through a lot, it's okay to be not okay. Are you sure you're happy being back in the office?'

'I couldn't stay at home any longer. I was going stir crazy. It's just a couple of days a week at the moment, mainly paperwork.'

'That's good. Just don't try to do too much all at once. We can't afford to lose you.'

Riley blushed. Although she didn't think of herself as a complete mess anymore, her self-confidence wasn't where it should be. She didn't quite understand why they valued her so much. 'I won't, and I won't go off on my own chasing phantom bad guys again. I promised I'd let you know if I thought I was reading too much into something. Seeing things that weren't there.'

'You said on the phone that you needed to speak off the record.'

Riley nodded. 'That's right. It's about Logan Palmer, is he working for us?'

'We haven't spoken to him since his son's funeral. We thought it would be better to let him work things out and come back in his own time. Have you heard from him?'

'He sent me an anonymous email asking me to do a little background on someone. A man with a lot of underworld connections. Someone who looks like an absolute nightmare to get involved with. I got Logan to ring me, and he's definitely working for someone.'

'Where is he?'

Riley passed over a yellow Post-it note. 'I traced the call. It was from that diner in Texas. I thought he was still in Indonesia.'

'Do you think this is something that we should be involved in?'

'I'm not sure, not yet. It's just that... if Logan isn't working for us then he might be on his own. If he isn't, why contact me for information?'

Thomson paused, looking at the diner's address. 'Palmer isn't an official MI6 asset. He's a private citizen. We can't help him.'

'But...'

Thomson held up her hand and looked at the diner's address again. 'What's he up to this time? Look, he's still one of ours and we will need him again. I'll put a few feelers out, see if any other agencies are using him. In the meantime, you're only in the office two days a week. Use the rest of your time to do some research, find out what you can. Don't go to anyone else with this. If anyone questions what you're doing, send them to see me.'

Riley made a gesture as if zipping her lips closed. 'I'll keep it secret. Just between you and me. Thank you.'

Thomson looked at her watch and sighed. 'I've got to go now. I'm briefing the foreign secretary while Edward is away. Bloody politicians, pain in the arse.'

Riley stood. 'I'll keep you up to date on anything I find.'

'When it all quietens down a little, we'll go for lunch and catch up properly.'

'That would be nice.' Riley opened the door and left the office.

Chapter 19

Palmer knelt between a parked van and a stinking dumpster outside a fast-food joint. The smell of rotting food and grease was overpowering, even the rats were staying clear. He looked down and crushed a cockroach under his foot, nothing was keeping them away. He seemed to be dealing with a lot of cockroaches recently.

His rental car was parked across the street under a broken streetlight. It was next to the photocopying shop that occupied the corner lot of the small shopping mall. He had been watching it for over an hour now. There was no sign of movement, and the car park was only overlooked by business premises. It was unlikely that anyone had had time to set up a stakeout, even if they knew the car was his, but he couldn't be too careful.

He turned to Zahrah and spoke in a whisper. 'When I give you the go, we're running over to the car, as quickly, but as quietly, as we can. Once we're in the car, I want you to tuck yourself into the footwell and stay there until I say it's okay. Are you ready?'

Zahrah got to her feet. 'Ready.'

Palmer checked along the street for any vehicles and took out his Glock, just in case. 'Three... two... one... go.'

They stayed low and stuck to the shadows as much as possible, which wasn't easy while they were crossing the street. They crouched behind the car park's perimeter fence and followed it around to the car. There was still no sign of movement, and no one seemed to be watching them. Palmer retrieved the keys from the top of the tyre, and they climbed in.

Zahrah followed her instructions and sat in the passenger footwell looking up at Palmer. He kept his head down, constantly scanning the street, as he pushed the keys into the ignition. Before he could turn the key, a vehicle turned left onto the road and drove towards them. At first, he thought it was the panel van again, but, as he looked closer, he realised that this one had a logo on its side and the words *Office Cleaning*. The van slowed, turned into the car park, and stopped twenty feet from them outside a real estate agent's office.

Palmer looked at Zahrah. 'Stay down. We'll wait until they're inside.'

The cleaners took no time at all to unload their equipment. Palmer watched as they switched on the office's lights and got to work. As soon as he was sure they weren't paying any attention to the outside, he turned the key in the ignition and crept out onto the road.

Palmer didn't know exactly where they were heading, but he had to get out of Texas. This was Carver's power base, and he held all the cards. The fastest route out of the state would take them past Houston and into Louisiana. It was a risk, but he also had to check in with Cody Wickes. Palmer didn't believe that he was involved in this, which meant he was in danger. If Wickes had managed to get out of harm's way, he might have a safe house they could use. Palmer turned on the headlights and headed east.

Zahrah climbed out of the footwell and put on her seatbelt. 'What are we going to do?'

'We can't go to the police, at least not around here. Looks like Carver has paid off the locals. We need to find somewhere to hide until we can guarantee your safety. It won't be easy.'

Zahrah pulled off her hoodie and took the necklace out of the pocket. She ran her thumb over the raised pattern on the silver jigsaw piece that hung from the leather cord. 'I can do it. It's what Dad would've wanted.' Her voice faltered. 'It's what Mom would want.' She tried to say something else but the tears that were now flowing down her cheeks stopped her. Instead, she simply nodded.

Palmer squeezed her hand. 'At least our clothes are drying out. Get some sleep. I'll wake you when I find another car.'

Zahrah put the necklace back in her pocket and closed her eyes.

Chapter 20

Cody Wickes raised his head off his chest and rolled his neck from side to side to try to alleviate the stiffness. He didn't know how long he had been asleep or what time of night or day it was. There were no windows in the room he was in. The light was coming from a single industrial light fitting hanging from the ceiling high above his head. His hands were handcuffed and padlocked to the chain that fastened him to the steel girder he was leaning against. He wasn't going anywhere anytime soon.

The steel door opened, and Carver entered the room. He grabbed an old wooden chair from one corner and dragged it across to where Wickes sat. 'Good morning, Cody. I trust you slept well.'

'Fuck you.'

'That's hardly the best way to speak to the man who controls your future.'

'You aren't in control of anything. You only think you are.'

Carver scoffed. 'It doesn't matter what you and Palmer do. The girl is my granddaughter, the authorities will be on my side. Although, there is a way for you to come out of this in one piece, with double the money I was going to pay you. Just to make up for the inconvenience.'

'Don't tell me, all I have to do is set Palmer up for you.'

'Listen, Cody, you barely know the man. You met him less than two weeks ago. Why would you want to lose your life to help him? I'm sure, wherever he is, he's not thinking about you.'

Wickes cleared his throat. 'I need a drink, and something to eat.'

Carver clicked his fingers at the guard who stood at the doorway. 'Get Cody some food and water and unchain him. This isn't how we treat friends.' He handed Wickes his phone. 'I want you to send him a message. Just tell him that you are arranging for him to come in. Tell him you'll send the details later. Tell him not to call you.'

Wickes took the phone and pressed his thumb against the fingerprint sensor. 'It would be easier if I just called him.'

Carver gave him a condescending smirk. 'Maybe I don't trust you enough, just yet.'

Wickes typed in the message and pressed send. He handed the phone back to Carver with a grin. 'And I thought we were friends.'

* * *

Palmer was woken by his phone vibrating in his pocket. He had folded his jacket up, once it was dry, and was using it as a pillow. He took the phone out of its waterproof bag and swiped the screen. The message from Wickes just told him to head for Houston and await further instructions.

Zahrah read the message over his shoulder. 'Does that mean it's nearly over?'

'I wish it did.'

'What do you mean?'

He turned in his seat to face her. 'We don't know the message was actually from Cody. If it was, he might have sent it under duress. We still have to be careful.'

'If you're not sure it's him, why don't we just go somewhere else?'

'He has resources. He'll be able to give us money and maybe somewhere to stay. We can't afford to miss out on a chance like that. It's a risk, but not one that you're going to take. I'll leave you somewhere safe and go on my own.'

'But what if something happens?'

Palmer put the phone back in his pocket. 'I'll make sure it doesn't.'

* * *

Wickes was led out of his cell and into an office where Carver was sitting on a leather couch smoking a large Cuban cigar. He waved to the guard. 'Wait outside. He's not going to try anything.'

The guard left and closed the door.

'So, Cody, they tell me you have a problem with my plan.'

'That's right, it's not going to work.'

Carver blew smoke into the air. 'I get the impression that you're just trying to go back on our deal. Trying to pour a little rain on my parade.'

Wickes looked around at their surroundings. 'I don't know where this is, but why would Palmer come here? He doesn't know it. He knows that I don't have an office in Houston, so where did I suddenly get this from?'

'This isn't something we can do out in the open. If we do

91

this in public, the cops will have to take him in. I don't want that when I can deal with him myself.'

'Look, he's not going to bring the girl to a meeting, so whatever you do, you won't get her. You need to make him feel secure and then follow him. Then, you can take him out away from prying eyes.'

Carver took a draw from his cigar and blew out another stream of smoke. He obviously didn't trust Wickes, but what he was saying did make some sense. If they cornered Palmer, he was a man who would go down fighting rather than give up the girl. 'What are you suggesting?'

'I'll get him to come to my hotel room. He knows where it is, and your trained monkeys can still keep an eye on me. I'll give him the address to a safe house, that you'll know about, and he'll bring the girl to you.'

Carver let out a guttural laugh. 'Holy shit. You really are willing to sell him out. You should come and work for me full time. You'd fit right in.'

'No thanks, I'm happy working for myself. But it's like you said, I barely know the man. Why should I lose my life over this?'

Chapter 21

The hotel that Palmer had booked them into was in his normal mid-priced range, Goldilocks would have been happy with this one, it even had a security guard at reception. He paid for two adjoining rooms for a couple of nights, in cash of course, then he went to the nearby Walmart and bought them some clothes and toiletries. No one paid him any attention, in that part of Southwest Houston, people minded their own business.

He had a shower but left his beard. He had a feeling that they were going to be on the run for a little while, he had to change his appearance. The clothes he bought made him look like any other guy from Texas. Jeans, a Houston Texans t-shirt and an Astros baseball cap. He also picked up some weak reading glasses. They blurred his vision a little, but nothing he couldn't deal with. He would just look over the top of them when he needed to.

He picked up his phone and checked Wickes's message again. The meeting was at a hotel on the other side of Houston, but not for another three hours. He wasn't going to turn up at the time that had been agreed. If he did that, he may as well just turn up waving a flag and hand himself over. He switched the phone off, time to go.

Wearing his new Texan look and sporting his glasses, he knocked on the connecting door to Zahrah's room. When she answered, he almost didn't recognise her. She had changed her hair and made herself up to look three or four years older. She was the spitting image of her mother. It was perfect, anyone looking for her would have a picture of a slightly awkward sixteen-year-old girl, not the confident, young woman who stood in front of him now.

Zahrah looked Palmer up and down. 'You look like a redneck.'

'Thanks. I do my best.'

Zahrah smiled. 'What's the plan for tonight?'

Palmer gave her the rest of the money he had. 'If I'm not back by midnight, don't wait for me. Check out of here and run. Hop on a train and get as far away as you can.'

Zahrah stepped forward and hugged him. 'I don't want to be on my own.'

Palmer wasn't expecting the sudden display of affection. 'You won't be. I'm coming back, I promise.'

She stepped back and wiped away a tear. 'You better.'

Palmer left his room, walked down the hallway and through reception. His sense of purpose was stronger than it had been since the death of his son. He knew what he had to do and why he had to do it. First, he needed to get Zahrah somewhere safe, then he had to find out why Carver wanted her so badly and neutralise the threat. This wasn't just a job anymore. It had become his life's purpose.

* * *

Cody Wickes sat on the bed in his hotel room and watched

94

Carver as he paced up and down. 'You can't be anywhere near the room. If Palmer suspects that this is a set up in any way, he'll run, and you'll never see him again. He's coming here because he needs money, and probably to figure out what's going on. He's bound to turn up early to catch us off guard.'

'I don't like you being alone with him. You could be cooking up anything.'

Wickes held up his phone. 'You'll be listening to everything I say, remember. You've checked what's in the bag and you've got the details of the safe house. You won't even have to follow him. He'll come to you.'

'One of my men will be nearby. If I think you're up to anything, I'll kill you both and tear this city apart looking for the girl.'

Wickes nodded. 'Understood. Tell me, why do you want her so bad? It can't be just to make you look good to voters, and I know you don't care about her.'

'You don't need to know my business. Let's just say there's a lot of money riding on this. Money needed for important projects.'

Wickes raised his eyebrows. 'Look, I'm going to have to sell this to Palmer so don't be surprised if I tell him that.'

'Tell him what you like, he'll never figure it out.'

Wickes couldn't believe Carver's arrogance. He was underestimating Palmer and that could be fatal. Maybe Carver spent so much time surrounded by his hired idiots, that he considered himself to be some kind of genius. 'You should leave now. There's no telling when Palmer will show up.'

Carver looked out of the window. 'Keep your phone switched on and keep the call open. No matter how long it takes.' He turned and marched out of the room.

Wickes closed the door behind him then sat back down on the bed.

There was a knock on the window. Unbeknownst to Wickes and Carver, Palmer had already entered the building. He had worked his way up onto the roof and climbed into the window cleaning cradle. With all of Carver's men looking in the wrong direction, Palmer had manoeuvred down the three floors to the same level as the room and watched the meeting while pretending to clean the windows.

Wickes opened the window just enough for them to hold a conversation. The safety lock stopped him from opening it any further. 'Are you okay, brother?'

'I've been better. What the hell is going on? Why did they kick off like that at the exchange?'

Wickes shook his head. 'There was never any money. He sent you in knowing that he wasn't going to pay the ransom.'

'Bastard. He could have got us all killed. But why go to all that trouble? He doesn't care about the girl. Why not just refuse to pay, bring the police in? Once the story broke, he would have scored just as many points with the public for not bowing down to kidnappers.'

Wickes shrugged. 'I don't know the details. All I could find out is that there is a lot of money involved. How? I don't know.' At least Wickes was able to sound convincing, it was all the truth.

'What are my options from here.'

'You need to figure out the reason he wants Zahrah, if you don't, she'll never be safe. He's informed the police and FBI of the original kidnap and told them that you double crossed him. As far as the cops are concerned, you are now demanding a ransom to release Zahrah.'

'Shit, can it get any worse?'

'Well, you're both witnesses to the whole thing. My bet is, even if he gets what he wants, you're both dead anyway.' He handed Palmer a small holdall. 'There's a hundred grand in there and details of a safe house. You need to run far and fast.'

Palmer took the bag. 'What about you?'

'Don't worry about me, I'm the reason you're in this mess. Don't come back here and don't get in touch, they'll be tapping my phone and watching me. Just get the girl away from Carver.'

Palmer squeezed his hand through the gap. 'Thanks, Cody. I'll see you again when it's all over.'

'It's been a pleasure working with you, Brother. Even if it has been a complete clusterfuck. Just make sure you take the bastard down.' Wickes closed the window and watched as the cradle disappeared up the side of the building. He picked up the phone, it was still connected. 'Did you hear all that…? I've done what you wanted, you just need to go to the safe house and wait.'

* * *

Palmer knocked on Zahrah's door. She answered and immediately hugged him. 'Thank God you're alright. I was so worried.'

'We need to leave, right now. Pack your things.' He went into his room and unzipped the holdall Wickes had given him. The details for the safe house were written on a sheet of paper with a key taped to it. He folded the sheet and put it in the same plastic bag as his passport. He also added another thousand dollars to the bag, for emergencies. He tipped the rest of the money into his backpack and slung it over his shoulders.

Zahrah knocked on the connecting door and walked in. She had loaded what little she had into her own backpack and had put on a hoodie with the hood up. 'I'm ready.'

Palmer took out his phone and threw it on the bed. 'Won't be needing that anymore, too easy to track if the police are involved. Okay, let's go.'

Chapter 22

P almer pulled their panel van into a trailer park just over the border in Louisiana. They had picked it up at a second-hand car dealership outside Houston and it still had the remnants of a building company's logo on the sides. It was a few years old and one of the doors was a different colour to the rest of the bodywork, but the engine was sound. Although a newer vehicle might have been a smoother ride, the main reason Palmer had bought it was that the previous owner had turned the back into a camper. There were a couple of soft seats and a table that turned into two single beds, and a small camping stove that ran from a gas canister. A bracket had been fitted that held two four-gallon water containers, and a small sink that looked like a steel dog bowl. It wasn't luxurious and the only window was in the back door, but it was safer than checking into a motel.

Palmer drove around to the back of the car park and pulled in behind a truck that would screen them from the road. He closed the curtain that ran along a wire behind the front seats, and they climbed in the back. The window in the rear door had been tinted to make it difficult for anyone to see in, but Palmer had also pinned an old sheet over it to be on the safe side. He cranked the handle on one of the wind-up lanterns he had bought and switched it on.

Zahrah was going through the other supplies they had picked up in the camping shop. Sleeping bags, first aid kit, cyalume glow sticks, and a couple of one-gallon containers of water. There were two weeks' worth of sealed military ration packs, useful if they had to carry their kit, and a box full of various tinned foods. She was holding up two tins. 'You want vegetable soup, or beans with sausages in?'

Palmer rubbed his chin and considered the options. 'Definitely the beans.'

'Really?'

'Absolutely. A staple of the British Military. You can eat them cold.'

Zahrah shuddered. 'No thanks. I'll stick to soup.' She poured the contents of the tins into two saucepans and placed them on the stove, then they sat at the table and waited for their dinner to heat up.

Palmer emptied his backpack onto the table. He took two thousand dollars out of the bundle of cash and wrapped the rest in cling film. He kept one thousand as ready cash and handed the other notes to Zahrah. All he kept from his backpack were the Glock, spare magazines, and ammunition. He had a feeling he was going to need those again. Everything else went back in his bag to be thrown away.

Zahrah put two plates onto the table. 'Dinner is served.' She sat back down and dug into her soup. She looked worried. 'Have you got a plan, or do we just run?'

The first thing we do is split the stuff we've bought into the two new bags. If we have to leave the van and move on foot, take one of them with you.'

Zahrah nodded. 'Okay.'

'Cody gave me the address for a safe house.' He held up the key. 'We can hide out there while I make some arrangements, but it won't be a long-term solution. I've got contacts, friends who'll help us. The best thing to do is try to get you out of the country. I'm not sure how far Carver's network goes, but I'm pretty sure it isn't international.'

'Can't we just go to the police in a different state?'

Palmer shook his head. 'This has all the hallmarks of a conspiracy, and we don't know how big it is. If it's organised crime, they could have gangs that are affiliated with them in every state. Unfortunately, some law enforcement agencies have people sympathetic to the white power cause within their ranks too. If we can't get you out of the country, our only real option is the FBI.'

'How do we contact them?'

'We could try a local field office, but that would hand control over to them. We need to do this on our terms. It's probably unavoidable now anyway. We've crossed the state border. If they think I've kidnapped you, that definitely puts it under the FBI's jurisdiction, if it wasn't already.'

Palmer picked up the Glock and expertly field-stripped it. Working meticulously, he cleaned every part and applied a couple of drops of oil where it was needed. One of the advantages of the Glock range of pistols was that they were easy to maintain. That made it perfect for a situation like this and was why military and law enforcement organisations around the world used them. He re-assembled the weapon and made sure the magazines were fully loaded.

Zahrah fished about in her hoodie and pulled out her necklace. 'You don't think you could fix this do you?'

Palmer looked at the necklace, turning it over between his

fingers. It was shaped like a jigsaw piece and made of solid metal. It was silver but had a dull finish. He thought it might be steel, but it was quite light so maybe some kind of alloy. The pattern on the surface was a deep engraving made up of random dots and lines that ended abruptly at the bottom. As if the pattern hadn't been centred properly. It hung from a black leather thong that had a hooked clasp. It was the clasp that had buckled.

Palmer picked up his multi-tool and opened the pliers. 'I think the hook has just bent a bit. If I can bend it back, it should be okay. You might want to get it looked at by an actual jeweller though.' He re-fastened the clasp and tested it for strength. 'There you go.'

'Thanks, I don't want to lose it.'

Palmer held it in the palm of his hand and looked at the pattern again. The series of dots and lines were drawn vertically down the face of the metal. There was something familiar about it. He turned it through ninety degrees and looked again. He got it. 'Your Dad gave you this?'

'That's right. It's all I've got that he gave me. It's all I've got left of him.'

'What does it say?'

Zahrah looked puzzled. 'It doesn't say anything, it's just some random pattern.'

Palmer moved the lamp, so it shone directly onto the necklace. 'It's a long time since I've done this, but these dots and dashes are Morse code.'

'Morse what?'

'Morse code.' He pointed at the pattern. 'You see the way it's made up of dots and dashes?'

Zahrah nodded.

'Just like the ones and zeros in a digital signal. Each combination of dots and dashes means a letter or number. I learned it in the army.'

A flash of understanding showed on her face. 'Like flashing a torch when you're in trouble?'

Palmer nodded. 'Exactly. It's an old system, but it works.' He pointed at the bottom of the jigsaw piece. 'This message is cut off at the bottom though.'

Zahrah nodded. 'Yeah, it carried over onto my mom's.'

Things suddenly clicked into place. It was starting to make sense. Carver's insistence that they were photographed, getting them to pose for the camera. He was trying to make sure that the necklaces were there. The two necklaces were literally the missing jigsaw pieces.

Palmer did his best to decipher the code. He was a little rusty, but he could see that the rows were made up of numbers and letters. The first row looked like the start of a grid reference. If he had to bet, he would say that this led to something that Zahrah's dad had hidden away. Something George Carver was willing to kill to get his hands on. Having met the old man, Palmer reckoned there was probably money involved. 'Was your dad in the military at all?'

'He did some weekends with the National Guard, is that important?'

'It just explains why he might put down a grid reference in Morse code. It's a pity that your grandfather will have the other one, but it also means he won't stop looking for us.'

'Please don't call him my grandfather. He never had anything for us other than hatred for our skin colour.'

Palmer nodded. 'I'm sorry, Zahrah. I won't call him that again.'

'It's okay, Logan. I just never thought of him as part of our family. I don't want to start now.'

'I understand.'

Zahrah smiled. 'What makes you think he's got the other one?'

Palmer looked at her, still worried by the way she was dealing with the death of her mother. Concerned that she might not have accepted it yet. 'When we had to leave your mom, he'll have searched her.'

'But she wasn't wearing it.'

'What?'

'The clasp broke on hers too. I guess my dad wasn't too good at picking out jewellery. She always meant to get it fixed but hadn't got round to it.'

Palmer handed the necklace back to Zahrah. What he really wanted to do was keep it in his emergency stash so they didn't lose it, but he could see that she wanted to wear it. 'Do you know where your mum's necklace is?'

'It's at our house. We had a safe in the garage floor. Dad had it put in. Mom always kept it in there.'

'Is it well hidden?'

'Yeah, if you don't know where it is, there's no way you're finding it.'

The smart thing to do was to stick to the plan and get Zahrah out of the country. Plan B was to contact the FBI and get her into some sort of witness protection. Plan C, D and E were all much better options than what Palmer was considering. What he was thinking of was probably plan Y or Z. Taking Zahrah home was an easy way to get caught in an ambush. Carver could have people watching the house, but whatever the necklaces pointed to, could be their only bargaining chip.

It could be the only thing that would keep them alive.

Palmer rinsed out their bowls with hot water from the kettle then made them a cup of coffee. 'We need to go and get your mum's necklace. We need to take you home.'

'Back to Texas? Isn't that a big risk?'

'It is, but it could be our chance to figure out what all this is about.'

Chapter 23

Carver unzipped the body bag and uncovered Simone Kalu's face. He hadn't set eyes on her for over fifteen years, but he still recognised her. She didn't seem to have aged. 'I don't know what my son ever saw in you. You are the one to blame for all this. If you hadn't turned his head, he'd be with me now, preparing to take over the operation.'

He unzipped the bag the rest of the way and uncovered the whole body. It was obvious that Simone wasn't wearing a necklace. Carver ripped open her shirt and checked it hadn't fallen inside. It wasn't there either. He emptied the small handbag that she had been wearing over her shoulder. Make-up, purse, hairbrush, tissue, but no sign of a necklace. Things were getting worse. If the people further up the tree found out about this, he was history.

He leaned over and rested his hands on the table, staring at Simone Kalu. 'Where is it?' He picked up the handbag and catapulted it across the room. As it hit the floor, a side compartment opened, and a small diary fell out.

Carver walked over and picked the diary up. It wasn't anything special, just something cheap Simone had probably picked up in a supermarket. It was black and had the usual useless information in the front. A street map of New York, the phases of the moon and the time zones of the world. Most of the spaces to add meetings and notes were empty but, at the back, Simone had filled in the next of kin details. First were Brandon's details at the prison, underneath was Zahrah Kalu's name and their address. Carver ripped out the page. If the necklace wasn't on the body, there was a chance it was at the house.

* * *

Danny Leech stood outside Carver's door, building up the courage to knock. Since Nate Buttermill was no longer in the game, Leech was hoping to take over the spot as Carver's number two. If the old man was elected, it would be a foot in the door for his political ambitions. He knew all about Carver's past and the rumours of organised crime links of course, but all politicians had something they would prefer didn't become public. It didn't mean it was all true. Most of the rumours were invented by political opponents. Leech took a deep breath, knocked, and went in.

Carver was just finishing a phone call. '... Stay on it and keep me up to date.' He put the phone back in its cradle. 'What is it, Danny? Spit it out.'

'Just an update, Sir. I've heard back from the police who went to check on your son's house. They said that they couldn't find any evidence but will keep a watch on it.'

Carver banged his fist on the table. 'Shit.'

Leech hesitated. This wasn't going as well as he had hoped. 'The other team say that they checked the other house, and no one has turned up yet.'

Carver jumped up and knocked his chair over. His face

turned red, and he pointed an accusatory finger at Leech. 'Find them. I don't care what we have to do or who we have to pay off or threaten. I want Palmer gotten rid of and the girl with me, here, now. Or I'm going to hold you responsible.'

'Yes, Sir.'

'And why am I paying hundreds of thousands of dollars for a professional and yet I'm surrounded by amateurs? I want him on this, tell him to get on top of this clusterfuck.'

Danny Leech hurried out of the room as quickly as he could. His ambition to become Carver's number two had reduced to zero in a matter of minutes. What had he got himself involved in? No one had ever mentioned getting rid of people. What did Carver even mean by that? Was he really suggesting that they should have Palmer killed? He started to wonder where Nate Buttermill had gone. They had all assumed that he had just been sacked.

Back at his desk, Leech picked up the phone and called the pro. No one knew who this guy was, but they all tried to stay away from him. 'Yeah, the old man says he wants you to find the girl, right away.'

'And what does he think I'm doing?'

'I… well… I…'

The Pro sighed. 'Forget it. Get someone else here to watch this place. I've got other things to do.'

Chapter 24

Palmer waited for the car to drive away. He had been watching them for over an hour and was sure it was the Pro conducting surveillance on the house. Why else would they have been sitting there? If they were leaving, they must have been pulled off onto something more urgent. Maybe they had given up on the idea of Palmer being stupid enough to turn up at the house. Whatever the reason, it was working in Palmer's favour. He wouldn't have attempted to enter the house with a team parked outside.

He checked his watch, it was two hours since the sun had set, it wasn't going to get any darker. There was no way of knowing how long they had, there was no sign of a second surveillance team taking over, but he could have missed another car, or they could be in one of the houses. They had to get on with it and get out of the area. He checked for traffic at both ends of the street then walked back to the van.

Zahrah Kalu was crouched behind the seats in the dark. When Palmer opened the side door, she jumped and almost banged her head on the table. 'Shit, you scared me.'

Palmer spoke in a whisper. 'Sorry. We have to do this now. Stay behind me. Don't move until I do. Do exactly what I say. Okay?'

She rolled her eyes. 'Okay, okay, I get it.'

Palmer didn't want to take her with him. He would have been much happier if she had stayed in the van, but he couldn't risk not finding the safe. She had given him directions to it and, if they had enough time, he could have gone in and found it. The problem was, he didn't know how much time they had. This had to be a quick in-and-out operation. Anything else could lead to them being caught or even killed. The fastest way to get this done was for Zahrah to open the safe while he kept watch.

They walked across the street and through the yard of a property that backed onto Zahrah's house. Palmer had already checked for signs that the owners had a dog that might sleep outside. There was no kennel or run, no sign of any chew toys, and no brown patches on the grass. So, probably, safe.

They quickly moved past the gas barbecue and swing set, around the single flowerbed, and up to the whitewashed back fence. Palmer checked the wooden panels for strength. They were stable and looked in good repair, but you could never be too careful. He picked a spot next to a shoulder high concrete post, gripped the top of the panel, and threw his legs over.

He landed in a crouch and checked around for anyone watching him. There were no lights, no sounds, the whole neighbourhood was quiet. He stood and turned around to give Zahrah a hand to climb over the fence, but she cleared it without any difficulty. Probably didn't want to be shown up by some old guy.

They approached the back of the house and its half-glass door. The entrance to the garage was just inside, halfway along the kitchen wall. Palmer shielded the light from his torch with his hand as he shone it through the window, the

110

room had been trashed. Whoever had been sent to search the house wasn't worried about hiding it. The good news was, if they were still watching the house, they hadn't found what they were looking for. It did confirm one thing though, the two jigsaw pieces were the key to this whole thing.

Zahrah was shining her torch at the rocks that marked out the flowerbed under the kitchen window. She mumbled to herself, counting them. 'One, two, three, four…' The fourth rock was a secure key box. After brushing dirt from the keypad, Zahrah punched in the four figures of the combination and the bottom sprang open. She smiled at Palmer and held up the key. 'Told you it was here.'

'Okay, let's get on with it.'

Zahrah unlocked the door and Palmer moved her to one side. He pulled out the Glock from his jacket and held his finger up to his lips.

Zahrah nodded.

Palmer turned the handle and pushed open the door. There was no beep from the alarm. It was unlikely that the people who had trashed the house knew the code. They had probably just smashed it. If they had been actual operators, they would have switched it back on as they left. He nodded to Zahrah, and they stepped in.

Palmer led the way to the garage door. 'Stay behind me. We don't know if there's anyone here.' The door opened with a creak, and he put his ear to the gap. There was no sound but there was a draft. It felt like one of the outside entrances to the garage was open. He pushed the door a few more inches until it stopped with a clunk. It felt like something was blocking it. He pushed harder but it wasn't opening any wider no matter what he did. He let out the breath he had been holding in and stepped back.

'What is it?'

Putting his shoulder back to the door, he tried one more time. 'The door's jammed.' He looked around the frame to see if there was any way he could force it, there was nothing obvious. 'It won't give.'

'There are some shelves just inside. They must have knocked them over.'

Palmer tried to squeeze through the gap, but he was going to have to lose a few pounds to make it. 'I'll have to go round the outside. See if I can get in that way.' Palmer wasn't happy with that plan. If anyone was watching the house, it would be a giveaway, but he had to do something to get them in there.

Zahrah pulled him out of the way. 'I can get through. I'm the one who knows where the safe is.'

'Okay, see if you can clear the door.'

Zahrah pushed her left leg through the gap, sucked her stomach in, and slid through. She barely touched the sides.

Palmer listened at the gap. 'Are you okay?'

'Yeah, it is the shelves. Someone's tipped them over and left the garage door half open. That must be how they went out.'

Palmer could hear her pulling at the shelves, trying to clear the door.

'They're too heavy. It's all the old engine parts and tools that belonged to my dad. I told Mom to get rid of them, but she wouldn't. She always said they would still be there when he got back.' Zahrah's voice began to falter. There were lots of memories here.

'Are you okay, Zahrah?'

There was a pause then she whispered through the gap in the doorway. 'I can't move them. I'll get the stuff out of the safe, but you need to do me a big favour.'

'What is it?'

'I need my laptop and my journal.'

Palmer just wanted to get out of the house. They had already spent too much time in there. 'No. You can get another laptop.'

'Please, Logan. It has all my photos on it. Pictures of me and Mom. Pictures of my dad. Please.'

'No. It's too risky. Just get the stuff in the safe.'

She went quiet again.

'Zahrah… Zahrah…'

'You don't care about me at all. You just want whatever my dad had. You're just like everyone else.'

Palmer felt guilty. Zahrah was sixteen and she had lost her whole family. She was in no fit state, mentally, to be doing any of this. 'I just want you to be safe. We can't stay here.'

'Fine. I'll just leave then. The front door's open.'

'No, Zahrah.' Palmer put his ear to the gap. He could hear her crying. 'It's okay. Tell me what I'm looking for, and I'll do my best to find it.'

Zahrah sniffed 'It's the last door on the right. My laptop bag is light blue with a pattern of yellow flowers on it. I normally leave it hanging on the back of the door.'

Palmer looked around at the state of the kitchen. If the rest of the house was like this, there was no telling if anything was still where it should have been. 'Be quick. Get the stuff and come back out this way. If I'm not back, don't come looking for me. If it takes me longer than ten minutes, get back to the van. You understand?'

'Yeah, I understand.' She stepped away from the door and back into the garage.

Palmer reached the top of the stairs and made his way along

113

the landing to the last door on the right, it was already open. The bedroom had been trashed in the same way as the rest of the house. The drawers had been pulled out and their contents tipped onto the floor. The wardrobe had been emptied and the bathroom cabinet pulled off the wall. It was a mess. Palmer checked the back of the door. Surprisingly, the bag was still there.

If Palmer had been given the job of finding something in the house, he would have taken the laptop. Even if the necklace wasn't in there, it could contain valuable information that pointed to its location. The fact that the searchers hadn't even thought to check behind the door heartened Palmer. These people were nothing more than hired thugs who couldn't think for themselves. It wouldn't surprise him if the searchers had just trashed the place and not really looked at all.

Palmer opened the bag. The laptop and journal were still in there and looked undamaged. He looked at the mess on the floor, he would have liked to have let Zahrah go through it all and at least take some clothes with her. He rolled up a couple of t-shirts and a pair of jeans and stuffed them into the bag. Sitting on the dressing table was a small jewellery box that had been emptied out, its contents strewn across the surface of the dresser. He didn't know anything about the value of jewellery, but he knew that a lot of sentimental value was often placed on the cheapest of rings and bangles. He put everything he could find back into the box and shoved it into the top of the laptop bag.

Palmer left Zahrah's room and checked the other doors. He was looking for her mother's room. If Zahrah had a jewellery box, she was probably mimicking her mother. The first door he tried was the bathroom, nothing to look at in there. The second door was the other bedroom. It had been trashed, just like the rest of the house, but worse. Things in this room hadn't just been emptied, they had been smashed. Ornaments lay in pieces and the mirror had a spider's web of cracks across the glass. The searchers must have been frustrated by the time they got to this room. Smashing things up for the sake of it, because of who it belonged to.

He picked his way over to the dressing table with the smashed mirror and moved some of the clothes that had been dropped onto it. Sure enough, Simone Kalu's jewellery was scattered in the same way Zahrah's had been. Palmer scooped up everything he could see and dropped it into the bag. That was all he had time for. They had to leave. Hopefully, Zahrah had found the necklace. Palmer picked his way back through the wreckage of the room and looked out of the bedroom window. Shit. He slung the bag over his shoulder and descended the stairs two at a time. He got to the garage door as quietly, but as quickly, as he could. 'Zahrah… Zahrah.'

Chapter 25

The Sheriff's car pulled up on the opposite side of the street. He had been told to keep an eye on the house, apprehend Palmer and free the girl if they showed up. He wasn't going to sit outside all night, one of his deputies could do that. He shouldn't even be out on patrol, he had much more important things to do. They might be a small county, but he still had responsibilities. All he was planning to do was swing past every hour or so and do a quick lap of the building. His office didn't have the resources to mount a bigger operation.

The Sheriff climbed out of his patrol car and crossed the street, he was sure he had just seen a light in the garage. The main door was half open. Maybe burglars had decided to take advantage, maybe it was Palmer. He pulled his gun out of its holster and stayed low.

He peered under the corner of the door. Zahrah was crouched on the floor closing the door of a small safe that was set in the garage floor. Over the top of it was a fake drain cover. No wonder his men hadn't been able to find it.

The Sheriff crawled forward and rolled under the main door and into the garage. He stood up, weapon in one hand, his other hand held out with its palm outwards towards Zahrah.

'It's okay, Miss Kalu, I'm the County Sheriff, I'm here to rescue you.'

Zahrah stepped towards the door where she knew Palmer would be. She didn't try to keep her voice down; she wanted Palmer to hear. 'I don't need rescuing, Sheriff. This is my house.'

'Whatever Palmer has told you, he's lying. He's demanding a ransom for you. Your grandfather has told us everything.'

Zahrah looked back over her shoulder at the other door. 'He's not my grandfather, and he's the one who's lying.'

Palmer was no longer at the door. He had already left the house and had worked his way around to the front. Being seen was no longer an issue. If the police were here, there were probably none of Carver's men watching, they could be on their way though. He had to act quickly.

He stopped at the corner of the house and dropped to the floor. Slowly and quietly, he edged forward and peered under the garage door.

Zahrah looked straight at him. She tried to create a diversion. 'Palmer isn't here. He dumped me and drove off.' She held her arms out and did her best to squeeze out a few tears.

Palmer rolled under the door and drew his Glock. 'Don't move, Sheriff.'

The Sheriff didn't listen, he spun around and levelled his weapon. 'No, you don't move.'

Palmer could see that the Sheriff's hands were trembling slightly. That could have been caused by any number of things. Fear, adrenaline, fatigue, even a hangover. Sheriffs were elected, he may not even have been an experienced police officer. The problem was, with his finger curled around the trigger, he could accidentally shoot Palmer at any second.

'Stay cool, Sheriff. We don't want any accidents.' Palmer lowered his weapon and placed it on the floor in front of him.

It had the desired effect. The Sheriff moved his finger back outside the trigger guard. 'Lie down and place your hands behind your back.'

Palmer did as he was told. He needed to disarm the Sheriff and that meant bringing him in closer.

'Miss Kalu, take my cuffs off the back of my belt and secure his hands, please.'

'I can't do that.'

'Don't worry, he's not going to do anything as long as I have the gun on him. Just take my cuffs.'

Zahrah stepped forward and reached out her hand. She pulled the taser clear of the Sheriff's holster and, before he knew what was happening, fired it into his back.

The Sheriff dropped to the ground like a felled tree. Every muscle in his body contracted as the fifty thousand volts coursed through him. His teeth clenched and his bladder emptied.

Palmer jumped to his feet. 'You can let go of the trigger now.'

She released the trigger and dropped the Taser at her feet. 'Sorry.'

'Did you get the stuff from the safe?'

Zahrah nodded. 'Did you get my laptop?'

'It's outside. Let's go.'

They both rolled under the garage door and sprinted towards the van.

Chapter 26

Anna Riley sat in an alcove at the Dharma Café. She had always liked it here. She felt all her anxiety leaving her body as soon as she sat down. The décor itself seemed soothing. It reminded her of a Buddhist monastery she had once stayed in for a weekend while she did a yoga course. The Dharma Café was also the place where she had first met Victoria Thompson, where her new life with MI6 and Logan Palmer had begun.

Thomson put their coffees down on the table and took off her jacket. 'Decaf soy latte for you, heavy-duty caffeine for me. I don't know how you drink that stuff.'

'Caffeine is bad for you. It stops you from relaxing.'

'It keeps me going, and I need all the help I can get. Insomnia's a bitch.'

Riley clicked a sweetener into her cup from a plastic dispenser. 'You should spend a little time at Yardley Manor. The therapists there are great.'

'I spent two years at Yardley. They did everything they could. This is as good as I get.'

Riley knew Thomson's background. Being abducted in Afghanistan would affect anyone's mental health, but Thomson had had it particularly bad. Beatings, torture, mock

119

executions, it was surprising that she had survived at all. 'Sorry Vicky. I forgot.'

Thomson shook her head. 'No need to apologise. You're right, I should go back for a visit. Maybe when things calm down a little.'

Riley was keen to move the conversation on. 'I'm glad you could spare some time for a coffee with me.'

Thomson shrugged. 'What can I say, I was in the area.'

'It's work, isn't it.'

Thomson reached into her bag and pulled out a sealed brown envelope. 'Not all work, Anna. I always enjoy our little get togethers.' She slid the envelope across the table. 'It seems that our mutual friend in Texas has come to the attention of some law enforcement agencies. I had to use an old contact to dig out the details.'

'What are they saying he's done?'

'Stole a twenty-million-dollar ransom and kidnapped one of the hostages.'

Riley frowned. 'He wouldn't do that. Not Logan. There must be a good reason why he's doing it.'

'The FBI is involved because the girl is a minor and he took her across the state border. Makes it a federal case.'

'I knew there was something wrong with the guy he asked me to look at.'

Thomson stirred her coffee. 'Did you find out anything else?'

'This guy, George H. Carver, is as corrupt as they come. He's a real nasty piece of work with ties to racist and fascist groups all over the place. He's also implicated in murder, drug smuggling and trafficking. Somehow, whenever the police get close to him, someone else crawls out of the woodwork and takes the fall.'

'So, he's got protection then?'

'It looks like it, but I'm struggling to find out where from. It can't just be organised crime. Not with the number of things he's got away with.'

Thomson checked no one was listening. 'You think it could be a connection within the law itself?'

Riley nodded. 'Maybe even government. This guy is running for governor of Texas and, although he isn't expected to get anywhere, he could end up with a solid platform to promote the shit he believes.'

'No one gets anywhere in US politics without money and backers. Someone must be promoting him in the right circles.'

Riley leaned forward. 'That's what I thought. This could be bigger than we think.'

Thomson raised an eyebrow. 'I think finding more on this guy could be in all our interests. Stay on it, Anna.'

Riley finished her coffee. 'I'll get right to it.'

'Remember though, this isn't official yet. Just keep it between us. As always, keep me in the loop.' Thomson stood and put on her jacket. She looked at the café's menu. 'Next time, we're meeting in a pub. I need a vodka.'

Riley smiled. 'See you soon, Vicky.'

Thomson turned on her heels and left the café.

Chapter 27

Palmer ripped a page out of his notebook and handed it to Zahrah. 'These are the first numbers on the necklaces. They look like GPS or map coordinates and I'm willing to bet they'll lead us to a bank or a secure deposit company of some sort.'

'Why do you think that?'

He pointed at the other numbers he had written down. 'The rest look like account numbers and PIN codes. I think your dad hid something, probably a lot of money, and this will show us where it is.'

'Is that why Carver wants us dead?'

Palmer shook his head. 'No, he wants us dead because we're witnesses. We can link him to everything that's gone on, but I think your dad hid something else. Some sort of evidence that shows that Carver is crooked. Maybe even who his contacts are in government and law enforcement. If we get it, it'll be the best protection we have. It might even save our lives.'

'What do you need me to do? I want to help.'

Palmer handed Zahrah her laptop bag. 'I'm going to go and buy us some burner phones. I need to talk to a friend of mine, see if she can help us out. While I'm doing that, I want you to go over to that diner and get onto their free Wi-Fi, find out where that bank is.'

'I can do that.'

'That's my girl.'

Zahrah put the bag over her shoulder then paused, looking down at her hands. 'I'm sorry I said you were just like everyone else. You're not. If it wasn't for you, I'd be dead.'

Palmer reached out and held her hands. 'I promised your mum I'd look after you, and I will, no matter what. I keep my promises.'

'I'm glad you're here. I don't want to be on my own.'

Palmer smiled. 'Don't worry. You won't be. Now, let's find this bank.'

They climbed out of the van and made their way across the car park. Zahrah veered off to the right towards the diner. The door stood open with a screen over the opening to keep out the bugs. When she pulled it open, an electronic bell chimed to warn the staff. It was a sign that they didn't get a lot of customers at this time in the morning.

A middle-aged man appeared through a door behind the counter. 'Good morning, what can I get you?'

'Two coffees please and do you have a password for your Wi-Fi?'

The man tapped a card that was stuck to the counter. 'That's the password there. Take a seat and I'll bring your coffee over.'

'Thanks.'

Zahrah took the seat in the corner opposite the counter. There was a small table with just enough room for two people. She sat down with her back to the wall. It gave her a view of the car park and the direction she expected Palmer to come from. She opened up her laptop and connected to the Wi-Fi.

Once she punched in the numbers from the note, the map

zoomed in on a small L-shaped building with a parking lot at the front that it shared with a burger joint. She zoomed in and wrote down the address, it wasn't too far away. She clicked on the directions button, forty miles. Even with the country roads they would have to use, they could still be there by early afternoon.

Two young men, the diner's only other customers, were watching Zahrah from the other side of the room. Were they there when she came in? She couldn't remember. She made a point of not making eye contact and concentrated on her screen.

The middle-aged man from behind the counter brought the coffee over and placed it on the table. 'Can I get you anything else?'

Zahrah lowered her voice. 'Those two guys over there, do you know them?'

The man looked over at them. One of the men waved. 'They come in here a lot. They can get rowdy when they've a mind to. Best for you to stay away from them.'

'Thanks.'

The man went back to the counter and busied himself with sorting out the pastries in the display cabinet.

Zahrah switched to street view on the map and checked out the front of the building. Painted on the large front window was the name, *Johnson Memorial Bank & Credit*. She typed the name into a search engine. It was a single branch bank and had been in the same spot since the First World War. Set up by a local business owner in memory of his son who had been killed in France. It was dedicated to helping returning GIs and had been in the same family ever since. She looked at their services. Banking, safe deposit, notary and document checking. All the standard things you would expect from a bank, but with a cheery smile and good old-fashioned family values. According to the website.

Zahrah jumped when one of the young men from the other side of the room pulled out the chair opposite hers and sat down. 'Good morning beautiful, ain't seen you in here before.'

'Someone is sitting there.'

The man looked around. 'I don't see anyone. Looks like you're all alone to me.'

Zahrah looked across to the counter, but the man wasn't there. He had gone into the storage room. 'He'll be here in a minute. You should go now.'

'Well, maybe we can talk until he gets here. You might even like me. I'm very popular with girls.'

Zahrah looked down at the screen. 'Sorry, I've got things I need to do. I don't have time for small talk.'

The man reached out and closed the laptop's lid. 'Whatever you're doin' it can wait. Me an' Bobby,' he pointed at his buddy at the other table. 'We're havin' a party. You'll enjoy it.'

The other man had walked over to join them. 'She looks like she enjoys a party, Wayne.' A broad grin spread across his face. It would have looked less sinister if it wasn't for the missing teeth.

Zahrah put the laptop back in her bag and tried to stand, but Wayne grabbed her arm. 'Where do you think you're going?'

She pulled away from him. 'Leave me alone.'

The electronic bell chimed as the screen door opened and Palmer walked in. 'You ready to go?'

Wayne grabbed Zahrah's arm again. 'We ain't finished talkin' to her yet.'

Palmer put his shopping bag down on the floor. 'Okay, fellas.

Here's the deal. You get your hands off her right now, and I let you keep what's left of your teeth.'

The middle-aged man was back behind the counter. 'Come on now boys, I don't want any trouble.'

Palmer held up one hand as a warning for them to back off. 'Neither do I but, if you don't let go of her, I'm gonna fuck you up.'

Bobby made his move. He took two steps forward and swung his huge fist like it was a club. Palmer ducked underneath the punch, grabbed Bobby's arm, and used his momentum to slam him into the wall. He followed up with two quick kidney punches, and Bobby was done.

Wayne's resolve appeared to be wavering. He had obviously never seen his much bigger friend dispatched so easily. He pulled a knife from a sheath he had attached to his belt and pointed it at Palmer. 'Back off, or I hurt the girl.'

It was the worst thing Wayne could have done. It raised the stakes and put Palmer on a life-or-death footing. Palmer was done talking, it was time to end this.

Zahrah spotted an opportunity. She twisted her wrist out of Wayne's grip and stamped as hard as she could on the top of his foot.

Wayne stumbled and swung the blade wildly at Zahrah, but Palmer had already closed the gap between them. He grabbed Wayne's wrist, twisted it, and took the knife away from him. As Wayne tried to throw a punch, Palmer spun him around and slammed his face into the table. Wayne collapsed into a heap spitting out blood and teeth as he went.

Palmer looked at the shock on Zahrah's face. 'I did warn him.'

She nodded. 'Yeah, you definitely did.'

Palmer pulled several notes out and placed them on the counter. 'Sorry for any trouble, Sir.' He picked up his shopping bag and led Zahrah out of the diner.

Back at the van, Zahrah shared the address and info she had found. 'It's about forty miles away, but I didn't have enough time to write down the directions before those two idiots...' She fell silent. She was clearly shaken by what had gone on.

Palmer placed his hand on her shoulder. He didn't cope well with situations like this. He had enough trouble dealing with his own issues. 'Are you okay?'

Zahrah nodded and a tear dropped from her eye. She leaned over and buried her face in Palmer's chest. Everything was catching up with her, all the emotion she had bottled up was on the verge of pouring out. Her sobs were stifled and her whole body trembled.

Palmer wrapped his arms around her. She was acting so grown up and seemed to be handling it all so well, it was easy to miss how devastated she was. She was just a kid.

They stayed like that for a few minutes. Palmer constantly watched the diner to see if anyone was coming after them. They couldn't afford to hang about. He waited until Zahrah had calmed down a little then lifted her head. 'We have to get away from here.'

Zahrah sat back and wiped her eyes, a little embarrassed. 'Yeah, I know.'

'When we've been to the bank, we'll go to the safe house. We'll be able to relax for a while and de-stress.' He reached into his backpack and pulled out a packet of tissues. 'Here you go.'

'Thanks.'

Palmer rummaged in his shopping bag and pulled out a box.

'Look, I got us a satnav. See if you can get it working.' He turned the key in the ignition and drove out of the car park, heading east.

Chapter 28

Special Agent Ethan Gault shook his head as he watched the CCTV footage that played on the laptop. He watched Zahrah Kalu arrive at the diner alone and the altercation between Palmer and the two men. He paused the footage. 'Anyone looking at this footage would say that she hasn't been kidnapped at all, that's obvious. What are the locals saying?'

The Sheriff leaned forward in his chair. 'They're not that interested in it. As far as they are concerned, two local troublemakers got what they deserved. They're on the lookout for the couple but I don't see them putting any major resources on it.'

'Good, it will save me the effort of warning them off. It's the FBI's case now.'

Carver shuffled in his chair. 'Alleged kidnapping?'

'The FBI will want to see all the information you have on Palmer and everything the Sheriff has. The Bureau wasn't involved with the original kidnapping, so my supervisor will want everything done by the book. If anything goes wrong, she'll want someone else's neck on the block, not hers.'

The Sheriff cleared his throat. 'I've done everything that I've been asked to do. I've cooperated in every way. I know this is your case now, but I can still find them.'

Ethan Gault turned to look at the Sheriff. 'Let's just summarize what happened when you got to the house. You went in without backup and somehow managed to corner and unarm Palmer, a miracle in itself, but then you got tasered by a sixteen-year-old girl. Pissing yourself in the process. Have I got that correct?'

The Sheriff looked suitably embarrassed. 'I didn't need backup, he's just one man, I...'

Gault cut him off. 'Did you notice anything out of the ordinary before you went all gung-ho and charged in?'

'Not really. I mean, there was a beaten-up old van I passed on the way to the house. It didn't fit in with the more expensive cars in that neighbourhood.'

'But you didn't think it was worth writing any of the details down. You didn't think it might have something to do with Palmer.'

The Sheriff looked at Carver and shrugged.

Gault pressed play on the laptop. 'Look at the end of the footage from the diner. Do you see a vehicle driving off just before the police arrive?'

'Yeah.'

'And what does it look like to you? How would you describe it?'

'It's a beaten-up old van.'

'Yes, it is. How about that... You can leave now, Sheriff. I think you've outlived your usefulness.'

Carver nodded and the Sheriff walked out of the office. 'He's a good man.'

'I'm sure he is, and you have a lot of influence with local law enforcement, but this is federal now, you need to back off.'

Carver stabbed his finger into the desk. 'I need to be kept in the loop.'

'You will be, as a relative of the victim, but the FBI has its ways of working and operating to the whims of a would-be politician don't figure in them. You can't buy off a whole federal agency.'

'Okay, but I want the girl brought to me. I'm her family.'

Gault stood and opened the door. 'The FBI are only interested in rescuing Zahrah Kalu, you can depend on that.' He walked out of the office and closed the door behind him.

The phone on Carver's desk rang. He picked it up. 'What is it?'

It was Danny Leech. 'There's someone here to see you, Sir.'

'I'm busy.'

Leech sounded nervous. 'I've told him that, Sir. He says it's important.'

'Whoever it is, tell them to come back another time.'

'I don't think…'

The office door burst open. 'You'll see me right fuckin' now.'

Carver gestured towards the chair in front of his desk. 'Do come in. Close the door, have a seat.'

The man who had burst in was known simply as The Preacher because of the number of people he had buried. He was the current president of the Lords of Texas MC, an outlaw biker gang renowned for their extreme violence. Carver had used them as muscle for some of his less legal enterprises.

'What's your problem, Preacher?'

Preacher squeezed his huge frame into the seat and put his feet up on Carver's desk. 'My problem is that I lost two of my foot soldiers last night. They were strung up by the Don's men.'

131

'I'm sorry to hear that, but I'm sure you can get plenty more recruits where they came from.'

'A lot of these cartels work together. If you piss off one group, you've got a problem with them all.'

Carver shrugged. 'I've told you before, if you're selling shit on their ground, you're gonna get retaliation.'

Preacher slammed his fist into the desk. 'It's not us who they're after, it's you. Whatever you've done, you need to make it right with them.'

'And if I don't?'

Preacher smiled. 'You don't get it, do you? If I can't operate, I don't make money. If I don't make money, neither do you. One word from me and every biker gang that you use as muscle walks away. With no security, who's gonna protect you from the Don?'

Carver stood up and walked around to the other side of the desk. He jabbed a finger at Preacher. 'Is that a threat?'

Preacher slowly got out of the chair. He towered over Carver. 'If you don't sort this, it's over. You don't control anything.' He turned and stormed out.

Carver watched out of the office window as Preacher and several of his gang cruised past on their bikes. Standing at the side of the road, watching Carver, were two Latino men in sharp suits. One of them lifted his hand and drew it across his tattooed throat. The other smiled and made his fingers into a pistol that he fired at the window.

Carver stepped back and closed the blinds. They were no longer interested in getting the money he owed them; it had gone beyond that. They wanted him dead. He walked over to his phone and pressed the number for Danny Leech. 'I'm going to my house on the coast. Get my car ready and move everyone, and I mean everyone over there. Now.'

Chapter 29

New Orleans, The Big Easy, Birthplace of Jazz, a favoured backdrop of countless films and books, was somewhere that Palmer had always wanted to visit. Not like this though. He had imagined himself staying in an old hotel in the French Quarter, standing on a balcony overlooking the Mardi Gras festivities. What he hadn't envisaged was being routed through some of the poorer districts by a satnav that seemed to be avoiding main roads.

Palmer, like a lot of people, assumed that all of New Orleans was how it was depicted in films and TV. He was expecting old French colonial buildings and jazz clubs, not neighbourhoods that looked like they hadn't been repaired properly since Hurricane Katrina. In common with a great many major cities around the world, the appearance of wealth was merely a veneer. Extreme levels of poverty existed just beneath the surface.

The satnav guided them to a T junction that led to a main road. The female voice told them to turn left and that their destination would be on the right, finally. Palmer followed the directions and pulled into the parking lot.

The Johnson Memorial Bank and Credit looked a little worse for wear. The building needed a coat of paint and one of the side windows had a crack in it. Obviously, not everyone in the banking industry was awash with money. Small banks like this were becoming rarer as they were vacuumed up by the larger brands. Bought out, closed down and the customer accounts transferred. The irresistible march of global banking.

Palmer steered them past the queue of customers for the drive-through burger joint next door and parked up in front of the bank. He made sure he had all the details he needed, and they walked across to the entrance.

The armed security guard inside the bank opened the door for them. He wasn't supposed to, he was supposed to focus on security, but it was in his nature. 'Good afternoon, folks. Welcome to Johnson Memorial.'

The inside of the bank was also looking a little dated and in need of a makeover. It was like a nineties time capsule of mahogany and brass. Etched glass framed the tellers' windows, and all the pens were chained to the desk. No sign of any high-tech touch screens of translucent plastic and chrome or wall mounted flat screen TVs that displayed an endless loop of bank ads. It all looked a little mom and pop quaint. A little too *Murder, She Wrote.*

Off to the right, several bank employees were packing files into boxes and adding them to a pile by the door. A couple of other people were busy shredding documents and filling plastic bags. It looked like they were in the process of closing down.

Palmer nodded to the guard and walked up to the counter. 'Hello. We'd like to talk to someone about an old account that we have with the bank.'

The teller smiled. 'No problem at all, sir. Have a seat, I'll see if someone can come and speak to you.'

As they were about to sit, a woman appeared through a door at the back of the bank and waved for them to follow her. The office she ushered them into had the same about-to-be-vacated feel as the rest of the bank. Empty filing cabinets lined one wall alongside a desk that had been turned upside down and the legs removed.

'Good afternoon, my name's Francis Johnson and I'm the manager of the bank.'

Palmer pointed at the logo that was painted on the office's back wall. 'I take it it's your family's bank.'

'That's right. We've been here for over a hundred years.'

'It looks like you aren't going to be here much longer.'

Johnson nodded. 'The time has come for me to retire and do some of those things on my bucket list. None of my kids want to be bankers. Apparently, we are evil incarnate. I've had to let the operation go to one of the big names. It's for the best.'

'I imagine some of your customers don't see it that way.'

Johnson shrugged. 'Most of our customers have been transferred to our new owners. Unfortunately, some decided to bank elsewhere. We do, however, still have a handful of accounts that we are unable to trace the owners of. It's why I was happy when you mentioned an old account.'

Palmer handed over the page from his notebook that had the decoded necklace numbers on it. 'I believe there are two accounts. They will have been opened by Brandon Carver around fifteen years ago.' He pointed at Zahrah. 'This is Zahrah Kalu, his daughter.'

Johnson hit a few keys on her keyboard and brought up the details. 'Mmm, these accounts are actually in the name of

Zahrah Kalu, which makes things a little easier. Have you got any photo ID Ms Kalu?'

Zahrah handed over her passport. 'Came prepared.'

Johnson checked the details. 'All good. I'll need to take a copy, but I'm happy to deal with you over the accounts. Bear with me a moment.' She stood and left the office.

Palmer whispered to Zahrah, 'Whatever is in these accounts, don't get upset about it. We need to get out of here as quick as we can, with no fuss, and get you to the safe house.'

'I'll be fine. I know Dad did this for a reason.'

Johnson came back in and handed Zahrah her passport. 'Thank you, Ms Kalu.' She placed a steel container the size of a family sized pack of breakfast cereal onto the table. 'That is the safe deposit box that makes up account number one. It's been in our safe for fifteen years. I've no idea what's in it, but, as you can see, it has a combination lock on it. Do you know the number?'

Palmer opened his notebook. 'I think so.' He turned the four dials on the front of the box to match the last number from the necklaces. The lock sprung open. 'Bingo.'

Johnson held up her hand. 'I'll leave you alone in a moment, you can go through it in private.'

Palmer nodded.

'Okay, account number two.' Johnson punched some more keys on her computer. 'Number two was an investment account. A portfolio of shares that we managed as part of our larger fund.'

'Was?'

Johnson nodded. 'As part of closing down, we liquidated our shares and placed the proceeds into new accounts for the customers we couldn't trace. You now have a deposit account at a different bank.'

Palmer looked at Zahrah. 'How much is in the account?'

'When we sold the shares…' She tapped a few more keys. 'It came to slightly more than thirty million.'

Zahrah gasped. 'Dollars?'

Johnson smiled. 'Yes, dollars. You're a rich young woman, Ms Kalu.' She printed out a letter to the new bank and handed it to Zahrah. That will let the new bank know that you are the account holder if you want to visit them. They have set up an online account so you can transfer the money to a bank of your choice.' She printed out the details and handed them to Zahrah. 'I'll leave you alone now to go through your deposit box. Just let me know when you're done.' She stood and left the office.

Zahrah stared at the printed sheet. 'Thirty million dollars. Where did Dad get that kind of money?'

'I would imagine he took it from Carver's white power organisation before he got sent to prison. A little insurance policy. It's why they left him alone for so long.'

She handed the paper to Palmer. 'I don't want any of it. It's hate money.'

Palmer took the account details and folded them up. 'We can decide what to do with it later. You could do a lot of good with that much money. It could buy us a way out.' He turned to the steel box and lifted the lid. 'Let's see what else he left for you.'

'What else could there be.'

Palmer shrugged. 'I don't know, but all of this has to be about more than thirty million dollars.'

'That money could have paid for me and Mom's ransom. He could have saved her.'

'Yeah, but he would have had to tell someone about the necklaces to get to it. He would have had to risk losing whatever else is hidden here. I don't think he ever cared what happened to you and your mom, and I think your dad had something on him.'

Zahrah sat in silence, shaking her head, and shuffling her feet.

Palmer leaned forward and looked inside the box. There was a collection of photographs bound together with an elastic band. He lifted them out. He recognised Simone Kalu and Brandon Carver, they were much younger, but it was them. He assumed the baby girl in the pictures was Zahrah. He handed them to her. 'These are yours.'

She took them, staring at each one. 'I don't remember these being taken.'

'You're less than one in those photos, you wouldn't.' Palmer reached back into the box. There was a memory stick, physically big by today's standards, but it would still work, and a leather cylinder about ten inches long. Palmer thought it looked like the one his grandad kept his telescope in. He unfastened the brass buckle and pulled out the contents.

The ten by eight photo Palmer was now looking at showed a group of men in combat uniforms. They weren't military though. The combats they were wearing weren't all the same and, the big giveaway, they were kneeling in front of a Confederate Stars and Bars flag, and a Ku Klux Klan banner. The picture had been taken in front of a rural cabin that showed all the signs of a white supremacist or survivalist compound out in the sticks. The image quality wasn't great, but the man in the centre was George H. Carver.

Zahrah looked over at the picture. 'Who are they?'

Palmer let go of the picture and it rolled back up. It didn't want to be flat after fifteen years in a cylinder. He unrolled the sheet of paper that it was stapled to. 'This gives the names of everyone in the photograph, and it's dated nineteen ninety-six.'

'Do you recognise any of the people?'

Palmer shook his head. 'No one other than Carver. Although, I'm willing to bet that if we searched for the names on Google, we would find several high-profile people. Maybe a politician or two, cops, FBI, bankers. I think this is what this is all about, not the money. Someone big is in this photo, and I think Carver is scared of them. It would also kill his budding political ambitions. Can you imagine this photo being aired on Sixty Minutes?'

'Is it genuine or photoshopped?'

Palmer tipped up the cylinder and a packet of negatives fell out. He held them up to the light. They showed the same men engaged in various training drills and, what they saw as, heroic poses. 'You can't photoshop negatives.'

'So, all of this shit, my mum, my dad, all so some politician can cover their ass.'

Palmer put the photo back into the cylinder and added the memory stick. 'We've got the evidence now. We can make sure they don't get away with it.' He checked the steel box again, in case he had missed something, but it was empty. 'Time for us to get out of here. We need to get to the safe house that Cody arranged for us. Even if it's just for a few days.'

'They're going to keep coming after us, aren't they? Even if we give them the money and the pictures.'

Palmer put the cylinder into his backpack. 'Not if we take

them down first. Let's go.'

They picked up their things and thanked the Bank Manager, wishing her well in the pursuit of her bucket list. The security guard opened the door for them again as they left, and they grabbed a coffee on the way back to the van.

Palmer typed the safe house's location into the satnav and pressed go. The map that appeared on the screen showed that it was a few miles outside the city on the edge of the swamp. 'You ready for a trip down to the bayou?' He tried out his best Southern accent, which was a bit rubbish by anyone's standards.

Zahrah shuddered. 'Just so you know, I don't like spiders, or snakes.'

Palmer gave up on his accent. 'You'll be okay. You're more likely to be eaten by an alligator before the spiders get to you.'

'What?'

'Nothing.' Palmer chuckled to himself as they pulled out of the carpark and turned south.

Chapter 30

Palmer and Zahrah held on as the van bounced down the rutted track towards Cody Wickes's cabin. The property hadn't been visited for a while judging by how overgrown the access track was. Anything left alone for long enough in this part of the world was soon reclaimed by the swamp. Palmer just hoped the cabin was waterproof. That was all they really needed. Somewhere safe to cook sleep and eat, anything else was a bonus. What they saw when they broke through into the clearing took them both by surprise.

The cabin wasn't the ramshackle wooden hut they were expecting. It was a modern building with a concrete base and a steel frame. The wooden exterior had been treated to withstand whatever the environment could throw at it and the windows had shutters across them to keep out the wildlife. An array of solar panels covered half of the corrugated steel roof and a water catchment system had been put in to collect rainfall from the guttering. Wickes had done a good job. This was a self-sufficient homestead. Somewhere he could live off grid, full time.

Palmer dug out the key that Wickes had given him back in the hotel room and climbed the three wooden steps to the front porch. The cabin door was stiff. The galvanised steel hinges needed a clean and the wood had swollen in the humid atmosphere. Palmer braced his shoulder against it and pushed.

The door opened with a metallic scrape, and they stepped in. The inside of the cabin was dark. The shutters that kept out the wildlife also kept out the light. Palmer fished out a torch and switched it on. It was still daylight so, if all was well, he was hoping that the lights would work directly from the solar panels. He shone the torch around the door frame and found a light switch beside the door.

The good news was there were no large predators who got spooked by the sudden light and came rushing towards them. The bad news was that it smelled like something had died. Palmer walked through to the kitchen and followed his nose. In the corner was a collection of bones wrapped in flea-bitten fur. Something long dead that he didn't recognise. He grabbed the dead thing's tail, peeled it off the floor, and threw it out the door.

Zahrah stepped aside. 'Oh my god, what was that?'

'I don't know, but I don't think it'll be bothering us. We just need to get rid of the smell.'

Zahrah looked around. The lights were dim, but enough for them to get in and prepare for the night. She walked through to the kitchen and checked the cupboards. There were plenty of pots, pans, and utensils, but no food. Having said that, she wasn't really expecting any. The small cooker was gas, she thought it must run from a bottle somewhere. She turned one of the knobs and pushed the ignition switch. The blue flame sparked into life. At least they could cook something half-decent. In the cupboard at the side of the cooker, she found a spray bottle of floor cleaner and some paper towels.

She sprayed as much as she could over the area where the fur bag of bones had been and hoped that would do the job. For now, at least.

As Palmer went back out to the van and started ferrying their camping supplies into the cabin, Zahrah decided to explore. She was hoping to find a modern bathroom and was hoping that the owners didn't wash in the bayou. There was a bedroom on either side of a rear corridor and, behind the last door, the answer to her dreams. She had never been so happy to see a shower cubicle in her life.

Once Palmer had brought in the stuff they needed for the night, they sat in the main living area with their sleeping bags and two of the wind-up lamps. They had decided it was better to stay in the main room until the morning. They could explore properly in full daylight and open the shutters. For now, they just needed a good night's sleep. It had been a rough few days and they were both exhausted.

* * *

One of Carver's hired goons sat in the undergrowth. It wasn't his idea of fun, why did he always pull the short straw? Being left behind just in case Palmer showed up was bad enough, what could he do on his own? But to make things worse, they now wanted him to go all the way up to the cabin to see if anyone was there. Absolutely pointless. At least, that's what he thought. He was around one hundred yards from the cabin when he noticed the light. It wasn't bright, but it was definitely there. Time to check-in.

Chapter 31

C arver's house on the coast was a world away from being a two-bedroomed vacation chalet by the sea. The imposing stone-built mansion sat on its own artificial island in the Gulf of Mexico. The original wooden house had been built in a nineteenth century French style in the thirties by a man who made his money during the prohibition era. Like so many back then, he had made his fortune and then gone legit. This was his winter retreat.

The house was extended several times, but disaster befell it when it was levelled by a hurricane in the sixties. By then, the original owner was an old man, and his business was on the decline. He retired to a small apartment in Los Angeles and the island house rotted down into a pile of wood and broken foundations.

In the late nineteen nineties, Carver bought the property for a knockdown price and had the current structure built to his specifications. The main house was still in the French style, but the island now included a wall and a separate building for staff. The island could only be accessed by the steel bridge that linked it to the mainland. A bridge that could be raised and lowered to improve the already formidable security. Carver felt safe here. Why wouldn't he?

The room he used as his main office was on the second floor at the top of an ornate staircase. Its large, shuttered windows looked over the impressive, sculpted garden and out across the Gulf towards Florida.

Like so much in Carver's life, the house didn't belong to him. It was registered as the property of a faceless corporation in the Cayman Islands. No one knew where the money came from to build it. Everything from drug runners to mafia and rogue states were rumoured to have put up the finances. All anyone knew was that George H. Carver was a minor cog in the white power movement then, almost overnight, he had money to spend on the house.

There was a knock on the door. Carver lit a cigar and blew out a stream of smoke. 'Come in.' He loved the feeling of power this place gave him.

Danny Leech opened the door and entered the room. He hadn't been told the details of what was going on, but he had the look of someone who was in over his head. 'We've had a message from the man we left in Louisiana. He said there appears to be some movement at the safe house.'

'It's about time. I was beginning to think our plan wouldn't work. Tell him to stay away.'

'Sir?'

Carver didn't like being questioned, especially when he was in his power office. 'Just do it. I don't want some incompetent idiot being seen and blowing it. If Palmer has arrived, it's because he wants to reassess things. Firm up his plan. He might only be there for a couple of days, but, while he is, we can take him. We're paying for a professional, get him over there with a team who can take Palmer out.'

'Yes, Sir.' Leech backed out of the room and closed the

double door behind him.

Carver took another long draw from his cigar. Things were starting to drop into place. This could all be over in a couple of days. Then it was back to normal, back to his election campaign.

Chapter 32

I t was mid-morning by the time Palmer woke up. He hadn't slept that long in years. He sat up and shielded his eyes against the daylight that streamed through the window. Zahrah had woken up earlier and was now outside opening the shutters. Palmer had to get up, there was a lot to organise. He rubbed his eyes and unzipped his sleeping bag.

Zahrah came back inside. 'Good morning sleepy head. I wondered when you were going to wake up.'

'Morning, Zahrah. How are you feeling?'

'A lot better than I have for the last few days, I'm just a bit hungry now.'

Palmer walked over to the kitchen. 'I'm putting the kettle on first. Then I can sort us out with some breakfast.'

'I'll do the breakfast if you figure out how the hot water and power works. I really need a shower.'

'Leave it to me. I'm better at fixing things than cooking anyway.'

It didn't take Palmer long to find the controls for the solar power system. Nothing needed fixing, it just needed to be turned on. He flicked the switches that allowed the batteries to charge, for night-time power, and checked that they were working. By the time Zahrah had rustled them up something to eat, Palmer had managed to switch on the cabin's main electricity circuit and figured out the hot water system. 'There you go, Zahrah. Give it an hour and you should have enough warm water for a luxurious shower.'

'Thanks, Logan. I'll feel much better after that.'

Two hours later, fed and showered, they sat at the table and looked at Zahrah's laptop. They had inserted the memory stick from the bank, and they were now scrolling through the files it held. There were copies of the photographs from the cylinder, Palmer expected that, but there was so much more.

He took notes as they opened the files. Most were digital scans of documents that went back twenty or twenty-five years. Some gave the details of donations to Carver's organisation. Many of the names were the same as those in the photograph, others were well known family names that Palmer recognised. There were details of contacts and communications between Carver and other ultra-nationalist groups across America and the rest of the world. Video files and audio from telephone conversations blew apart any argument Carver might have that the photos and documents were forged.

Palmer was stunned by what he was reading. He was aware that America was deeply polarized and, in some parts of the country, always had been. The thirteenth amendment to the US Constitution officially ended slavery, but it did nothing to end the racism that created it in the first place. Legislation was continually put in place, especially in the southern states, to ensure white supremacy. From the Black Codes immediately after the Civil War, through the Jim Crow segregation laws to the War on Drugs in the eighties. There are more than two million prisoners in the USA, forty per cent of them are Black men. Many prisons are run by private companies for profit and supply cheap labour for big corporations. Slavery in all but name.

The storming of the Capitol after Trump lost power showed how some sections of society could be mobilized with a mixture of fear and fake news, and it had emboldened far-right extremists, but that was just a small group, this was huge. The information, taken all together, showed the existence of a global, well-funded conspiracy to infiltrate multiple governments and economies with sleepers. This was a plan to try to rebuild nationalist influence. To bring about a resurgence of far-right power. Maybe not the Ku Klux Klan themselves, but, without a doubt, this was an organisation with the same ideology, the same goals.

Zahrah sat back. 'What does it all mean?'

'It means that Carver is a very small fish in a much bigger pond. He is the figurehead, but he'll also be the scapegoat for any problems. These documents could bring down their whole scheme, and he knows it.'

'Why didn't they try to get these back before now? Why wait if they're that important.'

Palmer looked down the list of names he had written in his notebook. 'I don't think they know.'

'What makes you think that?'

'If the big fish in this conspiracy had known that Carver kept this information and your dad had stolen it, they would have cut him up into small pieces and buried him in the desert. They would have restructured the whole thing, picked different sleepers, maybe even called it off altogether. Your dad knew what it meant and used it to keep you safe.'

Zahrah clicked on the photo of the men at the training camp.

'So, you think some of these men are the big names. The ones who were picked to join the military, the FBI, CIA, that sort of thing. They were going to try to make it to the top.'

'That's right. Some would go into politics, some into business. If they put enough people into it, the odds say that a few will have made it a good way up their chosen tree. It's something the KGB perfected during the Cold War. The more of them that made it, the more of their kind they could recruit.'

'And the ones who didn't make it?'

'It stands to reason that, in any group, some will have died. Illness or accident, it makes no difference which. Maybe a few were caught doing something they shouldn't. Hand in the cookie jar or succumbing to their baser instincts. There's a good chance that a lot of these names aren't in the game anymore.'

'But the ones that are left could be quite powerful.'

Palmer nodded. 'When your dad first hid this, I think Carver probably thought he could get it back quickly. He passed it off as an internal problem. Told them it was just money that was missing. He probably got new funds from them. As time went by, he couldn't risk the others finding out the truth. He knew they would kill him. If the big names know about it now, Carver is on borrowed time. He'll be running scared and desperate to save his own arse.'

'That's why he didn't just tell the kidnappers where they could get the ransom money. He had to get the cylinder and the stick before anyone else saw them.'

'Yeah, and we've messed it all up for him. We're in a different state now so the FBI will be involved. If that's the case, the news might have found its way onto someone on this list.'

Zahrah ejected the memory stick and dropped it back into

the leather cylinder. 'We need to hide this somewhere, keep it away from Carver.'

'I've written the names down. We can do a quick check on them, see what we're up against.'

'And then what? How do we get out of this, Logan?'

Palmer didn't want to put Zahrah at any more risk than she already was. 'I'll go into the city this afternoon. I'll make sure all the info is secure. It's best if you don't know where. If Carver finds you, you are still safe until he has it in his hands. That gives me time to come and get you.'

Zahrah's eyes widened when she realised what he was saying. 'I don't want to be alone. Don't leave me here. Everyone leaves me.'

Palmer put his hand on hers. 'You'll be fine. It's just better if I go alone. The police are expecting us to be together. It'll be easier for me to go about unnoticed if you stay here.'

'But you're coming back?'

Palmer smiled. 'Of course I am. I won't be long.' He put the cylinder into a bag and went out to the van.

* * *

The professional spread a map out across the table. He had marked it to show the location of the safe house, the access route, and the surrounding area. He handed a zoomed in copy to each of the three men who sat at the table. 'These maps show where each of your teams will be stationed before we go in. I'll be with Team Red 1. Your call signs are written on the back along with the radio channel you'll be using. Just so you don't forget it. You all need to brief your men before we make the assault.'

One of the men shook his head. 'It's one man. Why do we need four teams to take out one man?'

'We need four teams because that is the best option. All you need to do; is exactly as you're told. Don't make the mistake of underestimating this guy. Don't forget, he's ex-Special Boat Service, that's British special forces. He was trained by the best to be the best. Whereas you are all wannabe survivalists who were trained by some fat guy called Bubba in a camp in the woods. He's a combat veteran and has managed to last this long without too much effort. Be under no illusion, some of you might not make it through this.'

The three men looked at each other. Their expressions showed they hadn't considered the possibility that they might die.

The pro continued. 'Each team will travel to the cabin separately and approach from a different direction. Once the asset in situ confirms that they are in there, we make a synchronised assault. Quick and silent. Palmer dies and you bring the girl to me. Understood?'

The three men nodded.

'Good. Let's go.'

Chapter 33

Palmer parked the van and went into a copier centre. The best way to make this information safe was to have multiple copies in different locations. He copied all the files and loaded them onto three new memory sticks. Two of them went into a protective bag and then a padded envelope. He put the first one in his pocket, it always paid to have an extra copy to hand. A copy each went to Anna Riley, and Jerry Scarlett at the dive school. The original cylinder and memory stick were packed into a box and addressed to the proprietor of the pub he always drank in when he was back at home in Cumbria. He had often used it as a mail drop over the years, and he knew it would be kept safe until he collected it. Once he had posted them all, his next stop was an internet café.

As always, Palmer sat at a terminal at the end of a row that wasn't overlooked by anyone, and no one would be walking past. He logged into his secure email account and checked for any updates from Riley. She hadn't sent him anything new, so he inserted the memory stick and zipped up the files, so they were small enough to attach to an email. He added a generic note saying something about holiday snaps, added the number of one of the burner phones and clicked send.

Whatever happened, Riley would know what to do with it.

He pulled out his notebook and started at the top of his list of names. His first suspicions proved to be correct. Within minutes, he had found high-profile people who matched three of the names on the list. They were all dead. Two from cancer and one in a car crash. Several of the names were too common to find a definite hit without spending a few hours researching them. A couple were minor government officials working their way up the ladder, two were CEOs of listed companies, and then, he hit pay dirt. One of the names was a US congressman and another brought up the new Deputy Director of the FBI. It could be a coincidence of course. The real owners of the two names could actually be working at fast-food joints flipping burgers, but Palmer didn't think so. He wrote down the details and logged off.

Outside, the sun was going down. Checking the names had taken up more time than he had planned. It was getting late, and he needed to get back to the cabin before it was fully dark.

Palmer was making good time through the little traffic there was. It was time to check in with Zahrah, make sure everything was okay. He picked up his phone and dialled the burner he had left with her.

'Logan?'

'Yeah. I'm on my way back, I'll be about thirty minutes. Is everything alright?'

'Yeah, I'm good, I've made us some dinner. I just need to heat it up. Let me know when you're ten minutes away.'

'You're too good to me, Zahrah. Next time it's my turn to make you dinner.'

She laughed. 'It's okay, I like cooking. Used to do it a lot with Mom. Anyway, I wanted something more than beans

155

with little sausages in.'

Palmer scoffed. 'It is my speciality. I'll phone you when I'm almost there.'

'Okay. It's getting dark so I'll leave a light on for you.'

'Thanks. See you soon.' He ended the call and put the phone back on the dashboard.

* * *

The pro crawled through the undergrowth until he could just make out the safe house through the trees. It was well hidden off the track and not a place you would just stumble across. It was a perfect hideout. He pulled out a pair of binoculars, but they didn't make things any clearer. The vegetation was too dense to get a close look from that distance. He couldn't see anyone moving about inside and there was no vehicle. That didn't mean they weren't in there. Palmer could easily have disposed of the car or simply parked it out of sight. The one thing the pro could tell was that there was a light on.

Carver's men closed in on the cabin and took up their positions. Each team covered one approach, north, south, east, and west. The pro keyed the mic on his radio. 'All call signs, Red 1, listen in. Hold position, do not move until I give the order, confirm.'

'Red 2, confirm.'

'Red 3, confirm.'

'Yeah, got it.'

The pro closed his eyes. If he wasn't short of men, he would shoot these pricks himself. 'Red 4, say again, over.'

'Okay, okay, Red 4, confirm.'

'Red 1, maintain radio silence. Out.' He put down his radio

and phoned Carver. 'We're ready to go in. We can't confirm that Palmer is there but there is a light on... Yes... Will do.' He ended the call and cocked his weapon.

The pro keyed up his radio again. 'All call signs, Red 1. On my mark. Three, two, one ... Go, Go, Go.'

The four teams rose as one. Each was made up of three men wearing respirators and armed with AR-15s. They quickly made up the ground to the safe house and were on it in seconds. Two of the teams smashed a window and threw in a stun grenade while a third covered the back door. The Pro waited for the bright light and concussive blast of the grenades then cleared the front steps in one and smashed open the door.

* * *

Carver poured himself a large bourbon and waited for his phone to ring. Today was going to be a good day, his problems were almost over. He leaned back in his chair and answered the call. 'Tell me it's all over... What?' He stood up and threw his drink across the room. 'What do you mean they aren't fuckin' there?'

The Pro cleared his throat. 'Exactly what I said. They aren't here. There hasn't been anyone here for a couple of months at least.'

'I thought you said there was a light on.'

'It was on an automatic switch. Programmed to come on at dusk. Like the ones that people put in to convince burglars there is someone in the house.'

Carver swung a kick at his chair. 'Burglars and shit operators. What the hell am I paying you for?'

'Cody Wickes lied to you. He didn't give Palmer the details of this safe house. They could be anywhere by now. We need to know where he sent them, find out.' He ended the call.

Carver leaned on the desk. His whole body was shaking, his breathing shallow and harsh. He beat a slow rhythm with his fist. 'Fuck.' His rhythm increased. His fist pounding until his knuckles reddened and started to bleed. 'LEECH, GET IN HERE!'

When Danny Leech opened the door, he looked terrified. 'Yes, Sir?'

Carver rubbed his knuckles. 'Go and tell them to get Cody Wickes ready. I'm coming to question him myself. Tell them it's going to get messy.'

'Yes, Sir.' Leech closed the door and hurried away.

Chapter 34

Cody Wickes had been locked up and guarded ever since his meeting with Palmer at the hotel. First in the industrial unit and now in what looked like an unused section of a big house. The room they were keeping him in wasn't a dungeon by any means, but it was basic. What furniture there was had been covered over with dust sheets as if the owners had gone away for a long holiday. There was a toilet and shower cubicle through a second door, and he had an old army fold-up camp bed to sleep on.

He had thought of escaping, but the room's windows all had locked shutters on them. Except for the bathroom. The window in there didn't have shutters, it had a steel bar on the outside that ran top to bottom down the middle. It blocked the window from being opened fully and, even if he had smashed the glass, made the gap too small to squeeze through anyway. That left the room's door, which was solid wood and always kept locked with two guards outside. The only chance he had was to try to catch them by surprise, but that was unlikely. He knew he wasn't getting out of this alive but the least he could do was buy Palmer as much time as possible to get the girl to safety.

Once he had given Palmer the keys to his parents' cabin

instead of his, he knew it wouldn't take too long for Carver and his men to find out. To be honest, he was surprised they hadn't killed him already. He was as much of a witness in this as they were. They must have been planning to use him as bait to get Palmer to come in. He couldn't let that happen. As soon as the guards left him alone, he began to formulate a plan.

The old army camp bed that Wickes had been provided with was a long piece of canvas that was held taught by a number of flexible steel poles. With a bit of twisting and pulling, he managed to remove one of the poles and had spent the last day sharpening it against the concrete floor of the toilet. It wasn't as sharp as he would have liked, but it would do. He fashioned a handle at one end using his belt and one of his socks then hid it under the blanket they had left him. All he needed now was the opportunity to use it.

Wickes knelt in front of the door and put his eye to the keyhole. The solid door was an old-fashioned style, and the mortice lock wouldn't have looked out of place on the front door of a castle. He had spent hours monitoring the guards through it, waiting for his chance.

They were taking turns to guard the door for two hours at a time. One was sitting on a wooden chair directly in front of the door while the other lay on a leather couch against the opposite wall. They were both watching football on a small television they had rigged up in the corner.

Danny Leech was out of breath when he burst into the room and tried to blurt out his instructions. 'Mr Carver... He says...' He was fighting to catch his breath.

Guard number one, the one who looked like an orc, held up his hand. 'Calm down office boy. You'll do yourself an injury.

Catch your breath and start again. Slowly.'

Guard number two, the one who looked like an orc's uglier brother, sat up on the couch. 'You better check he hasn't shit in his pants for Christ's sake.'

They both roared with laughter at their orc humour.

Leech swallowed hard and slowed his breathing. 'Mr Carver says get Wickes ready. He is coming here himself to question him... Oh yeah, and it could get messy.'

That was enough to spur the Orcs into action. 'Why didn't you tell us that sooner you prick.? Switch that TV off.'

Wickes sat on the bed and slumped over like he was having a heart attack.

Orc One opened the door and walked in. He reached out and shoved Wickes' shoulder. 'Stand up.'

Wickes didn't move.

Orc One pushed him again. 'I said stand up.'

Orc Two shouted from the couch. 'What is it, man?'

'I don't know.' Orc One looked over his shoulder. 'He's not moving. I think...'

Wickes stood up and drove the metal bed pole under the Orc's rib cage. He pushed with his legs and put his whole body weight behind it. The thin pole, with that much force, went straight through Orc One. As he fell backwards, Wickes pulled the man's semi-automatic out of his shoulder holster and ran to the door.

Orc Two was still on his knees after rolling off the couch. Wickes shot him and swung his weapon around to aim at Danny Leech.

Leech held up his arms. 'No, no, please. I'm not like them. I just want out of here. I just want to go home.'

Wickes looked at the stain that spread across the front of

Leech's trousers. He wasn't a soldier. He was just a terrified young man who had found himself in a situation he wasn't equipped to cope with. 'Where's Carver?'

'Down the stairs and across to the other wing of the house. He's in the room at the top of the main staircase.'

Wickes lowered his sights. 'Get as far away from here as you can. You don't want to be in the vicinity when Palmer comes looking for Carver.'

Leech nodded. He'd already made his mind up. He didn't need any more encouragement.

Wickes sprinted for the stairs and charged down them. The sound of gunfire was sure to have alerted someone. At the bottom of the staircase, he skidded into the entrance hall as bullets zipped past him. He dived to the floor and rolled just as Carver came out of his office. Wickes saw his chance. He took aim and squeezed the trigger, but two of Carver's men ran out of the room next to the office and opened fire. Three bullets hit Wickes in the chest, and he fell backwards, slumped against the wall, a pool of blood spreading out across the tiled floor.

Carver climbed to his feet and looked at the aftermath in the hallway. 'I'm surrounded by idiots.' He let out a deep frustrated sigh. 'Clean this shit up.' He stormed back into his office and slammed the door.

Chapter 35

Palmer had finished his dinner and was sitting on the chair in the main living area, fed and happy. 'That was the best meal I've had since I got here. You should think about becoming a chef.'

Zahrah lay on the small couch and blew out her cheeks. 'I think I made too much though. I can hardly move.'

'Never pass up the chance to eat or sleep. You never know when you'll get the opportunity again.'

'That sounds like an army thing.'

Palmer stared at Zahrah. 'Army? Royal Marines, thank you very much.'

Zahrah laughed. 'How did it go today?'

'I managed to sort a few things out. I sent my friends in London some info to work on. Anna will do a real job of finding the people in the photo. We'll know exactly who they are within a couple of days.'

'Did you ask about the other stuff?'

Palmer nodded. 'In a way. I didn't want to go into details. I said that we needed an exit. She'll know what that means. It'll cost me though.'

Zahrah sat up. 'If it's money they want we've got thirty million to play with.'

Palmer shook his head. 'It's not money. They owe me a favour, up to a point, but, at some stage, there'll be something that they'll want me to do for them. A repayment if you like.'

'And you'll do it?'

Palmer shrugged. 'It's kind of my job. It's all I'm good at. They know that.'

'Is that why you were sent for me and Mom?'

'I came here because Cody Wickes told me about you and your mum. I wouldn't have come for just anyone. I also wouldn't have come if there wasn't money in it for me. That's just a reality of life.'

Zahrah lowered her eyes. 'I'm glad you came.'

'So am I, Zahrah. So am I.'

They sat in silence for a while. Each of them just appreciating the physical presence of the other. They both had trauma that they needed to deal with, demons they had to slay, but that would have to wait until this particular nightmare was over and done with.

It was the insistent buzz of the burner phone that broke the silence. The only person who had that number was Riley. She worked fast.

Palmer grabbed the phone and pressed the green button. 'Hello.'

'It's me. I don't have everything, but I have some.'

'Good. I just need the basics.'

'You were right about the Bureau guy and the politician. Looks like this thing is pretty big.'

'Not what I wanted to hear, but okay.'

Riley spoke fast, trying to get the call over quickly in case eavesdroppers picked up on it. Especially with the FBI involved. 'Another Bureau guy was involved but died during a hostage negotiation. There are other officials on the list, but low level.'

Palmer didn't like the way this was going. 'Do we have an exit?'

'I'll work on it, but you aren't official. They'll want payback.'

'I know. Just do what you can.'

There was a pause. 'I'll send you the details.'

'I'll arrange another number for you to call.'

The line went dead. Palmer removed the battery and took out the SIM card. If someone was already tracking that number, they were probably screwed. Although, in the rural area they were in, it was unlikely the phone had attached to more than one cell site. That made triangulating their position with any accuracy very difficult. Ultimately, getting rid of the phone and using another was just standard operational security. If he and Riley were using different numbers every time, the chance that someone could eavesdrop reduced dramatically.

'What did they say?'

Palmer threw the phone into the waste basket. 'We were right. This is big. The FBI Deputy Director and the Congressman are on the list and in the photographs.'

'That's bad, isn't it? What do we do now?'

'We need to be careful who we trust. If I handed myself into the wrong person, we could both end up dead. I'm hoping the Firm will step in and arrange something.'

'The Firm?'

Palmer nodded. 'Yeah. MI6.'

Chapter 36

Anna Riley tapped at her laptop keyboard. She had already found the names that Palmer had given her. Now she just needed to build a full profile of them and join the dots. She needed to flesh out the full scope of the conspiracy. How far did this thing go? Was it a worldwide force for evil, a shadow government, or just the delusions of a handful of racists?

Most of the names on the list were people who had amounted to nothing. Men who saw themselves as infiltrators into the US establishment but, in reality, were unable to even get onto the bottom rung of the ladder. She had traced a few who had died, some violently, and the rest were working normal jobs with normal lives. Many had given up on their fascist ideals and reformed, but a few were still heavily involved in various movements. With those names crossed out and with no burning need to follow up with more detail just yet, she concentrated on the dozen that were left.

She had told Palmer about the dead FBI agent. He was seen as a highflyer. Someone who would make it to the upper echelons of the Bureau. Whether or not he was still part of the conspiracy when he died was up for debate, but he had been killed trying to rescue a twelve-year-old girl from a child prostitution ring. There was no evidence that he had done anything illegal or questionable in his career. His record was exemplary. Maybe he had atoned for any mistakes he had made in his choice of friends. She crossed the name out. There was no need to involve him, or his family in this. The other FBI Agent was another matter.

Blake Macey had risen quickly through the ranks of the FBI and was now the Deputy Director. He had been in position for six months and was hotly tipped for promotion to the top job when his boss retired in a year. He was happily married to a woman from a well-to-do family and they had two teenage children. His record was also exemplary. There had been no mistakes on his journey up the ladder. No sniff of scandal or disciplinary action. Riley thought that in itself was a little unusual. Who doesn't make a few mistakes when they are starting out? This man was the perfect sleeper agent.

The last name on the list was Congressman Harrison Draper. One of the leading lights in the House of Representatives and a potential presidential candidate for the future. He was a married father of three, a regular church goer and charity fundraiser. As with Blake Macey, he was also a man who was perfect for the job. Another two stars went against him for further research and follow-up.

The big problem that Riley saw with the list was that it was at least fifteen years old. The photographs went back further. How did they know that Carver's organisation hadn't put thirty more sleepers into play since then? Palmer might be right about Carver hiding the loss of the data. It would be a risk to the plan and his backers wouldn't be happy. Then again, this could be a list of people who are no longer involved. This was too big to keep quiet, it had to come out sooner or later. If anything happened to Palmer, she would make sure it was sent to every news outlet in the Western world. It was time for another meeting with Thomson.

* * *

Riley sat on the park bench and tried to look as normal as possible. Just a young woman taking some time out from work and feeding the ducks. She threw a couple of handfuls of birdseed into the water and scanned the footpath to see if Thomson was approaching. There were a couple of people walking along the edge of the other side of the pond, but none of them were her. She checked her watch.

'Can't you feed them bread like everyone else?'

Riley jumped. Thomson had managed to walk up right behind her without being noticed. It wasn't the first time she had done it. 'Dammit, Vicky. I wish you wouldn't do that.'

Thomson walked round to the front of the bench and sat down. 'Just trying to improve your situational awareness, Anna. Always know what's behind you.'

'What am I supposed to do, attach wing mirrors to my jacket?'

'You'll get the hang of it. Try sitting with your back to a wall instead of out in the open.'

Riley felt a little foolish. It was the obvious thing to do, why didn't she think of it? 'Okay, I'll remember that next time.'

Thomson took some of the birdseed. 'Anyway, I thought I said we should meet in the pub this time.'

Riley rummaged in her coat and pulled out a ready mixed can of vodka and lemonade. 'It's the best I could do at short notice.'

Thomson smiled. 'I was joking, Anna, but thank you very much. It was more about getting you into a social environment. You work and worry way too much. I know you don't drink anymore, and that's good, but it doesn't mean you can't go out for a little fun.'

'I can't think of relaxing when my friend is in danger.'

Thomson's head dropped. 'I'm sorry, Anna. I'd forgotten how close you are to him. I've been in this business too long. I've stopped seeing people as anything other than an asset.'

'It's okay, Vicky. I'm your friend, and I know Logan likes you too.'

Thomson smiled. 'Well, that settles it. When this is all over, we're having a party. My treat.'

'That would be nice.'

Thomson threw some more seed to the ducks. 'Right then, Anna. Back to the job at hand. What have you got for me?'

Riley handed Thomson a red, plastic folder. 'It's all in there. Names, dates, personal profiles. There are two people we need to worry about. Blake Macey and Harrison Draper. They've got the power and influence to make Logan look guilty and lock him away, maybe even kill him.'

Thomson flicked through the sheets in the folder. 'Don't worry, Anna, powerful people like this won't want anything to shine a light on them. The real problem is still George Carver.'

'But can't we just put a stop to this now? Bring Logan home?'

Thomson shook her head. 'That's not how it works, unfortunately. We need Palmer and the girl. They are the only people who can link Carver with these documents and the people on the list. Without that provenance, these documents could have been made yesterday. They're just wild allegations that expensive lawyers will quash in the courts.'

Riley didn't understand the politics or the legal implications. 'Can't you do anything for them? We have photographs.'

'Now that we've got the information, we can start to exert a little influence. Put some feelers out, but for the photographs to mean anything, we need the negatives.'

'Does that mean we're official now?'

Thomson sighed. 'I think MI6 can get involved to a certain extent. We can't just confront these people though. As you said, they have the power and influence to bury the story and Palmer. We can let our CIA and FBI contacts know that he's one of ours. We can get them to bring him in under our protection. You'll need to convince Palmer to give himself up though.'

'I can't talk him into that. It's a decision for him, but I'll do my best. If you give me the details, I'll send him the message.'

Thomson put the folder into her bag and patted its side. 'Leave this with me. I'm used to navigating the ins and outs of the game. You let him know he's not alone.'

'Can we get them out?'

'I can pull some strings, get a false ID for the girl. We'll call it witness protection. Palmer will belong to us after this though. We don't normally pull assets out of a mess of their own making. He was on a private job when this hit the fan.'

Riley nodded. 'He knows that. He understands.'

'Good. I think it's time for Palmer to have some more practical help, in theatre as it were.'

Riley leaned forward and lowered her voice. 'You want me to go over there?'

Thomson shook her head. 'No, no. We… he will need you back here doing what you're good at. We need someone who's used to working in the field. Someone who can cover his back.'

'Who are you thinking of?' She looked around for any observers. 'Ruby?'

'You know how to get hold of her, and, technically, she doesn't work for us either. What she does in her own time is her business. I believe she's due a holiday.'

Chapter 37

Ruby Finn was bored. She had been shopping until her feet, and her wallet, hurt, seen countless tourist attractions she had never bothered with before, and watched every newly released film the multiplex had to offer. Twice. MI6 were paying her to be available, but they hadn't been in touch with any work yet. She had always fantasised about having a lifestyle where she was paid to do nothing, but this was driving her to drink, literally. For the third time that week, she was in the pub at lunchtime. She lifted the pint glass to her lips just as Riley came through the door.

Riley gave a little wave and walked to the bar to order a drink. By the look on the barman's face, this wasn't the sort of place where people popped in for a lunchtime mineral water. She settled for a diet lemonade and took it over to Finn's table.

Finn stood up and gave Riley a hug. 'It's so good to see a friendly face. How've you been?'

'I have more good days than bad, how are you?'

Finn sat back down. 'I haven't been this bored for years. I'm in danger of becoming a raging alcoholic.'

'You don't want that to happen. Trust me. I thought you might have gone to see some of your family. Catch up with them.'

Finn scoffed. 'Both sides of my family are what you might call traditional. They don't approve of my lifestyle choices, as they put it. They think I should settle down, get married.'

'Well, that isn't going to happen, is it?'

'Not unless you're here to propose to me.'

Riley blushed. 'I… I'm not…'

'I'm joking. How did you track me down anyway?'

'I went round to your flat. One of your neighbours said you might be here.'

Finn smiled. 'See, I told you I was in here too much. I take it this isn't a social call?'

'It's unofficial. I'm just here to catch up with a friend, let you know about some work that might be available.'

Finn took a drink. 'You've got me curious. Tell me more.'

Riley took off her jacket and threw it on the seat beside Finn. 'There's an envelope in the inside pocket. If you're interested, it has an open ticket to the US and a briefing note with info on the main players. There's a credit card in your name and some cash to keep you going. When you get there, buy a burner phone and contact me.'

'You're getting good at this stuff, Anna. You said this isn't official. Do The Firm know you're here?'

'Officially? No. This is a private job and, if we get into trouble, there's no cavalry coming to bail us out.'

Finn nodded. 'And unofficially?'

'Vicky sent me. You're going in as backup for someone who might be in trouble.'

'This someone, must be quite important for Vicky to send you to track me down. Did some politician's kid get caught at the airport with a bag of Bolivian marching powder, or did someone's secret lover get caught shoplifting?'

Riley drank her lemonade and checked that no one was standing behind her. 'It's much more important than that. It's Logan… Logan Palmer.'

Finn sat up straight. 'What is it, what's happened? I haven't spoken to him for a couple of months. He invited me to visit him in Indonesia.'

'He must have been bored too. He took a job for a company that specialises in kidnap resolution. Delivering ransoms, recovering hostages, stuff like that.'

'What went wrong? He took it personally, didn't he?'

Riley frowned. 'What do you mean?'

'It's what he does. Haven't you noticed? Every time he takes on a job, he gets emotionally involved. Is he in big trouble?'

'We don't know all the details, but it seems he's got tangled up with some corrupt politician who runs a white supremacist organisation, and the FBI want him for kidnapping, and theft as a minimum.'

Finn shook her head. 'For fuck's sake, Logan. You don't do things in halves.' She took the envelope out of Riley's jacket and put it in her own pocket. 'I'll pack a few things and get the earliest flight I can.'

'Thank you, Ruby. Be careful, both of you. You're the only real friends I have.'

'Don't worry. With the two of us on the case, we'll have it sorted in no time. Do me a favour though. Don't tell him I'm coming.'

'What? Why?'

'If he knows I'm there, he might drop his guard. I need to be able to move about without any of the players, including Logan, knowing, until it's necessary.'

Riley nodded. 'Okay, I won't tell him anything.'

Finn drained her pint and stood up. 'Don't worry, Anna. I'll bring him home.' She left her empty glass on the bar and left the pub.

Riley sat for a few minutes before remembering that she was in a dive bar drinking lemonade at lunchtime on a Thursday. Maybe that was why she was getting strange looks. Especially off the guy behind the bar. She was an obvious fish out of water. She didn't want to hang around and discuss it with the other patrons, they didn't look like people she would get on with. She picked up her coat and hurried out of the door.

Chapter 38

Palmer was back in New Orleans checking his email. This time he had Zahrah with him. She didn't like being left alone in the cabin and, as she pointed out, she had a laptop. They didn't have to worry about accidentally leaving data on one of the internet café's desktops or being overlooked. They could sit in a corner and tap at the keyboard to their heart's content. Palmer had said that he could just take the laptop with him, but Zahrah wouldn't let it out of her site.

Palmer went through his usual routine of logging in to his secure mail and checking for updates. There was one message in his inbox and, of course, it was from Riley. He double-clicked on it and opened it up.

Zahrah put two coffees and a piece of chocolate cake down on the table and sat next to Palmer. 'Are you sure you don't want some cake? You don't know what you're missing.'

'No thanks. I'm good.' Palmer was uneasy about being in such a public place together. It made it easier to pick them out of the crowd. He had already checked there was no CCTV inside the building, and although the chances of some spook happening to look at this diner while they were here were very small, he still didn't like it. 'Make sure you keep your hat on.'

'You think someone might be watching us?'

'It's unlikely, but you never know. I think that, as long as we don't end up in a fight like the last place, we should be fine.'

Zahrah whispered, 'I'll try not to start anything.'

Palmer hit the keys on the laptop, scrolling down through Riley's email. He was shaking his head, muttering to himself continually. 'I can't believe they're even suggesting this as a plan.'

Zahrah cut off a chunk of chocolate cake. 'Suggesting what?'

'They want me to give myself up.'

'No way, are they crazy?'

Palmer shook his head. 'They are saying that it's the best way to protect you from Carver. They send someone over to pick you up and, while the FBI are busy dealing with me, get you out of the country.'

'I'm not running away and leaving you to take the blame for everything.'

'I'll be fine.' Palmer was lying to her now. He thought he was likely to be anything other than fine. 'Once the Firm claims me as one of their own, the US authorities will back off to a certain extent. Special relationship and all that. I might spend a little time in prison while they sort out the paperwork and high-level spooks argue with each other, but, sooner or later, I'll just get deported. Especially with the evidence we have hidden away. The US won't want all of this being made public.'

Zahrah pushed her plate away. 'I think it's too risky. What if the people you hand yourself over to are part of this?'

'The key is publicity. If we can get the basic story out, show that Carver is being investigated by the authorities, their options for getting rid of us get fewer and fewer. We also have to believe that not everyone can be in on it.'

'You're actually thinking about doing it, aren't you?'

Palmer typed on the keyboard. 'I'm going to let them know that I'll consider it if they set something up. The FBI agent in charge of the case won't have been involved until we left Texas. They aren't one of his paid for local cops. The agents on the ground aren't going to do anything illegal just because they've been told to. I was following orders isn't a valid defence.'

'And you think you can trust them?'

Palmer closed the lid of the laptop. 'I wouldn't say I trust them. I'm not going to tell anyone where we are, even my friends. It could leak out by accident. If they set up a meeting, it needs to be out in the open and away from here.'

'Don't do anything stupid.'

Palmer put his hand on Zahrah's. 'I promise I won't. They aren't going to get back to us for a while so I think we should pick up the supplies we need and get back to the cabin. My turn to cook.'

Zahrah rolled her eyes. 'I'm getting some more cake to take back with us.'

Chapter 39

Special Agent Ethan Gault drove across the bridge to Carver's seaside fortress. One of the security guards stepped in front of the car and forced him to stop. Gault wound down the window and shouted at the man. 'You know who I am, get out of the way or I'm going to run you over.'

Recognition dawned on the face of the guard. He stepped to one side and raised the barrier. 'Sorry, I didn't recognise the car.'

'Idiot.' Gault drove through the imposing gates and parked up.

Carver came out of the front of the house and steered Gault to a small wooden building at the bottom of the garden. It was the kind of building that suburban office workers put in their gardens so they could work from home. In Carver's case, it was there to provide the staff a place to chill out and have a drink when they weren't working. Carver preferred them to stay on the premises rather than head off to the nearest bar. Most of them couldn't keep their mouths shut when they'd had a few drinks.

The inside of the building was simple, a bar at one end and a huge TV at the other. Four small tables were scattered in between with padded wooden chairs arranged around them. The walls were decorated with signed football and baseball shirts, movie posters, and photographs of motorbikes. It was more man cave than a home office.

Carver went behind the bar and poured himself a large bourbon. 'You want a drink?'

'Not while I'm working.'

'What have you got for me?'

Gault pulled out one of the chairs and sat down, putting his feet up on another. 'The FBI has had a communication from MI6 in London. Apparently, Logan Palmer is one of theirs. Did you know that when you hired him and his buddy to take part in this cluster-fuck of a kidnap?'

'Wickes just told me that Palmer had experience in hostage negotiation. I didn't see the need to check up on him any more than that.'

'Maybe if you had, we would have known sooner what type of man we are dealing with. I've got the full force of the FBI behind me, resources you wouldn't believe, and all we knew was that he is an ex-Royal Marine and bodyguard. There's nothing in his record about MI6.'

Carver emptied his glass in one gulp and poured another. 'What difference would knowing he was MI6 have made?'

'Even the FBI, with all our resources, have to focus our efforts in the most likely places that our target will be. We've been using completely the wrong profile for Palmer. I've had our people working up the likely behaviour of a combat soldier, not a spy.'

'You'll just have to look harder.'

Gault took his feet off the chair and kicked it across the room. 'Is there something you aren't telling me?'

'Like what?'

'Why are you so keen to get your granddaughter back? You don't strike me as a man who would be worried about a girl with her... racial mix.'

Carver walked over to the door and pulled it closed. 'Her father, my son, stole thirty million dollars from me fifteen years ago. Now that he's dead, she's the last one who knows where it is.'

Gault smiled. 'Now it all makes sense. This is all about money. You expect the FBI to find these two just so you can get it back.'

'In short, yes. This man has kidnapped my granddaughter, a minor, and taken her across a state line. That makes it a federal case. That makes it the FBI's business. Whether you like it or not.'

'Lucky for you that MI6 want this dealt with quickly. My boss has told me that I'm to meet Palmer in a place of his choosing to discuss his surrender. Looks like he's willing to come to us, but only on his terms.'

Carver clenched his fist. 'Yes. That's perfect. We can take him out as soon as he shows.'

Gault held up his hand. 'Hold your horses there. This is, as you said, FBI business. I don't want to see, hear, or smell you or any of your weekend warrior militia anywhere near this. You stand down and stick to hiding behind the walls of your pretend castle. Who are you hiding from? Are you scared the Girl Scouts will come after you for muscling in on their cookie selling territory?'

Carver poured another bourbon down his throat. 'It's nothing for you to worry about. You just find my granddaughter.'

Chapter 40

Palmer drove to an area off River Road, between New Orleans and Baton Rouge. He pulled the van into an abandoned industrial site and hid behind a silo. The former chemical plant that the silo belonged to was one of many that dotted the area along the Mississippi River and the reason it was known by some as Cancer Alley.

The silo they were behind was one of three that ran along the front of the property. The rest of the site was taken up by two large, corrugated steel buildings and a towering chimney supported by a rusty scaffold structure.

Palmer turned off the engine. 'Stay here and don't switch any lights on, not even your phone. We have to stay hidden for this to work.'

Zahrah agreed. 'Mind if I get some sleep?'

'No, climb in the back and keep your head down. That would be perfect.' He grabbed his binoculars and a burner phone and climbed out of the van.

The silo Palmer climbed was the middle of the three. It had been painted white at some point in its life with a bright orange and blue logo on the front. Now the paint had turned yellow as the rust underneath ate its way into the steel and bubbled through to the surface. The ladder up the side of the silo was no longer attached in some places, where the bolts had corroded so much they had fallen out, and it wobbled as Palmer climbed it.

He shifted his weight slowly as he reached the end of the ladder and moved onto the top of the silo. The domed roof was showing signs of corrosion but felt solid enough. He checked that it wouldn't collapse underneath him then crawled to the structure's high point. It gave him a perfect view of another industrial site on the north bank of the river. The nearest bridge was miles away. Even if they spotted him, he would be long gone by the time they got here. Unless they had air support. Palmer had everything crossed that they wouldn't. He was hoping that they would play this by the book and at least try to bring him in peacefully.

He raised himself up on his elbows and lifted his binoculars. On the other side of the river, two police cars and a black SUV drove along the road to the coordinates where Palmer had told the FBI he would meet them. The cars pulled up and everyone climbed out. He knew who they all were, one of his stipulations for the meeting was that everyone wore clear identification. Four New Orleans Police Officers and one FBI Agent. Palmer put in his earpiece and pressed the speed dial on his phone.

The light from Special Agent Gault's phone screen lit up his face. Palmer had blocked the number, of course, but its approximate location could still be traced given time. This had to be kept short.

Gault answered the call. 'Palmer?'

'You must be Special Agent Gault.'

'That's me. So, are you coming in, Palmer?'

Palmer chuckled. 'You didn't think it would be that easy,

did you?'

Gault looked around to try to pick out Palmer, but the area they were standing in was floodlit. It was impossible to see any details outside the throw of the lights. Palmer had chosen the perfect location. 'I was hoping we could get this finished tonight. I'm on your side, Logan. Can I call you Logan?'

'You can call me whatever you want, but don't try any of that amateur psych, we can all be friends, crap on me.'

Gault signalled to the police to stand down. 'What is it that you want, Palmer? I know this isn't about money for you. I'm not falling for Carver's bullshit.'

'On the other side of the car park is a red dumpster. Taped to the bottom of it is an envelope that contains some documents that show that Carver is part of a right-wing conspiracy.'

'That isn't going to surprise anyone. We all know his history.'

Palmer checked his watch. He was timing the call. 'Maybe not, but the people who are involved with him might raise a few eyebrows.'

'Don't tell me, it's the CIA.'

'It's a little closer to home than that, Gault. The FBI Deputy Director is on the list. You need to clean up your own house.'

Gault lowered his voice. 'You're shitting me.'

'No, we've got cops, politicians, and CEOs all running through the woods pretending to be revolutionaries and signing up to a fascist plan to take over the country.'

'If that's true there's no telling who we can trust with this. What do you want from us, Logan? How can I help resolve this?'

Palmer checked his watch again. 'Look at the documents and make up your own mind. I have much more evidence that backs up the accusations. I'll be in touch.'

Palmer watched Gault walk over to the first police car and knock on the window. There was a brief exchange then the two cars started their engines and pulled away. They drove in a wide arc and headed back along the road towards New Orleans.

Gault waited until they were out of sight then walked across the carpark to the red dumpster. He dropped to his knees, retrieved the envelope from the bottom of the dumpster, and went back to his SUV.

Palmer climbed down the side of the silo and went back to the van. Zahrah was asleep curled up in the back. There was no need to wake her, he knew she hadn't been sleeping well. It wasn't surprising, after everything she had been through, she would need some professional help, or the dreams would never stop. He knew that from personal experience, his nightmares still haunted him every time he closed his eyes. He pulled out from behind the silo and drove them back to the cabin.

Zahrah woke up as Palmer pulled onto the cabin's access track. She sat up yawning and rubbing her eyes. 'Did everything go okay?'

'As well as we could have expected. The FBI have the documents I printed out. That'll give them a taste of what we have. I told Ethan Gault about his boss being on the list.'

'Did he sound surprised? Do you think he'll help us?'

Palmer wanted to say yes, tell Zahrah that it would be okay, but he couldn't. After seeing some of the names on the list, it was possible that the conspiracy went much higher than they knew. He might have just handed over information to the very people who were looking for them. He sighed. 'We have to trust someone, sooner or later. This guy Ethan Gault sounded genuine. Once I'd told him about the Deputy Director, he sent the police away before he went to get the envelope. It looked like he was playing it safe.'

'That sounds promising, doesn't it?'

Palmer stopped the van outside the cabin. 'All we can do is see what the reaction is. I'll give them tomorrow to make sense of the evidence and realise they need to see the rest. They'll get permission to offer me a deal the next day and try to bring us in.'

'But you don't need a deal, you haven't done anything wrong.'

'Don't worry. Like I said, it's just a way to get me to give myself up. Once I'm officially in the system, they can't hide the story. You'll be safe.'

Zahrah climbed out of the van, and they walked up the front steps into the cabin.

Chapter 41

Carver stood with his back to the desk and stared out of the window across the Gulf of Mexico. 'What do you want? You should be out there tracking down Palmer. Why didn't you bring him in last night?'

Gault had the documents in his hand. 'You told me this was about money. Why did you feel the need to lie about that?'

'I didn't lie, I just kept the information I gave you to things you needed to know.'

'Things I needed to know?'

Carver turned round. 'Your job, the FBI's job, is to rescue Zahrah Kalu from Palmer. The reason he has her, why I want her back, doesn't matter. It's nothing to do with you.'

Gault scoffed. 'Okay, here's how it looks back in DC. First of all, you hid the original kidnapping from the FBI. Second, you sent an armed team of… whatever the fuck they are to kill the hostage takers, so you don't have to raise the ransom. Unsuccessfully, I might add. Third, only then do you finally contact the FBI but fail to hand over all the information.'

'I don't give a shit how it looks. Those papers belong to me, they are my private documents. You don't get it, do you?'

Gault threw the sheets across the desk. 'Why don't you explain it to me, Carver? From where I'm sitting, it looks like you've been working against us from the start.'

'There are men above me, powerful men, men who can kill people like you and me without a moment's thought and get away with it.' He pointed at the paper strewn across the desk. 'Those documents, and the rest of the information that was stolen, compromises those men. How long do you think they'll let this carry on?'

'I don't think you even know who those powerful men are.'

Carver slammed his fist on the desk. 'God dammit. Just do your job and find them.'

Gault turned and headed for the door. 'No more secrets. No more fuck ups. Understand?' He swung open the door and stormed out of the office.

Carver picked up the papers and read through them. Some of the information was out of date, no longer valid. Releasing it would just lead investigators down blind alleys that would tie them up for years, but the rest of the evidence was a different matter. Everything that Brandon had stolen, when looked at together, laid bare the whole plan.

The phone on Carver's desk rang. He knew who it was. He had been waiting for them to call. This was his chance to convince them that he was still in control. If they didn't believe what he told them, he could count his remaining lifespan in hours. They would do away with him and take over the operation. He cleared his throat and picked up the handset.

* * *

Ethan Gault sat, alone, in the secure meeting room of the FBI field office. The sheet of paper in front of him was a copy of one of the documents that showed FBI Deputy Director Blake

Macey's involvement with Carver's organisation. If it became public, the fallout would be catastrophic. The evidence that Palmer was holding onto was a time bomb.

The desk phone in the middle of the table rang and Gault answered it. The voice on the other end of the call belonged to his SAC, Special Agent-in-Charge Amy Caddick. Right from the start her anger was obvious. Her shouts caused the telephone's hands-free speaker to distort and made her sound like an extra in a sci-fi movie. Gault turned the volume down a little so he could at least understand what she was screaming at him.

'Carver is making us look like fools. He's making it appear that he is above the law, and people are beginning to notice. They want to know why he didn't report the original kidnap and why we didn't pick up on it. You're telling me that there was no hint of anything happening.'

Gault exhaled. 'There was nothing to point the Bureau in Carver's direction before he contacted us. He's said that he didn't want to risk the hostages' safety and tried, mistakenly, to deal with it himself.'

'And that led to the death of the mother and the daughter being kidnapped by the man he hired to resolve it?'

'That's how it looks at the moment.'

Amy Caddick's heavy breathing filled the silence. 'What is he hiding from us? What doesn't he want us to know about this whole thing? I'm coming under pressure to explain what this is all about.'

Gault glanced at the sheet of paper in front of him. 'Carver is telling everyone that this is about some money that was stolen by his son before he went into prison. An insurance policy to make sure no one hurt his family. Apparently, the girl knows where everything is hidden. Carver wants it back.'

'Why didn't we know about this missing money when we locked Brandon Carver up?'

'I was just out of training back then. I'd have to go through the files to find out, but I would imagine that no one reported it stolen.' The tone of sarcasm in his voice was unmissable.

Once again, minutes passed with Amy Caddick's breathing the only sound coming out of the speaker. Finally, she let out a frustrated sigh and sucked her teeth. 'I want this cleared up as soon as possible. I want Palmer dealt with. Let's not forget that Simone Kalu was killed during the handover. Murder during a kidnapping attracts the death penalty in Texas. MI6 can come and get their man dead or alive, I don't give a shit which. I want the girl in our custody and kept safe from Carver until we know what she knows. There's more to this than I'm being told, and I want it kept out of the public eye. Can I rely on you to do that, Ethan?'

'Consider it done. We're getting closer to him every day. We know he's somewhere in Louisiana, possibly out in the swamp. If we can pinpoint his exact location, we can bring him in. What do you want me to do with Carver?'

'We've got plenty to hold him on if he causes any trouble. We have an apparent shootout at the handover, but he says there are no bodies other than the girl's mother. The mother's body was moved from the crime scene to a private morgue, but there's no evidence that any investigation was carried out first. I'm sure there'll be enough evidence of wrongdoing to lock him away for a long time. We'll deal with him later.'

Gault ended the call and picked up his mobile. He needed to get his hands on the rest of the evidence that Palmer was hiding. It was time to call on the full resources of the FBI.

He pressed the speed dial and waited for an answer. 'This is Special Agent Ethan Gault. I want a full work-up for Cody Wickes on my desk ASAP. I want to know everything about him.' He hung up and tossed the phone back on the desk.

Chapter 42

T he minute that Ruby Finn cleared immigration, she was off and running. She couldn't afford to waste time acclimatising and she had already snatched a couple of hours sleep on the plane. That would have to do. She wanted to visit all the places that they knew Palmer had been, but the first thing she needed was a weapon.

In Texas, it isn't unusual to see signs on office doors that say *No Weapons on the Premises*. For that reason, some residents of Houston, who like to be armed when they leave the house, keep their pistols in their cars. All Finn had to do was figure out which vehicles were the most likely to have a weapon in them.

Many truck drivers carry a pistol in their cab for obvious reasons. Some of them were hauling valuable cargo and hijackings weren't uncommon. The problem with trucks is that they aren't that easy to break into. They have good security, and the doors are too high up to force open without someone noticing. There was also the problem of CCTV. The drivers tended to park up somewhere well-lit and either public or covered by cameras.

What Finn wanted was a specific type of vehicle driven by a particular type of driver. Older vehicles that were beaten up or had a few dents in them were less likely to have working alarms. Smaller cars that might be driven by a single parent or a student were unlikely to have any weapons in them. What Finn was looking for was a beaten-up, fairly old, pick-up truck or four-wheel drive vehicle.

In the same way, the type of person who carried a weapon when they went to the shops or off to work could also be broken down into likely categories. She needed to stay away from anything with a child seat in the back or any stickers that showed a preference for yoga, veganism, or the environment. These were, of course, sweeping generalisations but, in the main, it helped to improve the chances of finding a weapon quickly. She had been driving around the streets of Houston in her hire car for ninety minutes when she came across the perfect candidate.

She favoured car parks behind bars as she figured the type of person who would drink and drive was more likely to be armed. So, when she drove past a bar just outside the West Loop and spotted the old rusty pick-up parked at the side, she knew she had to check it out.

She parked her hire car out of sight in the parking lot of a supermarket half a mile from the bar. As she walked towards the target, she noticed a shooting range not far away. The owner of the pick-up might have been firing a few off to pass the time.

Walking around the perimeter of the car park, she picked a spot that wasn't overlooked by any windows. She pulled the collar of her jacket up, put on a hat, and vaulted over the fence.

The pick-up was adorned with stickers that showed an allegiance to the Stars and Stripes, Texas, and Donald Trump.

Most importantly of all, it had a window sticker that professed support for the Second Amendment. That part of the constitution that gives US citizens the right to keep and bear arms. All it needed to make it an even better find was for the doors to be open. Unfortunately, she wasn't that lucky. The truck did, however, have a toolbox in the back that looked promising. She opened the box and took out a screwdriver, had a quick check for anyone approaching, and smashed the passenger window.

It didn't take long to open the door and check the glove compartment. Jackpot. A chrome-plated M1911 pistol sat on top of a full box of .45 calibre ammunition. It was a heavy weapon, but it had stopping power. It was thinner than many models and good for concealed carry. Finn tucked the pistol into the back of her jeans and put the box of ammo in her jacket. She had another check for any onlookers then left the car park the same way she had entered.

Back in her hire car, Finn's next stop was Carver's office. Not his campaign headquarters in the glass tower, but his industrial unit. The campaign office building was, more than likely, secured by numerous cameras and a round-the-clock security team. There was no way Finn was getting in and out of there unnoticed. The industrial unit, on the other hand, was a much more attractive proposition.

Finn parked outside the corrugated steel warehouse and waited for the sun to set. Although the whole area had some floodlighting, there were lots of shadows and black spots she could stick to. In the two hours she had been watching the building, there had been no visitors and no security patrols. She left her car and made her way to one of the small side doors.

It didn't take long for Finn to pick the lock on the door. Either Carver didn't keep anything valuable in here or he was so arrogant that he thought no one would break in. Finn closed the door behind her and switched on her torch.

She stood with her back to the wall and surveyed the area. The inside of the warehouse was pitch black. She checked every sight line from her position and could see no tell-tale red lights of an alarm or camera system. It didn't mean there weren't any, it just made it less probable. Once she was sure there was no one else in the building, she took a direct line to the office that filled up one corner.

The office was basic but looked deserted. There were two filing cabinets with the drawers open and empty. She checked the drawers in the desk, but they were empty too. Just when she was thinking this was a waste of time, she noticed a year planner pinned to the back wall. The only thing Carver hadn't got rid of.

Most of the dates in the planner were blank. Carver wasn't very organised for a crook. There were a couple of mentions of meetings and TV interviews but little else. The one thing he had put onto the planner with any regularity was where he had blocked out whole weeks with the word Galveston. That must be the house on the coast that Riley told her about. It must be where he was hiding.

The sudden mechanical clunk and whirr of the big roller door opening made Finn drop to her knees. A panel van reversed into the cavernous space and two men got out. They opened the back doors and lifted something out which they carried over to a stack of wooden crates along one wall.

One of them covered the package with a tarpaulin. 'That'll do for now. We don't want to get caught with it in the van.

We'll come back tomorrow and get rid of it.'

The two men got back in the vehicle and closed the roller door on their way out.

Finn waited until all noise had stopped then crept over to the stack of boxes. She rolled back the tarpaulin and uncovered a black body bag. For a moment, she was terrified that she was too late, and Carver had already killed Palmer. Taking several deep breaths, she unzipped the bag and pulled it open. She felt a wave of relief when she realised it wasn't him.

From the descriptions Riley had given her, she was sure that the body was that of Cody Wickes. If things weren't bad enough already, this made them many times worse. Carver was already killing people to get what he wanted. Palmer and the girl were in imminent danger. She took a photograph of the body and sent a message to Riley, *Find Logan*.

Chapter 43

Riley was having breakfast when Finn's message arrived. She didn't realise what it was at first, but when she did, she dropped her phone as if it was somehow contaminated. Taking a couple of calming breaths, she picked her phone back up and looked at the picture. She recognised the man in the picture from the research she had done. If the man who had hired Palmer was dead, he was in serious trouble.

There was no time to waste. Riley logged on to her laptop and got started. She had to find a way of pinpointing Palmer's location and letting him know what had happened. She had to get Finn to him as backup.

All she had to help her was the number of the burner phone and the IP address that Palmer logged into his email from. She assumed that he had already destroyed the phone, but she sent a message to an old contact at GCHQ to see if they could tell her which cell tower it had last attached to.

Next, the IP address. It led her to a location on the outskirts of New Orleans. At least she now knew the rough area Palmer was in. Or had been in when he checked his email. She put a tracker on his account. If he logged in again, she would get an instant alert. She added a message to Palmer's account to tell him Cody Wickes was dead, and his location might have been compromised.

Riley put the kettle on and made herself another strong, black coffee. She needed to switch on. There had to be a way to find out where Palmer was hiding and get a message to him. A trawl of the US law enforcement databases gave her the details of the FBI Agent who was working on Palmer's case. If all else failed, she could try contacting him, but that was a last resort. She didn't want to lead the FBI straight to Palmer.

She picked her phone up and dialled Finn's number. It took several rings before the call was answered.

Finn sounded groggy. The time difference and lack of sleep must have caught up with her. 'Yes?'

'It's me. You need to get over to Louisiana. Our mutual friend has been using a place on the outskirts of New Orleans. He must be holed up in that area.'

'Okay. I'll set off as soon as it gets light. Keep me up to date on anything else that comes in.'

'I will.' Riley ended the call. She had forgotten about the time difference. She took a gulp of lukewarm coffee and a sudden thought hit her. Palmer was hard to find because he was using operational security to stay hidden. He didn't want to be found. What Riley had to do was look at the people around him. Their details weren't hidden or constantly changing. If she could locate the people Palmer was interacting with, she could find him.

She gathered together all of the phone numbers she could, all the major players. Cody Wickes, George H. Carver, Ethan Gault, and Palmer. The call logs for the past few weeks would show their movements. If she cross-referenced them, she could create a heat map that would show the most likely area Palmer was in.

Riley had already done a full background check on the main names included in the evidence, now it was time to go over the names she had discounted. The first one she looked at was the FBI agent killed before he could climb the ladder.

Travis Newlan was in the mid-nineties photographs that Palmer had sent and there were copies of documentation that showed his involvement, so he was definitely knee-deep in the conspiracy. He was already at the FBI academy when the photographs were taken and was on course to graduate top of his class. He must have been seen as Carver's jewel in the crown.

Ten years after the original pictures were taken, Newlan was a supervisory special agent with a reputation for integrity and getting the job done. He was sent to oversee an operation to bring down a child sex ring and rescue a trafficked, twelve-year-old girl. He had been killed in the crossfire between the traffickers and the SWAT team.

Riley scrolled through the reports. There were pages of them. Newspapers, TV reports, magazine articles, all commended Travis Newlan on his bravery. There were photographs of his family and his funeral. The flag-draped coffin and guard of honour, his grief-stricken protégé. Riley paused on the photo and caption underneath. How did she miss it?

She leafed through the pile of printed sheets she had amassed during her research. She had only just been looking at it. At last, she found what she was searching for. She held the printed sheet up to the screen. Staring back at her were images of the same man, ten years apart. Travis Newlan was

Ethan Gault's mentor.

Chapter 44

Ruby Finn listened in silence as Riley panicked over the phone. There was no point interrupting her, she wasn't listening. Instead, Finn just waited for her to stop for breath. 'Calm down, Anna. I understand what you're saying, but you need to stay focused. Just because Travis Newlan was Ethan Gault's mentor doesn't mean he's in on it too. You said yourself that the dead guy's record was exemplary. You need to do some more digging.'

Riley's breathing slowed. 'I'll do a background check on him. I've got a friend pulling off mobile phone call logs for me. They might show something.'

'That's it. Logan needs you to find the links. Get the information to him so that he knows what he's dealing with.'

'I'll send him another message. I need to find out what number he's using. I knew it was a bad idea to lose contact with him. Where are you?'

Finn looked through the car windscreen. 'I'm outside the place in New Orleans. The people inside thought they recognised Palmer, but they weren't a hundred per cent. No One knew where he was staying.'

'I've sent you the location of a cabin that Cody Wickes is shown as owning. I don't think they'll be there, it's too obvious, but it needs to be checked out.'

'I'll drive up there now. Keep looking, Anna.'

'I will.'

* * *

Finn parked her car at the side of the road and approached the cabin on foot. As she did a complete circle of the surrounding area, she noticed the tell-tale signs of disturbed and damaged vegetation. Someone had surrounded the cabin. Each team looked like it consisted of at least two men, possibly more, and all were wearing combat-style boots.

She looked at the tracks that had been made in the patches of mud. They were fresh, no more than a couple of days old, and had different treads. That ruled out the military. There were no spent cartridges, so there hadn't been a firefight, but she found at least one position where a bipod-mounted weapon had been set up.

With the circle completed, Finn retraced her steps, but this time in a spiral that ended at the front of the cabin. The same muddy boot prints were evident on the wooden steps and on the door. The frame of the door was splintered, and the hinges had buckled. Someone had forced their way in. She pulled her pistol out of her waistband and pushed open the door.

Finn had noticed the smell as soon as she walked inside. It was something she had become accustomed to while growing up in Belfast. It was the acrid smell of tear gas. It was clinging to the fabric of the curtains and the furniture. She moved one of the curtains to the side to reveal the broken window. From the looks of it, this was where the gas canister breached the building. She was looking across the floor to try to find the canister itself when she heard footsteps outside.

When the man kicked open the door and entered the cabin, he didn't look like someone who was expecting to come across anyone inside. As he stepped inside, Finn felled him with a strike to the back of his head that dropped him to the floor.

Finn dragged the man into the middle of the cabin and searched him. He had no ID on him. At least someone had told him not to carry any. She pulled up his shirt and removed the nine-millimetre semi-automatic he had clipped to his belt. At the back of his waistband, she found two extra magazines and a spring-loaded, telescopic baton. Both would come in handy if any trouble kicked off.

She had one last look around the inside of the building then, as the man was starting to come around, went out the door and back to her car.

Chapter 45

Washington DC is just like any other city that hosts a seat of government. Residents didn't bat an eyelid when they saw powerful members of the administration out in public. Convoys of black SUVs were common, and teams of bodyguards were evident in many open spaces. The Deputy Director of the FBI and a Congressman bumping into each other and deciding to stop for a chat over a coffee wasn't out of the ordinary. It was the way that many political deals were done in The District.

Harrison Draper was struggling to keep his anger below the surface. 'What the fuck is going on? If any of this shit leaks out, we're both finished.'

'As far as anyone else is concerned, this is about a kidnapping that went wrong and a corrupt wannabe politician looking for his stolen money. There's nothing that links it back to us.'

'But we know that there are photos and documents that will lead law enforcement directly to our doorstep.'

Blake Macey checked that their bodyguards were keeping members of the public out of earshot. 'We just need to stay calm and do everything by the book. I haven't spoken to the agent on the case directly. I've only issued orders via his SAC. That means I can deny having anything other than a passing knowledge of the case.'

'We need to take care of Carver, he has become a liability. If he gets arrested, he'll offload everything he knows to try to get himself a deal.'

'Agreed, it's time he wasn't around anymore. What about the others? The girl, the Brit that's with her.'

Draper paused, considering the options. 'I don't think there's any reason to leave them around to spill everything. Deal with them and pick up any evidence.'

'I'll take care of that side of things.'

Draper nodded and stood up. 'We should probably stop meeting for a little while. Just until the dust has well and truly settled. I'll look for the resolution to this story, alongside Carver's obituary, in the news.' He walked off along the path back to his car.

Macey reached into his pocket and switched off the voice recorder on his phone. If anyone was getting a deal out of all of this, it was him. He finished his coffee, threw the cup in the dustbin, and walked back to his office.

Chapter 46

Palmer drove them north, through New Orleans and across the twenty-three-mile-long Lake Pontchartrain Causeway Bridge to the small city of Covington. They needed some fresh supplies, and it was always a good idea to shop in different places. Just in case someone was tracking them at the malls they had used previously. It also gave Palmer a different location to contact the FBI from.

He had given Agent Gault enough time to look through the samples of evidence he had given him and come up with a plan to bring him and Zahrah in safely. It might still be doing the rounds to get full approval, but he should have the bare bones of a plan worked out by now.

Palmer slotted a SIM card into another fresh burner phone, his last, and clipped on a battery. The phone came to life and Palmer dialled the number he had written down in his notebook.

The call was answered quickly. 'This is Gault.'

'It's Palmer. I'm hoping you've got an update for me.'

'I was about to ask you the same thing. What else have you got for me?'

'That entirely depends on how you want to move on this. If you've got a plan to keep Zahrah Kalu safe and bring us in,

I'm all ears. If not, I'll ring off and you'll never hear from me again.'

There was a long pause. Palmer knew that Gault was trying to keep him on the call. Even if he couldn't trace his location, Gault would be determined not to lose contact. It was the only chance he had of bringing this case to a conclusion. They would, most likely, have narrowed the search to Louisiana after the meeting, but they still couldn't find them. That proved that if Palmer decided to vanish, the FBI, with all its resources, would have no chance of finding him.

'There's no need to get spooked and run off, Logan. I'm here to help you.'

'So, what's the plan?'

'We've looked at the information you've given us, but some of it is out of date. I'd like to meet up with you and look at the rest so we can truly judge the size of this conspiracy.'

Palmer chuckled. 'And why should I trust you? After all, your own Deputy Director is on the list of conspirators.'

'Not everyone in the FBI knows each other. You can check me out if you want. I don't know him. I've never even met him. We move in different circles.'

'And why are you on this case?'

Gault paused again. The trace shouldn't take much longer. 'I was told to deal with this by my SAC. That's the normal process. The Deputy Director doesn't speak to agents at my level.'

It all made sense to Palmer. He knew how orders flowed down the chain of command. The people on the ground were given tasks by their immediate superiors. The top brass dealt with the bigger picture. 'I don't want another clandestine meeting. It's too much of a risk. The only way you're getting your hands on the rest of the evidence is when you bring us in. That isn't going to happen until you prove to me that I can trust you.'

'How can I prove that I can be trusted, Logan? Nothing happened at our last meeting. I could have used air support and picked you up quite easily. What more do you want?'

'I've given you enough information for you to arrest Carver and hold him for questioning. I want it done publicly. I want to see it on the news and in the papers. If you do that, I'll come in and give you the rest of the evidence to take him down.'

Gault let out a snort. 'You know I can't do that. Getting a warrant to arrest someone like Carver, with his connections, without a great deal of evidence, is above my pay grade. Look, I know that you didn't kill Simone Kalu and you haven't kidnapped Zahrah. If you come in, we can put you into witness protection, even get you out of the country. Wouldn't you like to go home, Logan?'

'Believe me, there's nowhere I would rather be right now than sitting in front of a roaring fire in a British pub with a pint. Unfortunately, that's not going to happen until you show me that the FBI are taking me seriously. Arrest Carver and I'll come in. Anything else and I'm gone.'

Palmer ended the call. He didn't want to go on the run with Zahrah in tow, it was their last resort if all else failed option. He needed to contact Riley and find out what MI6 could arrange.

* * *

Gault's phone pinged as a message came in. The trace had worked. Palmer was in Covington. Gault had a team of men on standby in New Orleans, ready to rush to whatever location they were given. He didn't expect that location to be so far north though.

He dropped his phone on the desk. His quick reaction team were on their way but Palmer would be long gone by the time they got there. This was no good. He wouldn't catch Palmer by tracking his phone. The guy was too good for that. This was going to take something different, and some luck. He needed all the CCTV images from Palmer's location, and both ends of the bridge. If he could spot Palmer's vehicle, he might be able to use traffic cameras to zero in on their hideout.

He arranged for an analyst to download all the images and then looked at the file that had just been dropped at his desk. It was the workup he had ordered on Cody Wickes. If his suspicions were correct, there would be something in there that would point to Palmer.

Chapter 47

Palmer drove away from the bridge, and any team that the FBI might send after him and followed Interstate I-12 around Lake Pontchartrain to the city of Slidell. He stopped at a gas station next to the road and used the public telephone that stood outside to call Riley.

She sounded like a mother who had just got a call from a missing child. 'Where have you been, don't you check your email?'

Palmer was surprised by the tone of panic in her voice. 'Don't worry, Anna. I'm okay.'

'You might be, but I'm not.'

Palmer fed some more coins into the phone. 'Just take deep breaths and tell me what's happened.'

'I'm sorry, Logan, but it's bad news. Cody Wickes is dead.'

Palmer lowered the phone. He hadn't known Wickes for long, but he did like him. He was an easy man to get on with. Maybe it was the common military past that had something to do with it. He put the handset back to his ear. 'Was it Carver?'

'Yes. Cody's body was taken to Carver's warehouse. He was responsible.'

'I can't let him get away with this, Anna. I have to take him down.'

Riley took a deep breath. 'We'll both do it, Logan. I'm always here to help you.'

'I know you are, Anna, and I need to make it up to you. When it's over.'

'I'll look forward to it.'

'Is there anything else I need to know?'

'Yes. It's Ethan Gault. I've found something about him that means he could be involved too.'

Palmer couldn't believe how difficult it was to find someone who wasn't. 'Involved with Carver?'

'Yes. The other FBI Agent on the list, Travis Newlan, was his mentor. They were partners.'

Palmer was no expert on how the FBI was structured, but he didn't think it was unusual for a younger agent to be placed alongside an older one. 'That doesn't mean he's part of this. It could be just a coincidence. They both came from Texas, which could be why they were put together. Maybe they have a hometown in common or went to the same university.'

'That's what Ruby said, but I had to let you know. You have to be careful, Logan.'

'Ruby's working on this?'

Riley let out a gasp. 'I was supposed to keep it a secret, but yes. She's over there now. Tell me where you are, and I'll send her to meet you.'

'No. That's a bad idea.'

'She said that too. I really don't understand this spying nonsense.'

'It's okay, Anna. You're good at lots of things none of us can do. Look, at the moment, no one knows who Ruby is or what she's doing. That could be valuable to us. She can move around incognito.'

'I think I get it, mostly. You could still tell me where you are though.'

'Not over an open line, Anna. Remember, no locations. We'll go back to our base and pack everything up. I think it would be best to walk away from Ethan Gault for the time being.'

'I think that's a good idea too. I'm going to keep digging and see if anything else pops up.'

Palmer was out of change for the phone. 'I have to go now, Anna. Get Ruby to set up a new safe house and we'll come to her. It'll make it harder to track us if we don't arrange any of it.'

'I'll put that in place as soon as I can and let you know in the email. Take care, Logan… Logan?'

Palmer's money had run out. He jogged back to the van and jumped in. 'We've got to move again, Zahrah. We might have been compromised.'

'Is it safe to go back?'

'It's only for one night. We need to pick up the rest of our stuff. We'll move first thing in the morning.'

Palmer started the engine and pulled onto I-10 heading for New Orleans.

Chapter 48

Ethan Gault flicked through the documents in the folder. Everything had been thought of, bank statements, phone logs, military records, photographs, page after page, but nothing stood out. Until he got to the last few sheets. At the back of the folder was a photocopy of an adoption certificate.

Cody Wickes's parents had been killed in a helicopter crash when he was only twelve. His mother's best friend took in the young boy and she and her husband eventually adopted him. He didn't, however, take their name. That's why a casual background check hadn't flagged them up. The last document in the folder was a copy of a will.

The last will and testament of his adoptive mother. Her husband had died a year earlier so she, with no other family, left a sizeable chunk of money and a house. Probably where Wickes got the funds to start his business. As well as the house in Austin, which he had sold, his mother also left him a holiday cabin on the edges of the bayou outside New Orleans.

Gault logged into his computer and did a quick property check. The cabin was still in Wickes's mother's name. He hadn't changed the ownership. That's why they couldn't find Palmer. He picked up the phone and dialled Carver. 'I think I know where Palmer is hiding.'

'Where is he?'

'His adoptive parents had a holiday cabin in Louisiana. It's in a different name, that's why we couldn't track it down.'

Carver sounded happy for a change. 'And you're certain about this?'

'It's the closest thing to a lead we've got. If he isn't there, then we'll have to come up with a plan to bring him in quietly.'

'Why, what has he said?'

Gault paused. 'He has said that he might be willing to turn himself in if we can guarantee his and the girl's safety and prove to him that we're taking him seriously. He's probably thinking that his MI6 connections will step in and save him once he's in custody. He still doesn't trust anyone though.'

'When do we go up to the cabin?'

'There is no we. This is an FBI operation. You stay well away. If the storm hits tonight, he won't be going anywhere for a while. He isn't a local. He won't be expecting how bad the storm could be. There's plenty of time to set up an assault. The first thing I'll need to do is check the cabin out and see if he's there. Maybe I can talk some sense into him.'

Carver chuckled quietly. 'Make sure you keep me updated.'

* * *

At the same time as Gault was stumbling across Cody Wickes's inherited cabin, Anna Riley was processing the call logs she had received from her contact at GCHQ. The software, which she had written, was basic enough. It took lists of phone numbers and cross-referenced them by date, time, number called and location and churned out any patterns that it found.

She could have done it by hand, but it would have taken ages.

Her laptop screen flickered as line after line of call records scrolled past and were analysed by the software. It looked for numbers that regularly called each other and phones that were close to another on the list. The result was a heat map that showed the likely location of each phone and who owned it, against a list of their contacts.

Riley then put her hacking skills to use and pinpointed the live location of each of the numbers. She sent the output to her fifty-five-inch screen and sat back, pleased with what she had done.

A map of Texas and Louisiana was displayed with flashing, coloured dots for each phone. She could see that George Carver was on the coast and that he had spoken often with Ethan Gault. That wasn't a surprise. Special Agent Gault was on the outskirts of New Orleans as was Ruby Finn, but there was no sign of the phone that Palmer was using.

She brought up Palmer's call history by backtracking from the call he made to Gault. That was the last time that phone had been used. Riley needed Palmer to switch the phone on so she could track his location, but he wouldn't do that again until he had to. Riley started clicking through all the phones' location histories to see if she could narrow down the search area. That was when she spotted the anomaly.

She had already seen that Carver and Gault were in touch regularly. As the lead FBI agent on the case, it would be expected that Gault would keep Carver up to date on how it was going. The problem was, they had been in proximity and in contact with each other before Palmer even arrived in the country.

Riley zoomed in on Texas and overlayed Palmer's location

history onto the map. She then overlayed the call logs from the original phone he had. The one Cody Wickes had given him. It showed Palmer in Houston, which was the starting point, then showed him travelling across Texas to Austin and then on to the handover. All things she knew about, but there was another line that intersected with Palmer. That line belonged to Ethan Gault.

She zoomed in on the map and printed out the call logs. This showed that Gault had been on the phone with Carver at the time of the handover. It also showed that he was close to Palmer. Her heart started to pound. Ethan Gault was at the shootout on the plateau when Palmer rescued the girl, and on the phone to Carver at the same time. He was on the payroll.

Riley knew she had to get the information out. The first thing she did was send an email to Palmer. She put in all the info so that he would be in no doubt what she was saying, but what if he didn't check it? She sent a simple message to his phone, but that wasn't switched on either. She had to get Finn to Palmer, somehow.

Across the globe, analysts who work for the security services use similar processes for tracking down information. They hack into the same databases and download the same data. So, it wasn't surprising that Riley found Cody Wickes's parents' cabin. She picked up her phone and called Finn's number.

Finn sounded like she had just woken up. 'I need to buy you a watch that has dual time zones on it.'

Riley was talking too quickly and not breathing. 'Ruby, you need to get to him, it's… it's the FBI guy…'

'Anna, take a deep breath and calm down.' She could hear Riley's panicked breaths. 'Now, slowly, tell me what's wrong.'

Riley paused and gathered her thoughts. 'I've been going

through the files that Logan sent me and found out that the FBI guy, Ethan Gault, has links to someone on Carver's list. I know you're going to say that doesn't prove anything, but I've found something else.'

'What is it?'

'Gault was at the handover when they tried to kill Logan. He hasn't just joined the case. He's been involved from the start. He must be on Carver's payroll.'

'How certain are you, Anna?'

'One hundred and fifty per cent. Gault's phone was at the handover, within one hundred metres of Logan's, and connected to Carver at the same time. There's no other explanation for it. The FBI weren't aware of the original kidnapping.'

'Do you know Palmer's location?'

Riley zoomed in on the map. 'Cody Wickes's parents had a cabin which is within the footprint of one of the cell sites Logan's phone connected to. I'm betting he's there. I don't have anywhere else to look.'

'Send me the location of the cabin and I'll try and get there, but the storm might slow me down a bit.'

'Okay, Ruby, I will. Take care and let me know what's happening.'

Chapter 49

There was a loud knock that made Finn jump. She put her phone back on the desk and walked over to the door. The distorted face that she could see through the spyhole was wearing a hotel waistcoat. He knocked again. Finn took the chain off and opened the door.

The young man standing in the hallway looked like a character from an eighties high school movie. Spots, braces, and long hair in a ponytail made him look like the handsome hero's geeky friend. He was banging on the other doors along the corridor as he waited for them to answer. Finn wasn't the only person who now stood at their open doorway, so the young man addressed everyone at once.

He held up a card and read the words that were printed on it in big, bold, letters. 'There is a hurricane. All guests must come to reception and stay away from windows. Coffee and cakes are available. Thank You.' He gave a smile and rushed off to rouse another corridor.

Finn ducked back into her room and threw what few things she had brought with her into her bag. She was very much of the same school of thought as Palmer. Travel light, buy everything you need when you get there, keep your money and documents in a plastic bag. She threw her backpack over her shoulders and clipped its belt around her waist.

The hotel's reception area was chaotic. The skeleton staff that normally looked after the place at night were doing everything they could, but it was hard work. They had set up a few pots of coffee on a long table beside boxes of individually wrapped cakes and biscuits. A couple of baskets of fruit had been rustled up from somewhere and a trolley cage full of bottled water stood by the desk.

One of the staff, a young woman wearing a badge that said *Night Manager*, banged a stapler on the desk to get everyone's attention. 'Ladies and gentlemen…' Bang, bang, bang. 'Ladies and gentlemen…'

The crowd eventually fell silent.

'Thank you. There is no need to panic. We have plans in place for these sorts of things. Help yourself to coffee and snacks. We have a kitchen in the back and will be able to serve you a hot breakfast very soon. We have brought out comfortable chairs and mattresses from the rooms on this floor, and the windows in the main entrance have steel shutters.'

Everyone started to settle down a little. Some were old hands and had been through hurricanes before. One by one they started to pour cups of coffee and tuck into cakes. After a few minutes, the whole place developed a, *we're all in it together* atmosphere, and people began to chat and laugh.

Finn headed for the door. The electronic shutters were being lowered by a large security guard. 'Sorry. I can't let you out.'

'Yes, you can, open the door.'

The security guard kept his finger on the button. 'We've been told to keep everyone inside.'

'You can do that once I'm out of here. Open the door.'

'Sorry, Darlin', just doin' my job.'

Finn checked to see if anyone was watching her. Thankfully they were mostly distracted by the free cakes. She pulled the nine-millimetre from the back of her waistband and pointed it at the guard's chest. 'I'll say it once more. Open the fucking door.'

The security guard didn't know who Finn was, but the threat had its desired effect. He raised the shutters and let her out.

The car park was rapidly turning into a swimming pool. Finn splashed her way to her car and climbed in through the passenger side. The driver's door was facing the full force of the wind and she didn't want to flood the inside. She threw her bag into the back and set her phone up on the dashboard. The directions to the cabin looked pretty simple, but there was no telling how many roads were blocked or closed. She turned the key in the ignition and pulled out onto the road.

Chapter 50

Carver didn't contact Blake Macey. He had been given clear instructions never to get in touch unless it was critical. Leaving a traceable link between them was a sure-fire way to get caught. Carver left an anonymous message with his corrupt sheriff, who passed it on to Houston PD, who in turn sent it up the chain of command to the FBI. When Macey received the message, he left his office and used a public pay phone to call Carver's number. It took a few hours, but it worked.

The phone rang. Carver let it ring three times, a little game that gave him a feeling of importance. 'Hello.'

Macey sounded angry. Like he was speaking through clenched teeth. 'Have you cleared up your shit yet?'

'We've had some good news. Ethan Gault has tracked Palmer down. He's at a cabin in Louisiana. I told you I was reliable.'

'Have you got him in custody yet?'

'Not actually in custody, no, but there's a hurricane. He won't be going…'

Macey shouted down the phone. 'If you haven't got him yet, don't give me any shit about how reliable you are. He's got away from you before. I don't care what the weather's like, get it done.'

'You know, with the information I'm about to get my hands on, you might want to start showing me some respect.'

'Is that a threat?'

Carver panicked. What was he thinking threatening Macey? 'No, no, of course not. I'm just saying that I want to stay part of the operation. Once I've recovered any evidence the girl has.'

'We'll decide what your place in the organisation is when this is over. Don't contact me again until it's over.'

The line cut off. Carver didn't know if Blake Macey had hung up on him or if the wind had taken out the telephone line. He had to get hold of Gault while he still could. If the mobile networks went down, they had no way of communicating. The fallout of Palmer getting away again didn't bear thinking about.

Chapter 51

Hurricane Joshua smashed into the Gulf Coasts of Louisiana and Texas in the early hours of the morning. It had strengthened overnight and was a lot more powerful than expected when it made landfall. Memories of Katrina and the chaos and flooding it caused weighed heavily on the minds of the people who had lived through it. Was this hurricane going to be as bad? Only time would tell, but it was doing its best.

The power of the wind folded coastal buildings up like flat pack furniture while the storm surge flooded neighbourhoods that were unprepared for this level of damage. The driving rain turned even the major highways into fast-flowing rivers that were undrivable for cars whose wipers were overwhelmed. Trees and power lines collapsed into the street, boats were picked up from their moorings and smashed into matchwood on the shore, and yet, here and there, people were still moving about.

Palmer was checking the news for any mention of Carver being arrested, but all they were talking about was Hurricane Joshua. When he had heard the first warnings on the van's radio, he had closed the outside shutters on the cabin's windows and made sure everything was fastened down. They wouldn't be leaving to go to a new safe house today. It shouldn't be a problem though, no one would be coming after them in this weather. Or so he thought. Looking through the smallest of gaps in one of the shutters, he was convinced he had seen movement.

Zahrah came out of the bathroom and stood in the kitchen. 'It's really bad out there, isn't it?'

'According to the TV, the worst hasn't hit us yet. I wouldn't worry. This cabin has been built to survive worse than this.'

Zahrah looked up at the steel beams in the roof. I hope so. I wish there was an underground bunker though. What are you watching?'

'I don't know. I'm almost certain I saw some movement out there. In the trees by the track.'

Zahrah joined him at the window and tried to look through the same gap. 'How can you tell? Maybe it was just a tree blowing down. Nobody is going to be out there in this.'

'It's okay, you get something to eat. I'll just keep an eye out for a little longer.'

The wind outside was gaining strength, rattling the external shutters against the window frames. Water started to leak under the door as the rain was driven into the front of the cabin. Palmer changed eyes, but it was getting impossible to see. The rain was now being forced through the gap in the shutter and blocking his view. He was going to have to go outside.

He grabbed the jacket that hung by the door and put it on, not that it was going to do much. 'I'm just going to go outside and have a look. Close the door behind me.'

Zahrah walked over and stood behind the door. 'Okay, ready when you are.'

Palmer unbolted the door and stepped out. The wind drove him back a step and rain stung his face as he struggled to get down the steps. He leaned into the wind and headed for the first tree. Turning his back to it, he wiped his face then spun around it to the next one. One after another, he zigzagged his way through the trees towards the gate at the end of the track.

The padlock on the gate was still secure and the gate undamaged. There was no sign of anyone on either side of the track or the road past it. It must have been debris blowing past that had caught his eye. He took a deep breath then set off on another zigzag back to the cabin.

When he got back to the cabin, he didn't need to knock. The wind drove him into the door face first. Zahrah pulled back the bolt and Palmer fell in. The strength of the wind took Zahrah by surprise and almost blew her off her feet. She put her shoulder against the wood and pushed as hard as she could but couldn't quite get it closed. Palmer climbed to his feet and together they pushed the door shut and bolted it.

Palmer was drenched. Water rolled off his jacket and spread across the floor in a growing puddle. 'It's a bit windy out there.'

Zahrah turned around. The front of her t-shirt was soaked, and water dripped from the ends of her braids. 'You can say that again.'

* * *

Ethan Gault turned and crawled away. His camouflaged poncho did a good job of hiding him, but now it was flapping about and in danger of giving him away. When he reached the road, he crouched and pulled his head inside the material for a few seconds break before he stood up and walked, at an

225

angle, around the corner to his SUV.

Gault's vehicle was being rocked by the wind, even parking behind the trees wasn't enough to protect it. Four of Carver's best men were sitting in the vehicle with him. At least, the men he thought could carry out this operation without hurting themselves.

He took them through the plan one more time. 'He doesn't know who I am. He thinks I'm legit FBI. I'll walk up to the door and see if I can talk him into surrendering. While I'm doing that, you take up position around the cabin.'

All four men were nodding enthusiastically.

'Because of the storm, he has all the shutters closed, so we can't breech through the windows. All you have to do is stop him getting away. Do you think you can do that?'

The men nodded again.

Gault still wasn't convinced this was a good idea. Trying to take Palmer out in this weather could be suicidal. Visibility was down to a few feet. If Palmer got out of the cabin and got the drop on them, he wouldn't give them any quarter. With his life on the line, Palmer would shoot to kill.

Carver insisted that they go in now, but Gault wasn't doing it for him. He knew the old man was finished. The people who ran this organisation didn't tolerate incompetence. Carver would disappear, one way or another. Gault was going after Palmer to protect himself. Attack was the best form of defence. Besides, he had to think of his own future in the organisation. If he cleaned up this mess well, he might get a few more steps up the ladder.

The men were armed with AR-15s and enough ammunition to stage a coup in a former Soviet republic, but Gault only had his Glock. He press-checked it to make sure it was loaded and placed it back in its holster. 'If none of you have any questions, let's get this done.'

The men pulled up the hoods on their ponchos and they all climbed out of the SUV.

* * *

In the cabin, Palmer was still on edge. He was continually checking through various gaps in the shutters. He didn't want to get caught out by anything. He walked through the kitchen and up to the back door. The wind and rain didn't seem as bad on this side, and he managed to crack open the door without getting pushed back into the room. He stuck his head out, there was no one there. Maybe paranoia was getting the better of him, but he trusted his instincts. Something had spooked him. He pushed the door shut and bolted it.

The bang on the front door was loud. It was the kind of knock that only cops on a dawn raid do. Palmer ran through to the front and checked one of the gaps, he couldn't see anything. Zahrah stood with her back to the kitchen wall, shaking.

Gault knocked again, as loud as he could. 'Palmer. It's Special Agent Ethan Gault. I need to speak to you. Please open the door.'

Palmer put the battery into his phone. Riley had promised to get back to him if she found anything. Now was the time he needed that information. 'What do you want? How did you find us?'

'We're the FBI. It's what we do.'

Palmer looked at the phone. It was still trying to find a signal. He motioned to Zahrah to stand by the back door. If they needed to run, that would be the route. 'I told you I wanted to see the story in the news and then I would come in on my own.'

'That's not how it's going to happen, Palmer. I'm here to take you in now. I have authorisation to use force if necessary. You don't want that, do you?'

The phone buzzed in Palmer's hand. It had found a signal and received a message from Riley.

Ethan Gault was at the handover speaking to Carver on the phone. He's one of them.

Palmer was trying to process the information. He had felt there was something off about Gault, he wasn't expecting this. He was confident he could stay one step ahead of Carver's men, but he always knew he had to be wary of the pro. Now he knew who he was. Palmer couldn't believe that he hadn't recognised the FBI agent as the man on the plateau. Gault had fooled him into thinking he was one of the good guys. Now that he had tracked them down, the shit was really going to hit the fan.

Palmer shouted through the door. 'Back away, Gault, and show me your hands.'

He whispered to Zahrah. 'Unlock the back door. We're going to have to run for it. I'll create a diversion. Wait for me, I'll go out first. You keep hold of my belt and run. Okay?'

Tears were running down Zahrah's cheeks. Her eyes wide. She nodded slowly. 'I... I can do this.'

'Remember, they want you alive. They want to know where all the evidence is. They won't hurt you.'

There was another loud bang at the door. 'I'm getting pretty wet out here, Palmer. Let me in and we can discuss it.'

Palmer held up his fingers towards Zahrah. Three, two, one. 'Fuck you, Gault.' He fired six shots through the door then ran to the back.

Zahrah turned the handle and threw open the door. When Palmer got to her, she tucked her hand into the back of his belt and hung on.

Outside the back door, two of Gault's men were caught by surprise. The last thing they expected was for Palmer and the girl to burst out the door and charge towards them. As the first man raised his AR-15, Palmer shot him twice in the chest. The second man didn't fair any better. Palmer put a single round into his forehead. Before the man hit the floor, Palmer ran past him with Zahrah in tow.

The two men who had been at the front of the building raised their weapons and fired into the swamp, but Gault pushed them aside. 'You can't even see what you're shooting at you idiots. We need the girl alive. Get after them, they won't get far.'

Chapter 52

Ruby Finn stopped the car in front of the fallen tree that lay across the road. This was the fourth route she had punched into the phone's satnav. The first was blocked by the police and the next two were flooded. According to the phone, there was a track a hundred yards back down the road that would take her to within a mile of the cabin. She dropped the car into reverse and did a three-point turn.

The track was no wider than her car and had thick forest on either side. That meant it was quite sheltered from the wind, but water was pouring across the track, like a river, on its way to the bayou. There was every chance the car would get bogged down, but she needed to get as close as she could to the cabin. Walking in these conditions would be slow going and could be life-threatening.

Parts of the track had started to wash away. Finn went no more than ten miles an hour and picked her way through the potholes that were appearing in front of her. She zigged and zagged through the treacherous landscape. Her rear wheels spinning and the back of the car fishtailing as the tyres tried to get some grip. Just when she thought she was getting the hang of it, she came to a hole that stretched across the whole track.

Finn banged her hands on the steering wheel. 'Shit.' The hole was huge. Ten feet across and full of water. There was no telling how deep it was, and there was no way she was going to get through it. She checked the satnav on her phone, The cabin was just under one and a half miles away. There was no other way. Despite the risks, she would have to go cross country, on foot.

She climbed into the back of the car and unzipped her bag. Most of the things in there could be abandoned and replaced later. All Finn needed were items that would help her now. She emptied everything out and lined the backpack with a plastic bag from a supermarket she had visited. Her weapon, and a handful of extra ammunition, went into her jacket along with her phone. She rolled up one set of spare clothes. In this weather, dry clothes could be the difference between life and death. As an ex-army medic, she always had some sort of first aid kit with her. The one she tucked into the bag was medium size and in a waterproofed zip-up pouch. She wouldn't be able to start a fire if she got pinned down by the weather, and shelter might be no more than a tree branch, so the four space blankets and large nylon bivvy bag from the camping section of the supermarket went in the bag too. Finally, she added two one-litre bottles of water and a couple of chocolate bars.

With the backpack slung over her shoulders and the chest and waist belts fastened tight, she pulled up the hood of her waterproof coat and fastened the drawstring under her chin. She was ready to go. She kicked open the car door and stepped out into the tempest.

Chapter 53

Palmer's plans had disintegrated. The backpacks he had put together so they could grab them, and run were still in the van. Neither of them was dressed for a hurricane. Their jackets were water resistant, but far from being waterproof. It would only be a matter of time in this rain before they were soaked to the skin and in serious trouble. He had used half of the ammunition in his Glock and only had one spare magazine. They wouldn't be able to hold out for long if Gault caught up to them. Palmer had to think fast.

He knew if he headed North for long enough, he would come to a highway. There wouldn't be much traffic moving about they could hitch a lift from but travelling along the tarmac would be easier than the waterlogged undergrowth they were currently wading through. He made sure Zahrah still had a good grip on his belt and pushed on through the storm.

If he had been on his own, he would have stood a better chance of making it out of the swamp alive. Zahrah had no experience in her life that could have prepared her for this. She had been out camping a few times, in a compound where everything was safe and controlled, but this was different. She was doing her best, but all she could do was hang on and keep moving.

Palmer had spent a lot of time in extreme environments and his body, and mind, had been trained to adapt and overcome. The years he had spent learning escape and evasion techniques had given him an insight into how chases like this panned out, and they weren't moving quickly enough. Gault's men were catching up and he had to do something.

Up ahead, through the trees, Palmer could see the fast-flowing water of the river. There was no chance of crossing here, but, if they followed it, the map in Palmer's head told him it would lead to a road and a bridge. First, he had to deal with their pursuers or, at least, slow them down.

Palmer led Zahrah to a fallen tree and they climbed over its trunk, kneeling on the other side. He picked some leaves out of her hair and gave her a smile. 'You're doing great, but I have to stop them following us if we're going to get out of here. If we make it to the road, we might be able to flag down a car.'

Zahrah nodded. She was exhausted. The muscles in her legs were screaming and she was soaked to the skin. She couldn't keep going much longer. Flagging down a car sounded like a good plan.

'You stay here and keep your head down.' Palmer climbed back over the tree trunk and took up a position among some roots that stretched out towards the river.

Gault's two men burst through the trees and stood on the riverbank. Palmer didn't give them the chance to realise they had messed up. He fired three shots. The man at the front took all the rounds in his torso and dropped face-first into the mud. The second man dived to the side and rolled back into

233

the trees. Palmer fired the rest of the magazine into the trees around the man then re-loaded with the fresh one. These men weren't professionals and the thought of being shot would certainly slow the remaining guy down. Palmer went back to the fallen tree and picked up Zahrah.

They fought their way to the bridge where the road crossed the river. They had to keep going north if they were going to get away and this was the only crossing point for miles. Hopefully, they could get picked up by someone or, if not, maybe find some shelter along the road.

Zahrah was done. She sat with her back against the bridge support and her legs pulled up to her chest. She was trembling. Palmer knew that what she needed was to stop and rest for an hour or two, perhaps get some sleep, but that wasn't possible. They had a man following them and Ethan Gault was still out there somewhere.

Palmer crouched in front of Zahrah. 'We just need to keep going a little longer, then we can rest. I'm sure there'll be a house or a barn up there where we can get some sleep. One more push. Can you do that?'

Zahrah rolled onto her knees and struggled to her feet.

'That's it, good girl. Just hold onto my back and keep moving. One foot in front of the other. You'll be amazed what your body can still do after you think you're finished.' He gave her a hug and they moved out of the shelter of the bridge.

When they reached the bottom of the slope that led up to the road, Palmer checked behind them. He could see their follower moving from tree to tree, trying to stay undercover. Palmer fired two shots. He knew he was unlikely to hit the man, but it would remind him that he was risking his life by following them. Palmer turned and crawled up the slope to the road dragging Zahrah behind him.

* * *

Finn had made good progress through the undergrowth. It was a hard slog, but she was focused on getting to Palmer. She had made it through the first part of the swamp and was crouched at the side of the track that led to the cabin.

She watched Gault climb into his car and drive away before she broke cover and approached the cabin. She could see straight away that there were bullet holes in the door. From the shape of them, it looked like they had been fired from inside, but there was no blood. Whoever had been on this side of the door must have been standing to the side. She took the steps up to the entrance and stepped into the calm of the building.

Finn stood in the middle of the room for a few minutes just catching her breath. Her ears were ringing now that she was away from the constant roar of the wind. She checked the rest of the rooms. There was no blood inside either and, more importantly, no more bullet holes. Wherever Palmer was, he was probably still alive.

She picked up a towel from the bathroom, dried her face, then rolled the towel up and put it around her neck like a scarf. It might stop some of the water that was running down into her collar. Standing at the back door, she could see the two bodies lying at the bottom of the steps. It looked like Palmer had opened up through the front door and fought his way out the back. She pulled her hood up and set off back into the swamp.

Finn reached the river and found the third body. The tracks

that led away from him were going north, upstream. Palmer was still on the run and causing problems for the men who were after him. He was obviously looking for a way across the river. She picked up the dead man's AR-15 and searched the body, stripping him of the extra ammo he had. He wasn't carrying anything else she could use, so she checked the rifle was loaded and followed the tracks along the bank.

Chapter 54

They were halfway up the slope when Zahrah's legs gave way, and she dropped back down. She lay at the bottom, tears streaming down her face. Palmer could see that she wanted to keep going, but she couldn't.

Palmer grabbed the front of her jacket and pulled her to her feet. He bent over and lifted her onto his shoulders in a fireman's lift. His only choice was to carry her or to leave her where she was, and that was never going to happen. He took a deep breath, dug his feet into the slope, and pushed towards the top.

Their chaser appeared from the trees again. He was getting braver as he closed in on them. All Palmer wanted to do now was reach the road. From there, he could pick the man off and get Zahrah to some shelter. His legs ached and his back muscles burned as he climbed higher. Twice he lost his footing and skidded a few feet back down, but, after a final desperate push, his hands felt the tarmac of the road.

Two bullets thudded into the ground to his left. The follower was only one hundred meters away. Palmer knelt and lay Zahrah on the road, out of the line of fire. He turned and fired two more shots that sent the man running for cover under the bridge. If he had any sense, he would stay there. He was undercover while they were out in the open. Time was on his side.

Palmer looked along the road. Visibility was still terrible. All he could see was more trees and more swamp. There were no buildings. No houses, no barns, not even a bus shelter. He ran to the other side of the bridge to check on Gault's man. Palmer's instincts were correct. The man was trying to sneak out behind them. Palmer fired another two shots. That should keep his head down for a few minutes.

Zahrah had rolled over onto her knees and was now crawling along the road. Palmer shouted at her. 'Zahrah. Stay down. Stay the fuck down.'

She pointed along the road. 'Help us… Please, help us.'

Palmer looked to where she was pointing. He could make out a set of headlights. 'Holy shit.' He stood and waved his arms. 'Hey… HEY!'

The SUV skidded to a halt beside Zahrah. Palmer sprinted back to the southern side of the bridge. He grabbed Zahrah's jacket. 'Come on. You have to get up. We can make it.' He pulled her to her feet while still checking for the follower.

* * *

Special Agent Gault rolled down the window of his SUV and fired two shots.

The first bullet hit Palmer in his left shoulder and knocked him off balance. The second hit him in the back and tipped him over the guard rail.

Gault slid down the bank to the side of the river looking for Palmer. The man who had been following them stuck his head out from under the bridge. 'Someone went in the water.'

'What the fuck are you doing hiding under there?'

'He was shooting at me.'

'Get your ass down the bank and find his body. I want you to make sure he's dead. If he isn't, I want you to finish him off. Got it?'

The man nodded.

'Good. Then I want you to empty his pockets. Find everything he's carrying, even if you don't think it's important.'

Gault looked up and spotted Zahrah starting to walk away along the bridge. 'For fuck's sake.' He pointed down the river. 'Find him then get back to the cabin. I'll pick you up there.'

Gault climbed back up the slope and grabbed Zahrah. He opened the rear passenger door and pushed her in. She was in no condition to fight him. She curled into a ball and passed out.

Chapter 55

P almer had slammed into the water and been pulled under. The current was strong, and his left arm was useless. He broke the surface, gasping for air, but got dragged straight back under. His back started to spasm and blood clouded in front of his eyes. He kicked his legs and rolled onto his back.

He broke the surface again. Another deep breath caused him to splutter, coughing up muddy water. His eyes were blurred, but he could see that he wasn't too far from the bank. He rolled onto his right side and kicked his legs again. This wasn't a deep river, all he had to do was get to the shallows and he could push himself up the bank. He wasn't an expert on these swamps, but he knew there were gators around here. Getting eaten wasn't on his bucket list.

Palmer concentrated on one side stroke at a time. Swimming like he had been taught to at school when they did a lifesaving class in the pool. One arm around the drowning person to keep them afloat and the other to swim to safety. The only difference this time was that he was the drowning man. Another stroke. His back spasmed again. Another stroke. One more breath. Another stroke. His hand touched the bottom.

Palmer heard the unmistakable whine of an incoming round and saw the mud kick up on the bank. 'For fuck's sake. Give me a break.' Another round kicked up mud, but Palmer couldn't do anything to get out of the way. His best choice would be to push himself back into the river, but he knew he would drown. At least a bullet would be quick. Thankfully, the guy shooting at him was no sharpshooter. Palmer grabbed a root that was hanging over the edge of the bank and hung on.

He pushed with his legs until he was half out of the river. He couldn't get any higher up, but he was okay here. At least he didn't have to worry about sinking. Palmer saw movement up on the bank and tried to pick up his Glock. His left arm was numb and barely moved, no matter how hard he willed it to. He doubted his weapon was still in his waistband anyway. Didn't he have it in his hand when he went over the guardrail? He couldn't remember. His whole body was going numb, and his vision was starting to dim. Palmer knew who was up on the bank, he knew what was coming, but he didn't mind. He just wanted to rest. He didn't want to worry about anything anymore.

The follower stepped out from behind his tree and took aim. As he did, four bullets ripped into his back in quick succession. Finn's aim was perfect. The follower pitched forward into the water, his arms moving weakly as if he was trying to swim but blood was already pumping out of the holes in his back and spreading out across the surface of the muddy water.

Palmer's grip on the tree root loosened and the current started to drag him back in. Finn dived out from the trees and grabbed Palmer's hand before he sank back into the water. She struggled to her knees then gradually onto her feet. Using

Palmer's arm like it was a rope, she pulled him up the bank then gripped the back of his jacket. The higher she pulled him up the bank, the heavier he got, and her feet started to slip in the mud. 'Come on, Palmer. Help me. Push with your legs.'

Palmer tried, but he could barely move. Finn was losing the battle. She adjusted her grip again and planted her feet, leaning back like she was in a tug of war. 'Come on, Palmer. COME ON!'

Palmer's legs started to move. Not much, but it was enough. Once he was moving, the momentum gave Finn enough help to drag him clear of the water.

Finn collapsed on the bank, her breath heavy and rasping. She had to get them under cover. They wouldn't last long out in the open like this. She looked up at the bridge. There was no sign of anyone there. She would have preferred a log cabin and a roaring fire, but the bridge would have to do. She wasn't worried about the various species of predator that inhabited the swamp. All the animals would have scurried away into shelter. Only people were stupid enough to be out in these conditions.

She grabbed Palmer's one good arm and started to drag him along the riverbank. It was hard going. Palmer was heavier than she was, and the mud was clinging to his body. By the time she got him out of the rain, she was exhausted, but she couldn't stop yet. She set about treating his wounds. It didn't look like any major organs had been hit so all she had to do was stop the bleeding. Giving Palmer proper treatment could wait until the storm had ended.

Once Finn had stopped the blood flow and dressed Palmer's wounds, she rolled him into the bivvy bag and got in beside him. She wrapped them both in space blankets and zipped the bag up. With the hurricane howling and rain hammering down into the river, Finn put her arms around Palmer to warm him up. There was nothing else she could do until the storm stopped. She closed her eyes and tried to sleep.

Chapter 56

Special Agent Gault opened the cabin door and looked out. The rain had stopped, and the wind was back to being not much more than a stiff breeze. A big four-wheel drive pick-up truck carrying two of Carver's men was bouncing its way along the track towards him. The roads from New Orleans were passable in the right vehicle and he was eager to get back to Texas. The big problem he had was that the man he sent to finish off Palmer hadn't shown up yet.

He went back inside. Zahrah Kalu was sitting in one of the chairs in the main living area. Her clothes were still damp, and she shivered as the breeze entered the building.

Gault crouched in front of her. 'Where is the evidence? What did Palmer do with it?'

'I've told you already. Logan had it. He said it would be better for me if I didn't know where it was.'

Gault had already looked in the van and emptied the two emergency backpacks. He had searched the cabin and every pocket in any clothing he found. All a waste of time. He knew Palmer would have stored it all somewhere well away from him and the girl. He grabbed Zahrah's arm and dragged her outside.

Carver's two men finished loading the bodies of their

fallen comrades into the back of the pick-up and waited for instructions.

Gault pushed Zahrah into the back of his SUV and made sure the child locks were on. The last thing he wanted was for her to kill herself trying to escape out of a moving vehicle. He shouted over to the two men. 'One of you stay here in case someone turns up. The other one, come with me.'

The two men played rock, paper, scissors to decide who did what. The winner got to stay at the cabin. The unhappy loser got in the SUV with Gault and Zahrah, and they set off up the track.

* * *

Finn had been awake for most of the night. She had slept for no more than an hour at a time, then checked on Palmer. He was stable and the bleeding had mostly stopped. There was still some blood oozing out, but it wasn't pouring. That told her that the wounds weren't as bad as they could have been. He had been very lucky.

She unzipped the bivvy bag and climbed out. The storm was dying down and she had to get moving. The swollen river was full of debris from the damage caused upstream. There were dozens of tree branches and logs floating along with bits of wood from houses, advertising hoardings and picnic tables. Occasionally, a dead animal floated past. That worried Finn. The predators she hadn't been worried about the previous night would be out now, looking for easy pickings, but that wasn't her biggest problem.

She knew that, when his man did not return, Gault would come looking for him and Palmer. He needed to check for any evidence that Palmer had on him, and, if nothing else, he would want to make sure Palmer was dead. No one in their right mind would want the threat of a pissed-off Palmer hanging over them. The bridge was the obvious place for Gault to start the search and the last place they wanted to be.

Finn rolled Palmer onto his back and sat him up. He was groggy and looked like he belonged on a mortician's slab. She took a bottle of water out of her bag and held it for him to take a drink. He coughed and spluttered but kept it down. Who knew what he had swallowed when he had been in the river. Next, she removed the towel from around her neck and poured some of the water onto a clean part. Gently, she wiped the mud from his face, cleaning his eyes and ears. He looked a little better, but she had to get him somewhere he could hide. Somewhere he could recover.

She had a drink herself, then packed everything away. 'Do you think you can stand up?'

Palmer tried to speak but all he managed was a weak croak. He swallowed and tried again but then settled for a nod of his head.

Finn stood over him and braced herself. He got onto his knees then grabbed her arm. His first attempt failed but, with a lot of grunting, his second attempt was a success. He stood still, rocking slightly and his legs trembling.

Finn steadied him and waited for him to get his balance. 'You ready?'

He nodded. 'Where are we going?' Another coughing fit threatened to send him back down to his knees.

She steadied him again. 'Just concentrate on not falling over. We need to get away from here and find some shelter. Looks like dragging your arse out of the fire is becoming a full-time job for me.'

Palmer smiled and patted her arm.

'Come on. Let's go.'

Palmer put his good arm around her shoulders, and they climbed up to the road.

Chapter 57

Gault drove his SUV over the vegetation that littered the road. He weaved around the bigger branches and other bits of wreckage that had been blown into the swamp from the surrounding area. The hurricane had caused severe damage out here, but nature would recover. He wasn't sure the same could be said for some of the urban areas inland. Hurricane Katrina had shown them how fragile the infrastructure of civilization was. It wasn't something that should be allowed to happen again.

Up ahead, Gault saw the guardrail that ran along the sides of the bridge. A few branches were sticking out of the rails and a tree was covering one side of the road, but the bridge was still intact. He pulled up next to the top of the slope and switched off the engine.

His passenger unclipped his seat belt and opened the door to step out, but Gault grabbed his shoulder and dragged him back in. 'You stay here.' He motioned to the back seat. 'Keep an eye on her. Do not let me down.'

'Okay, boss. No problem.'

Gault cocked his nine-millimetre and got out of the car. If Palmer was alive, underneath the bridge was one of the best places to shelter. He didn't want to be caught out and get his head blown off as he reached the riverbank. After a check over the guardrail, on both sides of the bridge, he stepped off the road and slithered down the slope.

Underneath the bridge, the signs of someone hiding out there were obvious. Gault could make out lots of tracks leading to and from the area and the unmistakable shape of a body. Someone had spent the night here. He turned and looked at the drag marks that followed the river. Palmer had help. Gault put his weapon away and followed the tracks.

It wasn't long before he saw a pair of legs on the bank, the rest of the body submerged in the river. He grabbed it by its ankles and dragged it back up onto dry land. The bullet wounds in the corpse's back were well grouped and aimed to kill quickly. When he turned the body over, he recognised the man he had sent after Palmer. Whoever was helping Palmer had ambushed the man and killed him professionally.

Gault knew that Palmer had survived and escaped from the swamp. He wasn't going to find a body and he wouldn't get his hands on any documents. He had to keep hold of the girl, it was the only thing that would bring him in. At some point, Palmer would be in touch. Gault picked the body up by the arms and rolled it back into the river. Nature was good at getting rid of evidence. He walked back to the car and drove off.

* * *

Ruby Finn waited until the car was no longer in sight. They had only got a couple of hundred metres down the road before Palmer had collapsed again, but it was enough. Gault didn't have enough men to search the whole swamp.

Finn had to get help. There was no way that she could get Palmer away from here on her own. She pulled her phone out of the plastic bag she kept it in, but who was she going to phone? Cody Wickes was dead, she knew that. Riley could organise help, but she wasn't here. She put her phone down and sighed, she was going to have to carry him.

Palmer unbuttoned the map pocket in his trousers and pulled out the bag that he kept all his important stuff in. He passed it to Finn and pointed at the matchbook inside.

Finn opened the bag and took out the matches. On the front, in bright red lettering, it said *Ernie's Sports Bar.* She thought Palmer must be delirious. There was a phone number on the back, but what good would that do? Finding a bar to have a pint in would have been nice but it wasn't at the top of her priority list.

Palmer pointed at the number. 'Ask for Asher.'

Finn still wasn't sure.

Palmer pointed again and nodded. 'Asher.'

Finn raised her eyebrows. 'Okay.' She picked up her phone and dialled Ernie's.

Chapter 58

Anna Riley had never been a big fan of pubs. When she was still drinking, she drank on her own. She wasn't doing it to be sociable, she was drinking for the effect it had on her. Drowning her sorrows and drinking herself into oblivion helped her cope. At least, that was what she told herself. It was what a lot of alcoholics thought. Her therapist had explained to her how wrong that was. How it would only make her worse. Now she avoided drinking anything.

She watched the bubbles in her mineral water burst on the surface and picked at a packet of cheese and onion crisps as she tried to blend in. This wasn't a rough drinkers bar like the one she had met Ruby Finn in. This was a hipster bar. They sold craft beers, flavoured gins, and vegan sandwiches made with artisan bread. No one was interested in what she was doing, and she wasn't the only one sitting on her own, but she still felt out of place.

Victoria Thomson pushed the door open and headed straight for the bar. 'Double vodka and lemonade, please. No ice.'

The bartender nodded and had the drink mixed in a matter of seconds. 'Vodka, lemonade, no ice.'

Thomson looked impressed. She paid for her drink and

joined Riley at her small table. 'Good evening, Anna. How are you feeling?'

Riley gave her a forced smile. 'I'm really worried about our friends. I still haven't heard anything.' She was trying to get across how serious this was without giving anything away. Why did she agree to meet here? She wanted to scream and shout about how scared she was.

'No news is good news, Anna.'

Riley suspected that Thomson was just trying to make her feel better, but nothing helped. 'What if something bad has happened?'

'The authorities over there know that Palmer has worked for us. We made it clear that we were to be kept in the loop however things turned out. None of the law enforcement organisations know where they are.'

'But if Ethan Gault is collaborating with Carver, he could have hurt them and kept it hidden.'

Thomson took a large sip of her vodka and shook her head. 'The thing he wants, more than anything, is to stay in his job and stay hidden. That's the best thing for the conspiracy. Palmer is a wanted man. If Gault had killed him, he would have no reason to hide it. He could say that he and Finn resisted arrest and were killed in the process. He could then claim the credit and score brownie points.'

'Maybe. I've been trawling around all the usual networks, and nobody is saying anything. Most agencies are still cleaning up after the hurricane.'

'Well, there you go then. Palmer will be in touch when he's ready. From the looks of it, the Americans don't even know that Finn is involved. They're just lying low. Give them time.'

Riley wanted a drink. Her therapist told her that her former coping mechanism would resurface when she was under a lot of stress. 'If Palmer hasn't got in touch by next week, we need to do something.'

Thomson finished her drink. 'We will, Anna, we will. Now, I'm having another drink, do you want a mineral water, or something else?'

Riley thought about it. She almost said gin. 'I'll have a coke.'

Thomson stood up and went to the bar.

Chapter 59

The last thing Palmer could clearly remember was falling off the bridge. Everything after that was just a collection of blurred images. He had a faint memory of Finn being with him, of being loaded into a car and being driven somewhere, but none of it made any sense, there were too many gaps.

He pushed himself up onto his one good elbow and looked around. There was a fresh dressing on his shoulder and his left hand was bandaged. He tried to sit up, but a sharp pain shot up from the middle of his back and across his shoulders causing his muscles to spasm. He cried out and fell back onto the bed.

Finn opened the door. 'About time you woke up.'

'I feel like shit.'

'That'll be the morphine I gave you. Help you with the pain. Didn't want you screaming like a little kid when I stitched you up.'

Palmer laughed, then winced. 'How bad is it?'

'Well, your shoulder is just a flesh wound. I've done worse shaving my legs.'

'And my back? When can I go after Zahrah?' He tried to sit up again.

Finn put her hand on his chest. 'Whoa, take it easy there, tough guy. The bullet that went in your back went in at an angle and cracked one of your ribs. It deflected from there and came out of your side. Left a groove in the fleshy part of your thumb on the way out.'

Palmer lifted his bandaged hand. 'That explains this. So, you were telling me that I'll be up and about by tomorrow.'

'Not a chance. Look, you lost a lot of blood, mainly from your shoulder. The bullet that went in your back would have been much worse if it hadn't hit your rib. You were lucky and you need to rest, for a few days, at least.'

Palmer's head was spinning. He knew that if he tried to stand up, he would just fall flat on his face. He had to listen to Finn. 'Okay, doc, you're the boss.' He looked around at the room he was in. 'Where are we anyway?'

Finn pulled a chair over to the side of the bed. 'Your friend Asher certainly came through for us. He sent someone to pick us up and brought us back here.'

'Where's here?'

'We're in a trailer park back in Texas. There are quite a lot of people here who were made homeless by the hurricane, so we don't stand out. I've been telling them that's how you were hurt. Asher even got a friendly doctor to visit and check you out.'

Palmer smiled. 'He struck me as a man who needs a no-questions-asked doctor occasionally. Probably one of the services he provides.'

'How do you know him?'

'He supplied me with some hardware. Strictly off the record. He's a friend of Cody Wickes.' Palmer let out a long sigh. 'Is he really dead? I mean… There's no chance…'

Finn shook her head. 'I saw the body. I'm sorry, Logan.'

'It's alright, I barely knew him, but I can't help thinking he died trying to help me in some way.'

'He's still helping you. Asher's doing this because of him.'

They both fell silent. A mark of respect for the brother they had lost.

Palmer was the first to speak. 'Do you have a phone?'

'Yeah, something else courtesy of our new friend. Mine bit the dust. Thought I should get rid of it. Who'd you want to call?'

'I can imagine Anna is tearing her hair out about now. We should check in.'

Finn dialled the number, as Palmer dictated it to her, and put it on hands-free.

Riley answered before the second ring was finished. She must have been waiting with the phone in her hand. Her voice sounded sharp and panicked. 'Logan?'

'Hello, Anna, it's Ruby.'

'Oh my god, are you alright, where's Logan, is he okay, where are you…?'

Finn cut into Riley's stream of questions. 'Calm down, Anna, calm down. We're both fine. Palmer has a couple of extra holes in him, but he'll get over it. He's here with me.'

Palmer sounded rough. 'Hi, Anna, how's tricks?'

'Don't how's tricks me, Logan Palmer. I've been worried sick. Don't ever disappear on me like that again. I thought you were both dead, you arsehole.' The tremble in her voice was obvious.

'I'm sorry, Anna. We both are. Although to be fair, I did get shot and fall off a bridge during a hurricane.'

'That's no excuse.'

Palmer felt like a ten-year-old being scolded by his mother. 'I'll make it up to you when I get home. I promise.'

'You'd better.'

'Thank you for the warning. You saved my life, Anna.'

They could hear Riley blowing her nose. 'I'm just doing what any friend would do. What do you need from me now? How can I help?'

'I need you to do me a favour, Anna. I need you to find out where George Carver and Ethan Gault are and keep track of them. Wherever they are, that's where Zahrah will be.'

'That won't be a problem, Logan. I know where they are already.'

Chapter 60

Carver sat in his power office, feeling a little less powerful than he usually did. He couldn't believe that one man could cause so much shit. His security was down to a minimum thanks to Palmer killing several of his men. His tame law enforcement resource had suddenly found some integrity and walked away, and he still didn't have the documents in his hands.

Gault sat on the couch opposite Carver's desk. 'I've got field agents and cops all over three states looking for Palmer and there's still no sign of him.'

'He must have died in the river.'

Gault shook his head. 'No. Someone took out your man. Whoever that was, got him away and hid him.'

'Do you know who?'

'It has to be one of his MI6 contacts. Maybe not an official operative, but definitely an asset.'

Carver flicked through the report that Gault had put together. 'There are big gaps in this. Periods where no one seems to know where he was or what he was doing.'

'There's a lot more to him than meets the eye. You fucked up when you didn't check him out before allowing him in.'

'So, what do we do now?'

Gault smirked. 'We change identities, and we go and live in Tibet.'

Carver banged on the table. 'I'm serious.'

'So am I. Palmer is taking this personally. He's still out there and he isn't alone. All we've managed to do so far is piss him off.'

'You think he's coming after us?'

'I guarantee it. He wants the girl.'

Carver pulled the top from a crystal decanter and poured himself a drink. 'Maybe we should get rid of her.'

'That's the last thing you want to do. She's our insurance. If we hand her over in exchange for the evidence, he might let us live. If you kill her, you will die screaming.'

'I guess this'll cause a blip in your stellar FBI career.'

Gault shook his head. 'My career? If I'm still alive at the end of all this, I'll consider it a good outcome.'

'Maybe you should go and sort out my security detail.'

Gault got up off the couch. 'You just make sure that we have an exit strategy.' He left the room.

Carver decided it was time to liquidate his assets. It would take time. Shares had to be sold off and cash moved to a new anonymous account. He needed enough to live on. There was no coming back after this. He would also need new ID papers and tickets to another country. Maybe Tibet wasn't such a bad idea. He picked up the phone and made a call.

Chapter 61

P almer stood up and stretched his back. He had spent two days lying in bed and he was going stir crazy. He could move his left arm again, although a little stiffly, and the stitches in his back weren't restricting his movements too much. His cracked rib was still causing him pain, but the painkillers helped, if he didn't jump around too much. He pulled on his jeans, put on a clean t-shirt, and walked through to the main part of the trailer.

He moved the net curtain to one side and looked out of the window. Their trailer was on the end of a row of twelve. Kids played outside some of the others while their parents unpacked their trucks. All the possessions they had left in the world were piled up in a collection of cardboard boxes. Some were even less fortunate and had arrived at the park with only the clothes they stood up in. Palmer was glad he had the lifestyle he did. Never staying in one place too long. No possessions to speak of. It made him resilient. Able to adapt and cope with upheaval. It suited him.

Finn stood behind him in the kitchen area stirring the contents of a large pot. Occasionally she added spices and tasted it as she went. 'How are you feeling?'

'Like shit, but I can't just lie there. Zahrah needs my help.'

'You can get a good meal inside you before you plan on doing anything else.'

Palmer sat at the table. 'That smells incredible. What is it?'

'Old family recipe. My grandmother used to make it when she came over to visit us.'

'It's Indian?'

'That's right. The family moved to Belfast in the sixties and opened a restaurant.'

Palmer knew that Finn was from an Asian background, but he had never really spoken to her about it before. 'It can't have been easy for them, during the troubles.'

'I don't think it was too bad until my mum and dad met. My mum's family wanted her to marry a nice Indian boy. My dad's family wanted him to marry someone white.'

'It's certainly a clash of cultures.'

Finn smiled. 'Yeah, and I didn't fit into either of them.'

Palmer had spent time in Belfast himself. He knew how tribal it could be back then. 'Not Catholic or Protestant.'

'Not Asian or white. The subject of everyone's bigotry. That's why I got out of there as soon as I could, joined the army.'

'Have you been back since?'

Finn put two dinner plates on the table. 'Only my grand-mother really cared for me. Once she died, I had no reason to go back. That's who I'm named after.'

'Your grandmother was called Ruby?'

Finn smiled. 'My real name's Rubina. Rubina Ishani Finn. When I joined up, everyone just called me Ruby. It's been that way ever since.'

Palmer took a knife and fork from the holder at the end of the table and put them beside each plate. 'Rubina is a nice

261

name.'

Finn turned the heat off on the cooker. 'It hasn't been my name for a long time.' She lifted the pot over to the table. 'Dinner is served.'

Palmer was on his second plate full when the phone rang. 'Who's that?'

Finn picked it up. 'Number blocked. I think I know who it is though.' She answered. 'Hello... Yes... Okay, see you then.' She hung up and put the phone down. 'I contacted Asher again like you asked. He says he'll come here and see us. Less of a risk.'

Palmer finished his meal and sat back. His rib was starting to hurt again, and his stitches pulled. 'It's about to start again. Are you ready?'

Finn nodded. 'Whatever it takes.'

* * *

Blake Macey and Harrison Draper sat on another bench in a different park drinking more lukewarm coffee from cardboard cups.

Macey took a sip. 'I thought you said we should stop meeting.'

'That was back when I thought you had a handle on this. It's starting to look like I'll have to step in.'

'You don't need to do anything. Gault will do what I tell him to. Carver has outlived his usefulness. We'll use him as bait to lure Palmer in, then dispose of them both.'

Draper looked at his watch. 'I have a meeting to go to about my presidential run. I don't have time for this shit. What about the evidence? Do we know where it is?'

'If we kill Palmer, Carver and the girl, there'll be no one left to talk about it. We can dismantle Palmer's life and track down the original photos in our own time. If there are any digital copies, we can discount them as fake news. Photoshopped fakes from far-right groups to disrupt the democratic process. If we put our social media experts on it, we can create enough doubt to deflect the mainstream media.'

Draper took the lid off his coffee and poured it on the ground. 'This stuff tastes like dirt.' He threw the empty cup into the trash. 'How are you going to kill everyone without raising suspicions?'

'Gault is still an FBI Agent. He can kill them all and claim self-defence. We'll confirm his story that he was deep undercover inside Carver's organisation. No one will question it.'

Draper stood up. 'I do hope you're right, Blake. If I go down, everyone is coming with me.' He headed back to his car and his presidential campaign meeting.

Macey switched off his voice recorder. 'I won't be going down alone either, Congressman.'

Chapter 62

Asher pulled his car up to the end of the line of trailers and parked it behind a pick-up truck. It wasn't an expensive car or new, even though he could afford both. He preferred to stay low-key. That's why he didn't have a driver or a bodyguard. He didn't need one. The number of guns he sold didn't upset the big dealers and they left him alone. He didn't deal drugs, so had no reason to fear the cartels. Keeping his clientele to a small group of professionals and private military organisations meant the police and FBI weren't on to him either. He was just a guy who owned a bar.

He got out of the car, removed two holdalls from the boot, and walked up to the trailer's wooden porch.

Finn opened the door. 'Asher?'

He nodded once.

Finn stepped back, and Asher followed her inside.

Palmer was still climbing out of his seat. 'Good to see you again, man. Thanks for coming.'

'Don't get up. You look like you need the rest.'

Palmer sat back at the table. 'I'm sorry about Cody. I know you two were close.'

Asher put the two holdalls on the couch and sat down. 'Yeah, we served together in the Sandbox. He saved my life.'

'Like I said, I'm sorry.'

'This isn't on you, Palmer. That fucker Carver and his FBI stooge. They need to be dealt with.'

Palmer nodded, slowly. 'They will be. They have a lot to answer for, but that can wait. Unless the opportunity presents itself, I'm only interested in Zahrah for now. Did you manage to get the hardware?'

Asher pointed at the holdalls. 'Two bags. M4s plus ammunition, side arms, tac vests, everything you asked for is all in there. You're not planning on going in quiet.'

'Hard and fast. Some of these weekend warriors will shit their pants and bail out. I could do with reducing their numbers though.

'I know a couple of guys, ex-military, good solid operators. We could come with you. Even the odds a little.'

Palmer shook his head. 'No, this is my fight. Finn's only coming with me because I can't stop her.'

Finn scoffed. 'Damn right.'

Palmer smiled and nodded at Finn. 'See what I mean.'

'What do you need from me?'

'A little distraction. It'll help us get into Carver's house.'

'Happy to help, what's the plan?'

'I'm going to contact Gault, tell him I want to meet, arrange to exchange the evidence for Zahrah.'

Asher shook his head. 'He won't turn up. It's too risky for him. As long as he has the girl, he knows he has the upper hand.'

'Yeah, but he'll send some of his men to try to bring me in. You could be there to make sure they don't cause me any trouble.'

'I like the sound of that.'

Palmer paused. 'You probably won't like the sound of what I want next.'

'That doesn't surprise me at all. What is it?'

'I want a meeting with the Cartel.'

Asher sat back and let out a long sigh. 'You're crazy.'

'That's never been in any doubt, but I want to make sure they stay away from me and Zahrah. The last thing I want is to be watching over my shoulder in case some cartel sicario comes after me. They take things personally.'

'I hope you're not relying on your good looks to get them on your side. They can be unpredictable with people they don't know.'

Palmer smiled. 'I've got Carver's money. I'll give them that. He does owe it to them after all. I might tell them where he is too. They probably want a chat with him.'

Asher laughed. 'I like your thinking.' He stood up and walked towards the door. 'I'll leave you to it. I'll be in touch when I've contacted the Cartel.' He nodded to Finn. 'Good to meet you, Ruby. If you ever get tired of saving his ass, let me know. I'll give you a job.'

'Thanks. I will.'

Palmer stood up. 'There is just one more thing.'

Asher turned around. 'Name it.'

'If I don't make it through this, make sure Carver and Gault don't either.'

'It'll be a pleasure. By the way, Asher is my middle name.'

Palmer smiled. 'I'll speak to you soon, brother.'

Asher opened the door and walked out.

Chapter 63

In a small industrial area off State Highway 290, Asher had
a unit that he used when moving merchandise between
Houston and Austin. It wasn't his main storage, but it
was big enough to house a box truck. It was a solid, concrete
building with no windows and a single roller door at the rear.
There was a small steel door at the side and only one way to
approach by road. With all-around floodlights and cameras
above each of the entrances, it was a secure location for a
meeting.

Inside the building, a handful of crates sat in one corner
covered over with a tarpaulin. Asher wasn't worried about the
Cartel's men seeing where he kept his stock, he'd told Palmer
that he had dealt with this particular gang before, and he fully
expected to do business with them again. Still, there was no
need to take risks. One of Asher's armed men was under the
tarpaulin watching events through a spyhole. Elsewhere in
the building, he had another man hidden, ready to burst in
should anything happen, and two more waiting outside.

Palmer took off his jacket and placed it on top of the
tarpaulin with his nine-millimetre. All he needed to pull this
off was the memory stick he had in his hand.

Finn had tied her hair up into a ponytail and put on a

baseball cap. She was standing in a shadowed corner of the warehouse and, from the well-lit area in the middle, it was impossible to identify her. If anyone did spot her, they wouldn't be able to pick out the scar on her face or even be sure of her gender. None of the big players in this operation knew who she was, and Palmer wanted to keep it like that.

There was a loud bang on the roller door. One of the outside guards letting them know that the Cartel had arrived. Asher nodded to Palmer then pushed the button to raise the door.

The SUV outside waited until the door had opened all the way up, then paused, before creeping forward. The occupants were in the same frame of mind as Palmer and Asher. They shouldn't be expecting trouble, but no need to take unnecessary risks. The SUV rolled to a halt inside the warehouse and Asher closed the roller behind it.

The first passenger to get out was dressed in the same outfit as the suits at the handover. He had the cold stare of someone who had been involved with the cartels since he was a child. The tattoos that crept out from under his suit covered his hands and spread across his neck and face, adding to his intimidating appearance. For him, though, this wasn't just about business. One of the sicarios killed at the handover was his younger brother, and he wanted Carver to pay. He walked across to the roller door and stood with his back to it. From there, he would be able to see every part of the warehouse.

The driver's side window of the SUV rolled down and another heavily tattooed hand beckoned Palmer over to the open rear passenger door. Palmer took a deep breath and walked over to the vehicle.

The driver was another suit. He looked just as cold and hard as the first. Beside him was a younger man that Palmer recognised from the plateau. It was the guy who had checked Nate Buttermill's memory stick. Somehow, he had kept his head down and gone unnoticed in the chaos. He was a lucky man. He probably escaped while everyone else was looking for Palmer and Zahrah.

Sitting in the back was a man who looked to be in his sixties, although it was hard to tell. He had the same covering of tattoos as the others and, if he had been in the cartel since he was a child, the life he was involved in would have prematurely aged him. He nodded to Palmer and pointed to the seat beside him.

Palmer exchanged glances with Asher then climbed into the truck and closed the door behind him. 'Thank you for agreeing to see me, Don Miguel.'

'I have dealt with Asher before. I know he is trustworthy. That is enough to get you into that seat. What happens next, is up to you.'

Palmer held up the memory stick. 'This will give you the money you are owed by George Carver.'

Don Miguel pointed at the younger man in the front seat. 'Check this out. See if it is as he says.'

'Ci, Don Miguel.'

Don Miguel turned back to Palmer. 'Are you an honourable man, Mr Palmer?'

'I was a Royal Marine. It comes with the job.'

Don Miguel nodded. 'I have done a great many things in my life that I don't consider honourable. I have killed men, women... Children. All these things had to be done on the orders of my Don. There was no questioning the orders. You understand?'

'I understand that you've had a violent life, and I understand that you had to follow orders. If you wanted to survive.'

'This is true. Now I am the Don, and I am in a position to issue the orders. Anyone who crosses me will die, painfully, but I no longer allow the hurting of innocent people. Women and children especially.'

'I hope that means the girl is safe.'

Don Miguel smiled. 'You understand me, Mr Palmer. The man who organised this kidnapping was not acting under my orders. This man is now hanging from a bridge in Guadalajara with his balls in his mouth. The girl has nothing to fear from us.'

Palmer could only imagine the horrific nature of the man's death. He had heard stories of the cartels skinning people alive and hacking limbs off with a chainsaw. It was the stuff of nightmares. 'And me, Don Miguel? Do I need to stay one step ahead of your sicarios?'

'You killed one of my men in that clearing, Mr Palmer. He had a family.'

Palmer knew that a lot of importance was put on respect and honour in Don Miguel's world, but it was also a business. 'The money I'm giving you is the twenty million that Carver agreed and another ten. In reparation for the man I killed and for the disrespect shown to you during this whole thing.'

Don Miguel spoke to the man in the front seat. 'Do you have it?'

'There is thirty million as he says. All I need is the password and I can transfer it.'

Don Miguel turned back to Palmer. 'I will take the twenty million because Carver promised it. The extra ten will be useful for the families of my men. A great many children will have a better life because of it.'

'The password is Zahrah Kalu.'

'Thank you, Mr Palmer. That shows great trust. I could take the money and you would never leave the building.'

Palmer was gambling. If it didn't come off, they were all in trouble. 'My life is in your hands, Don Miguel.'

Don Miguel smiled and nodded. 'I asked if you were an honourable man. It is clear to me that you are. I know you only killed my man to protect the girl. He would have killed you. Our business is complete, Mr Palmer. You have nothing to fear from me.'

Palmer's muscles unclenched. 'Thank you, Don Miguel. Once I know where Carver and his men are, I'll let you know. When I've rescued Zahrah, you can do whatever you want with the rest.'

'That is a good gesture. I will take you up on it.' Don Miguel held out his hand. 'Good luck, Mr Palmer.'

Palmer took the Don's hand. 'It has been an honour.' He climbed out of the truck and closed the door.

The suit standing behind them got back into the passenger seat and Asher opened the roller to allow the truck to reverse out. He watched it drive away then closed the door.

Finn walked over to Palmer. 'How did it go?'

Palmer wiped the sweat from his forehead. 'That is one of the scariest things I've ever done. I was shitting myself all the way through it.'

'I don't blame you. They are all pretty scary. Is it done?'

Palmer nodded. 'He isn't looking to hurt us. His argument is with Carver and his men. I don't see them surviving for long.'

Asher joined them. 'I've never seen Don Miguel Vásquez come to a meeting away from his compound. Shows how

271

seriously he's taking it.'

Palmer nodded. 'He's not a happy bunny over all of this. Sounds like he had some internal strife that he had to deal with.'

'Not unusual. There's always someone younger who wants to be in charge. I'll bet the guy didn't die easy.'

'You're better off not knowing. Now, didn't you say you had some beer in the office?'

Asher smiled and gestured towards the door in the corner. 'Follow me.'

Chapter 64

Anna Riley was watching the dots on her screen as her software hack tracked various mobile phones. She wasn't worried about Palmer and Finn. Now that she knew they were alive and could contact them, she was happy. She had tracked them from their hideout to the meeting at the warehouse and knew they were still together.

The other dots she was interested in belonged to Carver and Gault. They had been at the house on the coast for days. She did begin to wonder if it was just their phones that were there, but she had tapped into the house's landline too. There were no cables running to the house. Instead, the landline used voice over IP technology and fed the traffic through several microwave links to the nearest exchange. It made it easier than a physical analogue line to tap into.

Carver and Gault obviously had no intention of leaving the house. Riley had to assume that was where Zahrah Kalu was being held. It made sense. If Gault knew Palmer might come after him, he would want her close by to use as a shield.

Riley tapped at the keyboard and brought up a map of Washington DC. Two new dots were flashing at her. They belonged to Harrison Draper and Blake Macey. It had been quite difficult to track down their personal numbers, but, now she had them, she was recording all their mobile data. The evidence it would give them could be priceless. Their call and location histories showed how often they had been together in a coffee shop or park. More often than would have been expected. Riley had also hacked Macy's cloud storage and now had several audio files of them discussing the whole conspiracy.

Her phone rang. She picked it up and swiped the screen. 'Hello, Logan.'

'How did you know it was me?'

'I'm tracking your phones. I can see every time you make a call. It didn't take much to narrow it down.'

'I knew blocking my number wouldn't be enough to stop you, Anna. How's my favourite computer hacker today?'

'Stop trying to butter me up, Logan. You still owe me a face-to-face apology.'

'I promise. As soon as I get home, I'll…'

'Just make sure you get home. That's all I want for now. You and Ruby.' Riley wasn't cut out for the realities of operations in the field. She suspected that Palmer had, long ago, come to terms with the idea that he could be killed. It was just part of what he did. An occupational hazard. She assumed Finn was the same, but for Riley, it was something she tried not to think about.

'You can help us there, Anna. Have you managed to find out where they are keeping Zahrah?'

Riley clicked back onto the map of Texas. 'It has to be the house on the coast. Ethan Gault and George Carver haven't moved from there for days. There has been lots of other traffic from phones that seem to come and go, but they never leave.'

'What's the house like, is there an obvious way in?'

Riley brought up the plans for the latest building. 'It's a fortress. It sits on its own island with one bridge to access it. Looks like the bridge is raised for extra security when needed.'

'What about access from the water? Is there anywhere a boat can dock?'

'It doesn't look like it. The whole property is basically a concrete platform that several houses have been built on over the years. At this time of year, the platform only sits four feet above water level at high tide. There is a narrow ledge all around before the walls start. The walls are twenty feet high and three feet thick at the bottom.'

Palmer spoke like he was thinking out loud. 'We'll have to do a recce of the house before we go in. The bridge is too obvious for an assault and would be where most of the security was focused. We need another way in. Can you send us the blueprints and any photos you have?'

'Will do. They'll be with you within the hour. Be careful, Logan.'

'Don't worry about us, Anna. We won't take any stupid risks.'

Riley ended the call. She knew she was a little naive when it came to this kind of thing, but even she could see how difficult attacking the house was going to be. She had to make sure that she did everything in her power to help. She selected Thomson's number from her contacts list and pressed the call button.

Chapter 65

Palmer and Finn unloaded their equipment from the truck. It had taken a while to find it all, but almost everything they needed was readily available in outdoor pursuits stores.

Asher unrolled the blueprints he had printed out and laid them on the table. 'It's not going to be easy.'

Palmer looked at the photographs. 'It's our only real option. A helicopter into the garden would give away our element of surprise. An airborne assault runs the risk of leaving us dangling from our chutes like targets in a fairground shooting gallery if we get spotted. The bridge is too easily defended unless we create a diversion.'

Finn looked at the map of the coastline. 'Are you going to be able to swim that far with all of the equipment?'

'The SBS have gills and webbed feet, didn't you know that?'

'I'm serious, Logan.'

Palmer pointed to the map. 'I'll enter the water here, out of sight of the house. It's only a mile. It won't be easy in that current, but I've done it before.'

'You weren't injured before. It's going to take timing and a lot of luck. It could go wrong at any stage.'

'If we get into position early enough, we'll give ourselves

the best chance of pulling it off.'

Asher nodded. 'Agreed. So, when do we go?'

'I'll call Gault now and set up the meeting for tomorrow night. He'll be expecting me to make contact so it shouldn't be a big surprise to him.'

'You think he'll turn up?'

Palmer shook his head. 'I don't think he will, but he'll send someone to take me out. If he does turn up, you can deal with him while we grab Zahrah. Either way, it helps us.'

Finn pulled the blueprints of the bridge over to her side of the table. 'I haven't been climbing for a while. This could get interesting.'

'For all of us.' Palmer picked up his phone and called Gault's number.

* * *

Gault picked up his phone. 'Who is this?'

'It's Palmer.'

Gault waved to Carver and pointed to his phone. 'I knew you weren't dead, Logan. How the fuck did you survive?'

'I have a guardian angel.'

'Your angel is a pretty good shot. Took out our men without too much problem.'

Palmer laughed. 'Let's cut out the shit, Gault. Where's Zahrah Kalu? If you've killed her, I'm coming for you.'

'Why would I kill her? It's just the money, documents, and photos that we want. All the originals.'

'We need to meet up and talk about an exchange. You give me the girl. I'll give you your shit back.'

Gault scoffed. 'You think I'm stupid? I'm not coming to a

meeting and giving you the chance to kill me from long range. I've seen your records.'

'What do you suggest?'

'I'll send some of our men to your meeting. The ones I can trust. You show them the evidence. Once they confirm it's all there, I'll leave the girl somewhere for you to pick up. We all get what we want.'

Palmer let out a long breath. 'Okay. I can agree to that. I'll send my guardian angel to pick up Zahrah. Where do you want to meet?'

'I've got somewhere in mind. Have you got a pen?'

Gault gave Palmer the details of the meeting's location then ended the call. He looked at Carver. 'He's falling for it. He's even agreed to separate himself from his backup. We'll have the evidence in our hands by tomorrow night and we can dispose of all the witnesses.'

Carver lit a cigar. 'Things are starting to look up, Ethan. With that much money injected into my election campaign and some renewed backing from the congressman, I'll be in the Governor's Mansion before you know it.'

Gault wasn't interested in politics. He viewed all politicians as self-serving and in it for what they could get. He had never met one who cared about the people once the election was over. That didn't bother him too much, as long as he got something out of it too. Blake Macey had already told him to deal with any liabilities when it was over, and when he said they could dispose of the witnesses, that list included George H. Carver.

Chapter 66

Palmer had picked a spot where the road was close to the shoreline and there were no buildings. It was just after dark when he and Finn pulled up. They grabbed a bag each and headed for the beach.

While Palmer pulled on his wet suit, Finn unpacked the second bag and loaded the equipment into a waterproof sack. The sack was fitted with a flotation device that would give it negative buoyancy at a depth of three metres. It would make it effectively weightless at that depth and allow Palmer to drag the equipment along behind him on the swim to the artificial island.

The lights of the house were visible in the distance. Carver wasn't worried about advertising his presence. He must have felt safe in his island fortress. The lights would make it easier for Palmer to keep his bearings as he swam. All he needed to do was surface occasionally and adjust his heading, but it would also make the assault more difficult. No shadows to hide in.

He pulled on a small single dive tank. He didn't plan on being underwater for long and the single tank was more than enough for the swim. Pulling the sack behind him would be hard, but if something went wrong and he ran out of oxygen, he could finish the swim on the surface. There was a risk he could be spotted, but it was better than drowning.

It was then that Finn noticed a set of headlights coming over the horizon back along the road. 'You get in the water. I'll distract whoever this is. Good luck. I'll see you in there.'

Palmer put on his mask. 'We've got this. I'll wait for your signal.'

Finn walked back up to the truck and waited for the car to reach her. It was when it was fifty meters away that the blue and red lights came on. Finn looked back along to the beach. She could see the silhouette of Palmer dragging his bag to the water's edge. She had to create a diversion. She pulled out a knife and stuck it in the truck's tyre.

The highway patrol car stopped directly behind the truck and the trooper climbed out, putting on his hat. 'Is everything okay, ma'am?'

Finn kicked the tyre. 'Got a flat. Don't know how to change it.' She put on her best damsel in distress act.

The trooper looked around to make sure he wasn't being set up. 'I can help you with that ma'am. We'll get you back on the road in no time.' He took off his hat and threw it back into the car.

'Thank you. You're really kind. I've heard that about people around here.'

'We do try to be neighbourly. You're not from around here, are you?'

Finn smiled at the trooper. She kept him distracted for half an hour while he changed the tyre. By the time she was waving him off, Palmer was nowhere in sight. She got back into the truck and drove towards the house.

* * *

At the same time as Finn was distracting the Highway Patrol trooper, Asher and five men he had hired were arriving at the meeting location. The men were all ex-forces. Marines, and Rangers. They were private military contractors used to supplying security in hell holes from Baghdad to Kabul. They all knew what they were doing, and Asher had used them before.

The meeting was taking place on the ground floor of a deserted warehouse just off I-69 on the outskirts of Sugar Land. Asher wanted to get there early and do a search of the area. He knew that the men he was using were much more highly trained than Carver's, but it was always possible to be caught unawares.

The plan wasn't to kill Carver's men. Asher was happy to tie them up and hand them over to the FBI, but his men were under instructions to defend themselves and not take any risks. If that meant taking out the whole of the white power brigade, so be it.

Asher looked at his watch. The meeting was in ninety minutes. Finn would be giving him a heads-up once Gault's team left the house. All he and his men had to do was set the trap. He gathered them together.

The ceiling above them was constructed by slotting thick wooden planks between a frame of I beams. It was a quick and easy way to create several levels if they didn't have to support too much weight. Since the warehouse had been abandoned, the roof had started to leak and some of the planks were rotting. Others had been broken, by accident or by bored kids, and some had been stolen. They were ideal for building a deck in the garden.

Two men positioned themselves up on the second floor aiming their weapons down through holes in the floor. Two other men built hides from empty crates, rubble, and old sacks on the ground floor. With one in each corner facing diagonally towards the entrance it was a perfect killing zone. The fifth man waited outside. Once Gault's team entered the building, he would cut off their exit. There was nowhere for them to go. If they had any sense at all, they would surrender quickly. *If* they had any sense.

Chapter 67

Dealing with the trooper, and the flat tyre, had held up Finn, but they had allowed enough time in the plan to cope with delays. She had driven to within half a mile of the house and parked the truck out of sight, then made the rest of the journey on foot.

She stood under the bridge that joined Carver's beach fortress to the mainland. A stone tower rose on either side of the approach road and supported the first twenty feet of the bridge. The deck then extended out to a stone arch which supported the middle of the structure. At the house end, a large wooden platform that resembled a medieval drawbridge was lowered down to the stone arch to grant access to the island's gate. The drawbridge was currently raised, cutting off the island from the mainland.

Finn donned her climbing gear and ascended one of the stone towers. The underside of the deck was built with a mesh of steel girders that resembled a kids' climbing frame. Swinging from strut to strut like it was a set of monkey bars, she made her way out to the stone arch. She fastened two straps to the last girder before the arch and settled back into her harness to wait.

Her forearms and shoulders were aching from the climb

out. It was a long time since she had had to do that, but at least this time she didn't have a grizzled sergeant screaming at her. She turned her wrist and checked the time. Bang on schedule.

The muscles in her legs started to tingle. Hanging in a harness wasn't the most comfortable thing she had ever done. She was just about to reposition herself when she felt the steel frame start to vibrate. The drawbridge on the house side was being lowered.

The powerful winch that controlled the lowering of the platform gave out a mechanical creak followed by a rhythmic clunk as it let out the thick cables that took the weight. Inch by inch, foot by foot, slowly and surprisingly smoothly, the deck lowered until it settled on top of the stone arch above Finn's head.

She immediately unhooked her harness and climbed across onto the house side as the house's gate opened and two vehicles drove across the bridge. She knew she had to get as far across to the house as she could or there would be a risk of being spotted. One girder at a time, one after another, she swung across. When she was halfway, the bridge began to rise again.

Finn was now in plain sight clinging to the underside of the bridge as it raised. Anyone of Carver's men looking back at the house could have seen her. Fortunately for her, they were too excited by the thought of taking down Palmer to worry about what was behind them. Finn waited for the bridge to reach its highest point then climbed down the frame, so she was hidden from view. Once again, she fastened her harness to one of the girders and waited.

Finn's phone vibrated in her pocket. She swiped the screen

and checked her messages. It was from Asher. He'd got her message, and the meeting was about to start. It was time for her to get ready. She unclipped her harness and climbed up on top of the bridge.

The security post for the house was inside the gate. Two men sat in a shelter and watched images from the cameras positioned around the house. Finn was standing in a blind spot. The only camera on the bridge was positioned above the gate and pointing along the approach to the bridge. As long as she stayed under it, and close to the gate, they couldn't see her.

She took off her backpack and removed the shaped, explosive demolition charges that Asher had sourced for them. The shape of the charge focussed the power of the explosion in one direction. Demolition companies used them to cut through steel beams when dropping a condemned building. The ones Finn was using were smaller than usual and only needed to cut through a small amount of metal.

Finn worked quickly. She fitted a charge to each of the gate's hinges and one to the electronic locking mechanism. She pressed the switch to activate the wireless detonator on each one then stood back against the wall, outside the gate's archway, and away from the path of the shock wave. She wiped the sweat from her face and relaxed. All being well, Palmer should be reaching the concrete platform in a few minutes.

Chapter 68

Palmer was in trouble. There was a rip current running parallel to the shore and away from the house. It was hard work, but he was a strong swimmer and had been making headway. Then, problem two hit. His equipment sack had sprung a leak. The buoyancy device relied on the bag being full of air. Without it and coupled with the extra weight of the kit inside, the bag had dragged him to the bottom. Luckily the water was only a few metres deep, but his oxygen wouldn't last long. With the extra exertion, he had burned through it quicker than planned and had to get back to the surface. There was no other way. He pulled out his knife and cut the strap that fastened him to his equipment.

Palmer broke the surface as quietly as he could. He had lost his bearings when he was dragged down and didn't know how close he was to the house. He unfastened the harness on his almost empty air bottle and pushed it away. It was of no use now. The house was no more than two hundred meters away and he struck out towards it. His problem now was that he had none of the equipment that he needed to get over the wall and breach the house.

He reached the concrete platform and clung to its surface like a limpet. It wasn't a smooth surface and had bumps and cracks that he could use as hand and foot holds. He took off his flippers then climbed the four feet to the ledge that ran around the base of the wall.

The ledge was only two feet deep and sloped so that water would run off it. Palmer managed to sit on it and get his breath back, but a strong gust of wind could have blown him off and back into the sea.

He looked up at the wall. The outside was built from red brick and had no bumps or cracks he could use to climb it. It was newer than the concrete of the platform and hadn't weathered as much. If he couldn't find a way up, he would have to swim to the front and join Finn on the bridge. He bent his knees and pushed himself up onto his feet.

Palmer edged his way around the ledge to his left. Its surface was curved like a massive lighthouse. Probably to help it withstand storms. After a few minutes, the gentle curve ended, and the wall turned sharply towards the beach. Palmer looked along it and up to the roof of the building it surrounded. There was no way of climbing up. Worse than that was the gap in the ledge. The weather had eaten its way into the concrete and caused a large chunk to fall off. He wasn't going any further. He shuffled around and headed back the way he had come.

Edging back the other way, he almost slipped off the ledge twice. Of all the things he thought might go wrong, this wasn't one of them. He made it to the other end of the curved wall and looked around the sharp turn.

This side of the island must have been shielded from the worst of the weather. The concrete was in better condition and had no big chunks missing. Better still, ten feet from where he was standing, there was a drainage pipe. That was his way up. He shuffled along to the pipe and wrapped his hand around it.

The pipe was metal and about three inches in diameter. The fixings looked solid, and it barely moved when he shook it. Looking up, it came out of the wall just beneath the top, next to a window. It didn't look like it was for rainwater. Maybe a new bathroom had been fitted in one of the rooms and the drain was for a shower or sink. Either way, it was sturdy enough to climb.

Normally, he would have climbed the pipe in no time, but all he had on his feet were neoprene dive boots. They had a little bit of tread on the sole, but they weren't ideal for shinning up a drainpipe. He grabbed hold of the pipe with both hands, braced his foot against the wall, and pushed.

It was slow going but his boots were better than he had expected. He reached the top of the pipe and pulled himself up onto the wall. He had a quick check in all directions and couldn't be seen from any part of the house. He let his arms hang loose and breathed deeply. His bullet wounds and cracked rib were screaming out for some painkillers, but that would have to wait.

The original plan was to listen for Finn's signal then they would both go into the house hard and fast. The element of surprise was everything. That plan wasn't viable anymore. All his weapons, and his phone, were at the bottom of the sea. He had literally brought a knife to a gunfight.

He crawled over to the window he had seen from the ledge. There was no light shining from it, so he took the chance and looked in. He had been right. The pipe was coming from a bathroom. He had to get inside the house quietly and get his hands on a gun before Finn made her entry. The window had a steel bar that ran from top to bottom on the outside. Palmer took out his knife and started to work on the bar's fixings.

Light suddenly flooded out of the window as someone flicked the switch and opened the door. Palmer ducked down below the sill. Caught off guard and unable to crawl away without risking being seen. He put his hand over his face in an attempt to camouflage it. His black neoprene gloves and wet suit covered up the rest of him. He looked up through his fingers and watched as the shadow of someone was thrown across the window.

Zahrah pressed her forehead against the cool glass and looked out at the sea. Palmer dropped his hand from his face and smiled at her. The shock caused Zahrah to gasp and step back. The last thing she had expected to see was a man in a wet suit curled up under the window. Palmer stood up and held his finger to his lips. He pointed to the window lock and made an unlocking gesture. Zahrah checked behind her then turned the latch.

Palmer carried on digging at the brick where the steel bar was fastened. After a few minutes of digging and pulling, the attachment gave way, and he moved the bar upwards and clear of the window. He pulled the window open, lifted his leg over the sill and climbed in.

Zahrah threw her arms around him and whispered in his ear. 'I knew you were alive. I just knew it.'

'Don't squeeze too hard. I've got a couple of extra holes since you last saw me.'

She pulled away. 'Are you okay?'

'I'm fine. I got patched up and Ruby has been looking after me.'

Zahrah frowned. 'Who's Ruby?'

'She's a good friend of mine. You'll meet her later. First,

289

we've got to get you out of here. How do you feel about a little climb and a swim?'

'I can't.'

Palmer pointed out of the window. 'It's only twenty feet down a drainpipe. The sea isn't rough. I'll keep you afloat.'

Zahrah shook her head. 'It's not that.' She lifted her t-shirt to reveal a steel chain fastened around her waist. 'I'm chained to the bed.'

'Why have they done that?'

'Probably to stop me climbing out of the window. I did try to escape a couple of times when I first got here.'

Palmer smiled. 'Keeping them on their toes? Good girl. Who's got the key?'

'It's always Gault that comes and unlocks it.'

That was exactly what Palmer didn't want to hear. 'Do you know how many guards there are?'

She led him back through to the bedroom and pointed at the door. 'There's always one guy outside the door, and the door is always kept locked. Whenever Carver sends for me, the guard unlocks the door, but has to wait for Gault to come with the key for the chain.'

Palmer inspected Zahrah's restraint. It was like the ones used to transport maximum security prisoners to their court appearances. Hardened steel with built-in handcuffs. A steel cable was padlocked to the back of it and fed through holes in the frame of the bed. There was no way they were cutting through it.

Palmer looked at his knife. It was damaged from digging at the wall, but it was all he had. 'When the guard comes in, does he have his gun out?'

Zahrah shook her head. 'No.'

'Good. I want you to bang on the door and get him in here. I'll do the rest.'

She nodded and banged on the door as hard as she could. 'You need to get in here.'

The guard stirred in his seat. 'Shut up. It's not time for you to eat.'

Zahrah banged again. 'I can smell smoke. I think something's on fire.'

The guard didn't reply.

Zahrah banged louder. 'It's getting worse.'

'Shit. Okay, okay. Get back and sit on the bed.'

Zahrah did as she was told.

The guard pushed the door open. 'What is it now? I don't smell anything.'

Zahrah raised an eyebrow. 'Oh, there is definitely something going on.'

Palmer stepped out from behind the door and clamped his left arm across the guard's throat. His right arm came down in an arc and buried the diving knife up to the hilt in the guard's chest.

The man struggled. Who wouldn't, but it was already too late. He was bleeding out. As the man fought, they both fell backwards. Palmer let out a grunt through clenched teeth as the weight of the other man's body landed squarely on his cracked rib and damaged it even more. The guard's struggling weakened and then stopped. Palmer pushed the body off and grabbed his side. He was in agony. There was no way he was climbing out of the window and down the drainpipe now.

Zahrah rushed over to him. 'Logan, are you okay?'

Palmer nodded, but it was obvious he wasn't. 'I think he broke my cracked rib, maybe even two of them.'

291

'I'll help you up.'

Palmer rolled over onto his knees. 'Close the door and find me something to strap up my ribs with.'

Chapter 69

Asher put away his phone and switched on the headlights of his pick-up. If he stood in front of them, Carver's men would only see him in silhouette. He was roughly the same height and build as Palmer so they wouldn't realise anything was wrong until it was too late.

The first mistake that Carver's goons made played right into Asher's hands. The two vehicles that Carver had sent drove straight into the warehouse. They didn't even leave anyone outside to watch for someone closing off their escape route. Absolute amateurs.

The two vehicles pulled up next to each other and switched off their engines. They also switched off their lights. Another mistake. Six of the weekend warriors climbed out of the vehicles and walked around to the front. None of them checked the perimeter. They didn't even have weapons drawn. Mistake number three. All the cards were now in Asher's hands.

One of the warriors stepped forward. 'Here's how it works, Palmer. You give us all of the evidence and hand yourself over to us…' he threw a pair of handcuffs at Asher's feet. '… and we let the girl go.' One of the men behind him held up a phone.

Asher took off his cap and pulled a nine-millimetre out of

his shoulder holster. 'Good evening, gentlemen. As you can see, I am not Logan Palmer. Let me explain to you what is going to happen. You will all place your weapons on the floor, my associates will handcuff you, and we will turn you over to the authorities. If you do this with no fuss, I'll let you live. I'll leave you to imagine what happens if you don't do it.'

The warriors were frozen for a moment. They had expected to be in control of this process. Gault must have told them it was all arranged. A simple pick up. The man at the front, obviously their leader, looked like he was going through things in his head. Things he realised he had got wrong. He looked in all directions, there was no one in sight. The plan he came up with was a good one. At least, it was in his head.

The leader held up his hands. 'Okay, boys. Do as he says. All weapons on the ground.'

The warriors looked at each other, questioning, but they complied anyway.

The leader put his hand in his jacket and gripped the handle of his Colt. It was now or never. Fast and accurate. He pulled out his weapon, but, before he could level it at Asher, a shot rang out from the men above and dropped the man to the floor like a marionette with the strings cut. The other warriors looked at their dead leader and threw up their hands. Placing them behind their heads.

Asher's men crawled out of their hiding places and proceeded to shackle the men together. They were made to kneel on the floor and the last man in the chain was cuffed to one of their vehicles.

Asher walked over to the man with the phone and took it from him. The call was still active. He held it to his ear and listened as Gault demanded to know what was going on.

Asher said nothing. He ended the call and dialled 9-1-1.

Chapter 70

E than Gault threw his phone across the room. 'SHIT!' Carver sat up in his chair. 'What is it?'

'It's a set-up.'

'I don't understand. How can it be a set-up? He's one man, injured. He's maybe got one person helping him.'

Gault shook his head. 'I sent six men to pick Palmer up. I was on the phone to them. They said he was in the warehouse.'

'What happened?'

'I heard a shot. Someone picked the phone up and it went dead.'

Carver clenched his teeth. 'How long will it take him to get here?'

'You still don't get it. Palmer couldn't have taken six men on his own. He has to have multiple people working with him.'

'Where would he get them?'

Gault poured a drink and sank it in one gulp. 'Palmer has been in the private military business for a long time. He has a lot of contacts. It wouldn't surprise me if these people weren't all mercenaries. Ex special forces. Able to take out your security without breaking a sweat.'

Carver picked up the phone and barked orders into the mouthpiece. 'Get my car ready.'

'Where the fuck do you think you're going?'

'We have to get out of here before Palmer arrives.'

Gault smiled. 'What makes you think he isn't here already?'

Finn's three demolition charges triggered in quick succession. The muffled thumps were unmistakable. Carver stood up. 'What the hell was that?'

'I think the question of whether or not Palmer is here has just been answered.'

Carver walked to the door of the office and listened. The first gunshots came as the reverberation of the explosions was dying. There was a pause, then all hell let loose. He backed away across the room. 'I need to get out of here. You need to do something.'

* * *

In the other wing, Zahrah had ripped the bedsheet into strips and strapped Palmer's upper left arm to his chest to try to protect his broken ribs.

The explosions and gunshots alerted Palmer to Finn's assault. 'That's Ruby. She was supposed to blow the gate while I attacked the house. She'll be heading for the front door.'

'You're in no condition to do anything.'

Palmer picked up his pistol and pushed himself up off the bed. 'I have to help. She'll be expecting me to be there, and I need to find something to get you out of those shackles. Go and hide in the bathroom and I'll be back as soon as I can.'

Zahrah nodded. 'Just be careful.'

'I will.' Palmer gritted his teeth and went out. He descended the stairs keeping his right shoulder and back against the wall. There was no sign of any movement inside the house, all of Carver's men must have gone outside when the shooting started. When he reached the last step, Palmer looked up at the landing outside Carver's office. What he wanted to do was go up the main staircase and take out the old man, but there was no guarantee he was still in there, and Finn needed help.

Palmer reached the front of the house and peered out of the window that sat beside the door. Finn had blown the gate and, by the looks of it, taken care of the first two guards already, but that was when the good luck and the element of surprise ran out. She was now pinned down by a hail of bullets coming from Carver's men.

On the right-hand side of the courtyard, three men were set up in a firing position behind a stack of sandbags. To the left, another two men were crouched down behind the four-foot wall that ran in front of their accommodation block. Between them, they had Finn in a crossfire. She had tucked herself into a corner of the gatehouse but couldn't return fire. The temporary building's wood and fibreglass walls wouldn't give her any protection.

Palmer couldn't see the men behind the sandbags, it was only the noise that told him they were there. He looked across to the accommodation block. He could see the men crouched behind the wall and had a clear line of fire. He pulled open the door and emptied his magazine into their position.

When Palmer engaged the men behind the wall, Finn was able to get to her knees and take on the men behind the sandbags. With Finn giving him covering fire, Palmer picked up an AR-15 from one of the dead men and skirted around the courtyard into a deep doorway entrance that looked like it hadn't been used for a long time. He took cover behind its stone archway and waited for Carver's men to show themselves.

* * *

Up in the power room, the only weapon Gault had was his FBI issued Glock and one spare magazine. From the sound of the gunfire he could hear, that wasn't going to be enough to get him out. He had to get himself some insurance. If he had Zahrah, he could at least negotiate an exit. Carver was on his own, this was about his survival. He opened the door and went out on the landing.

He ran down the main staircase two steps at a time and slid across to the wall beside the door. When he looked outside, all he could see were the bodies of Carver's men. He would have to find another way out. Keeping below the level of the windows, he ran across the hallway and up the steps.

Gault kicked open the door to Zahrah's room and almost fell over the dead guard. He wasn't expecting that. At least he knew Palmer had been here, the girl hadn't done this. 'You can come out now.'

Zahrah stayed where she was.

Gault grabbed the steel cable and followed it from the bed to the bathroom. He grabbed the shackles around Zahrah's waist, lifted her onto her feet, and slammed her against the wall. 'You do exactly what I say and maybe we'll both make it out of here. If not…' He tapped the barrel of his pistol against Zahrah's temple to leave her in no doubt what he had in mind. 'Yes?'

Tears ran down Zahrah's face and her answer was little

more than a whisper. 'Yes.'

'Good.' Gault unlocked her shackles and dragged her out of the room.

Chapter 71

Palmer was breathing heavily. His adrenaline rush was wearing off and the pain was becoming unbearable. They had to finish this quickly and get back inside. He signalled to Finn that he was going to rush the sandbags and ditched his AR-15. He was having trouble using it with one arm anyway. Finn changed her magazine and nodded back to Palmer. As soon as she stood up and opened fire, Palmer ran out of his doorway and closed on the sandbags.

Of the three men who had been crouched behind them, only two remained. Finn had managed to pick one of them off. One of the two that were left saw Palmer coming and swung his rifle around. That gave Finn the perfect shot and the man crumpled to the floor, dead as soon as the round hit him.

The last man, realising he was alone, vaulted over the pile of sandbags and ran towards the gatehouse. He just wanted to get out. Finn could have shot him but there was no reason to, he was unarmed. The man pushed the button to lower the bridge and sprinted out into the night.

Finn looked at Palmer strapped up with bed sheets. 'How are you doing?'

'I'm not sure how much longer I can keep going.'

Finn reached into a pouch that hung from her belt and

pulled out a shot of morphine. She removed the cap and stuck it into Palmer's leg. 'That'll ease the pain, but you'll crash and burn at some point.'

Palmer took two magazines for his pistol from the back of Finn's tac vest and put them into his pocket. 'I think there's only Carver and Gault left. We need to get back in the house and get Zahrah but be careful. We could still bump into stragglers who've been hiding out.'

'Okay, let's do it.'

Palmer and Finn burst into the hallway from the front door. Ethan Gault was on the landing trying to get into Carver's office, but it looked like the old bastard had locked him out. 'Let me in, Carver.'

Palmer set off up the steps. 'You just can't rely on people anymore. Can you Ethan?'

Zahrah screamed. 'LOGAN!'

Gault pulled her in front of him as a shield. 'Don't be stupid Palmer, you'll hit the girl.' He dragged Zahrah along the landing towards the attic and the access to the rooftop fire escape.

Palmer held his fire. The morphine was kicking in and affecting his vision. Finn didn't have that problem. She raised her M4 and fired a single shot that hit Gault just above his right kneecap.

Gault fell and pulled Zahrah down with him. He crawled around the corner of the landing and pushed her into a corner. 'Back off. I'll kill her if you come near.' He forced Zahrah through the door and up the steps towards the attic.

Finn put her hand on Palmer's shoulder. 'It's over. He can't get away. We can wait him out.'

Palmer shook his head. 'I can't risk him hurting Zahrah. I

need to do this. I'll let you take care of Carver.'

'Okay, watch your back.'

Palmer was still in a lot of pain. The sweat was pouring off him. He wiped his hands on his trousers and dried the grip of his weapon. The trail of Gault's blood was clearly visible and made him easy to follow, but Palmer had to be cautious. He didn't know the layout of this part of the house and Gault could ambush him at any time. The only thing in Palmer's favour was Gault's obvious sense of self-preservation. He would much rather run than fight.

Palmer reached the attic window in time to see Gault's legs disappearing around the corner. He was working his way around to the other side of the roof on all fours, or threes if you took his injured leg into account. The roof had a slope, and it was raining again. He was pushing Zahrah ahead of him towards the roof's ridge.

The way Palmer was facing, the window was on his left-hand side. He swapped his weapon to his left hand and fired two shots, but, with his upper arm strapped to his chest, he couldn't aim. The shots smashed roof tiles but didn't hit Gault.

Gault's progress was slow. As well as keeping hold of the Zahrah, the pain as his foot bounced off the surface of the roof must have been excruciating. At one point, he stopped and raised his face to the now torrential rain and breathed in the cold air. When they reached the ridge, he forced Zahrah to climb over to the other side, but, before he could move, Palmer's hand clamped down on his wounded leg. Gault screamed and lashed out with his other leg.

The kick hit Palmer square in the face and knocked him backwards. Palmer lost his footing and began to slide down the rain-slicked surface. His hands searched for any purchase to stop his descent, but there was none. He was accelerating towards the edge.

Gault crawled over the ridge and disappeared onto the other side of the roof.

Palmer's neoprene dive boots skidded on the tiles as he tried to stop himself. At the edge of the roof, just before he fell into the void, slammed into the platform at the bottom of the wall and rolled into the sea, one of his feet caught in the steel guttering. He braced his leg and started to glide sideways but was able to grab the gutter with his good arm and stop his fall. He shook his head to get the rain out of his eyes and started to climb back up to the ridge.

Through the rain that bounced off the roof tiles, he could see Gault threatening Zahrah. He had hold of her collar and was forcing her onto the fire escape ladder. Zahrah was too scared to stand up. Gault pointed his pistol at her head. 'Stand up and get on the ladder now.'

'Let her go, Gault.'

Gault kept his Glock pressed against Zahrah's temple and turned to face Palmer. 'Drop your weapon or I'll kill the girl.'

Palmer didn't move.

'Drop it, Palmer. I've got nothing to lose. Do it now or she dies.'

Palmer lowered his arm and dropped his pistol. It clattered onto the roof tiles and tumbled away from him.

Gault smiled and took his Glock away from Zahrah's head. 'You lose, Palmer.' He raised his arm and aimed at Palmer's chest.'

Zahrah screamed. 'NO!'

Palmer pulled his dive knife out of his belt and threw it at Gault. He had never been much good at throwing knives and this time was no different. The knife hit Gault handle first just below his left eye. It wasn't going to kill him, but it did knock him off his aim and his one good leg slipped in the rain.

Palmer took his chance and fell forward. He slid down the roof, grabbed his pistol, and fired three shots.

Two of the bullets missed completely, but the third hit Gault in the chest. He tipped over to one side and grabbed hold of the ladder as he fell off the roof.

Gault hung from the top rung, but he didn't hang for long. His strength had left him. Blood loss and exertion took their toll. The new wound to his chest was spurting blood and there was nothing he could do about it. He looked up at the sky, rain splashing off his face. With a look of resignation in his eyes, Ethan Gault let go of the ladder and plummeted down to the courtyard.

Chapter 72

C arver emptied the money out of his safe into a small holdall along with his fake passport. He had a private plane waiting for him at the airfield, all he had to do was get there. He reached under his desk and flicked the switch that was hidden in the corner. The bookcase to his left clicked and swung outwards to reveal a narrow staircase. He took one more gulp of his favourite bourbon then stepped onto the stairs and closed the bookcase behind him.

At the bottom of the narrow, secret staircase was a rusting steel door. Carver forced open the bolt that secured it and pushed. It was stiff. No one had opened it in a couple of decades. He braced his shoulder against the wood and drove with his legs against the bottom step. Gradually, with a scraping sound, the swollen wood of the frame gave way and the door swung open.

Outside the door, one of Carver's men who had stayed out of the gunfight was waiting with an SUV. The vehicle had the tailgate open and the engine running. Carver ran the few feet towards the vehicle then stopped. The sound of Gault landing on the cobbles of the courtyard was like nothing that Carver had ever heard before. He looked up to the roof but couldn't see anyone. Gault hadn't even screamed on the way down.

Carver looked at his driver. 'Get me out of here. I'll pay you a big bonus when I'm safe.' He dived into the back of the SUV and the driver closed the tailgate.

* * *

Ruby Finn tried to kick the office's door open, but it wouldn't budge. She emptied half a magazine of M4 rounds into the lock. The wood of the door was splintered, and the lock buckled. She kicked the door again and again. On the third kick, it gave way and opened.

The room was empty. There was no sign of Carver at all. She couldn't understand it. Somehow, he had got out of the room and past her. He must be heading for a vehicle to get him out. She left the room and ran back down the stairs.

Finn ran out of the front door and saw the vehicle pulling away. It had to be Carver. She dropped to one knee and aimed at the tyres. Several of her rounds hit their target, but to no effect. The tyres were run flats. Designed to withstand being punctured. She moved her aim to the body of the car. It was no good either. The bullets didn't seem to be doing enough damage. Her last option was to blow out the windows and try to hit the driver. She managed to shatter one of the rear windows, but the car had made it to the bridge. All Finn could do was watch as the taillights of the SUV vanished into the rain on the other side.

In the distance, Finn could hear sirens. She had to find Palmer. It would be better if they weren't there when the police arrived.

Finn ran back into the house. Blue flashing lights could now be seen approaching the bridge. She looked up at the landing and shouted. 'Zahrah. Palmer. Where are you?'

Zahrah ran down the stairs into the hallway. 'Are you Ruby?'

'Yeah, that's me. Where's Palmer?'

Palmer tried to stand up but was in too much pain. 'I'm up here.'

With Zahrah's help, Palmer had managed to get back inside the house and onto the landing outside Carver's office, but he was done. The injuries he was carrying and everything he had done over the past few weeks had sapped him of energy. He sat with his back to the wall and held onto his ribs.

Finn sprinted up to the landing. 'We need to get out of here.'

Palmer shook his head. 'There isn't time. I'll have to let the cops take me in. Where's Carver?'

'He got away. Don't worry about him. There's nowhere for him to hide. Even his own people want him dead.'

'Ruby. You need to take off your tac vest and get rid of your weapons. The cops don't know who you are. If you aren't armed, you can pass yourself off as a victim. Say you were abducted by Carver's goons when you were in the wrong place at the wrong time. Just an innocent tourist caught up in a nightmare.'

Finn took off her vest and threw everything over the balcony. 'Zahrah, we have to get in front of Logan. They can't shoot him if we're in the way.'

They heard the sound of boots in the entrance hall below. 'FBI. Drop your weapons. Come out with your hands above your head.'

Finn knelt in front of Palmer. 'Here they come. Look terrified.'

The first members of the black-clad FBI SWAT team reached the top of the stairs. 'FBI! DROP YOUR WEAPONS!'

Zahrah had managed to squeeze out a few tears. It wasn't all acting though. She was genuinely frightened.

Finn had her hands on her head. 'Thank God. You have to help us. We've been kidnapped.'

The seeds of doubt had been sewn in the minds of the SWAT team. 'Face down. Hands behind your head. Interlace your fingers.'

Finn and Zahrah did as they were told. Palmer gave it his best shot but ended up half lying half kneeling.

They were all handcuffed and taken out of the building. Finn and Zahrah to a waiting FBI car and Palmer to an ambulance.

Special Agent in Charge Amy Caddick stood outside watching the rain bounce off Ethan Gault's corpse. She looked around at the wreckage and the other bodies that littered the courtyard with her arms outstretched. 'What the fuck went on here?'

As the other FBI agents started to catalogue the scene of chaos that had been left behind, one of the paramedics closed the back door of the ambulance that carried Palmer. With its blue lights on, it swung around and drove across the bridge followed by Zahrah and Finn's car.

* * *

Carver cowered in the back of his SUV. He had flinched as the bullets struck the strengthened metal around the trunk. It was always best to plan for these things. He banged on the lid of the armoured box and shouted to his driver. 'Let me out.'

The car pulled to a halt, but his driver didn't open up. What was the idiot doing? He banged on the lid again. 'Let me out of here you idiot.'

There was the unmistakable sound of gunshots. Carver pulled his legs up to his chest as if that would protect him. What the hell was going on out there? He had to get his story straight for the FBI. He was the victim here.

The trunk of the SUV was finally opened. The lid of the armoured box was lifted up and its rear flap dropped down. A strong pair of hands reached in and grabbed Carver's ankles. He was pulled out of his SUV hiding place and thrown, roughly, into the boot of another car. Carver didn't understand. Was it Palmer? What did he want? 'I can give you money, Palmer.'

The rain that had been pouring down onto him suddenly stopped. Carver wiped the water from his eyes and looked up. Two tattooed Latinos in sharp suits and carrying golf umbrellas stared down at him. One of them smiled. 'Hola, cabron.'

Now Carver understood. He held out his hand. 'No... Wait...'

The boot was slammed shut before he could complain or negotiate. He knew what Don Miguel would do to him. Knew how hard his death would be, but he couldn't do anything about it. All he could do was lay in the darkness and scream.

Chapter 73

P almer spent two weeks in the prison hospital. His injuries were never life-threatening, but he did have broken ribs and two infected bullet wounds. Doctors wanted to keep him under observation before he was released into the prison's general population.

Now, in his orange jumpsuit and white t-shirt, he walked out of the prison block and into the heat of the exercise yard. This was a maximum-security federal penitentiary. It was a place where only the strong survived. The tension between the various groups and gangs within the prison was palpable. Palmer could handle himself, but some of the men inside these walls were cold-blooded killers with nothing to lose. That gave them an edge.

Palmer stood with his back to the wire. A lot of eyes were on him. He was being assessed. Was he a killer? Was he a threat to anyone, or would he become someone else's punk? The first person to approach him was a Latino man with skin that was taken up by what seemed to be a single tattoo. He was covered head to toe in prison ink that showed his gang affiliation. Tattoos that showed which gang he was in, that he had killed for them on the outside and since being incarcerated, and that he was serving life with no parole. He was exactly the type of prisoner who would easily kill Palmer just to prove a point.

Palmer changed his stance. Ready for any attack that came, but still keeping his back to the wire so no one came at him from behind.

The Latino man stopped a meter short of Palmer and looked him up and down. 'Look over my shoulder, gringo. The man on the right is El Jefe. He owns this yard. Do you understand?'

Palmer nodded. They were feeling him out. 'I'm no threat to him, but I don't work for him either. I'm my own man.'

The tattooed man gave him a smile that was more like a painful grimace. 'We have heard of you, Logan Palmer. Don Miguel Vásquez has issued instructions that you are not to be harmed in any way. Anyone who comes at you will be dealt with by us. You understand?'

Palmer nodded. 'I am grateful.' He nodded to the boss in the distance.

The tattooed man turned and went back to his gang.

Palmer breathed and started to feel a little more relaxed. The prison was still a dangerous place, but now he could live with the threat.

That was how it went for the next three months. A couple of times a fight broke out as scores were settled, but nothing Palmer couldn't deal with. On the one hundredth day of his imprisonment, he got a visitor.

Special Agent in Charge Amy Caddick came into the interview room and sat opposite Palmer. She opened a folder and flicked through the documents inside. After a few minutes, she finally spoke. 'You've got quite the record, Mr Palmer.'

'Thank you. I do my best.'

Caddick looked up. 'This is serious, Mr Palmer. Be under no doubts about that.'

Palmer smiled. 'And what is it you want?'

'My superiors would prefer it if this… sequence of events wasn't made public. It would cause us… problems.'

Palmer laughed. 'No shit. This isn't institutional racism. We're talking about hardcore white supremacists at the heart of the establishment. Can you imagine what the social media will do with that one in the current climate?'

'There's no need for people to know any of this. It would lead to mistrust of the government. It could damage our very democracy.'

'And let's not forget it could embarrass some high-up arses.'

Caddick slid a piece of paper across the table. 'Congressman Harrison Draper and FBI Deputy Director Blake Macey have resigned to spend more time with their families. They've been told what will happen if they do anything else.'

'The politicians get away with it, as is always the case. What about Carver?'

'We found his torso in the desert. God knows where his arms and legs are, but the autopsy showed they were removed before he died.'

Palmer whistled. 'I'll bet that hurt.'

'The cartels would normally get rid of the body. This was left as a message. Maybe you should be worried.'

Palmer grinned. 'Who do you think protects me in here?'

'Why would they do that?'

Palmer shrugged. 'I'm a popular guy.'

'Let's stop with the small talk, Palmer. You are about to go to court for killing Simone Kalu and abducting Zahrah Kalu. Trafficking of a minor, weapons smuggling and the murder

313

of an FBI Agent. There's also conspiracy to commit murder, obstruction of justice and several other charges that we can probably pin on you.' She pushed more paperwork across the table.

Palmer nodded slowly as he looked at the contents of the folder. 'Looks like an open and shut case. When's the trial? I've got a lot to get off my chest.'

Caddick gathered up the papers. 'Look, all we want is the original evidence and the photographs. We know you've got them. Tell us where they are, and we'll let you go.'

'If I did have anything like that, I'd make sure that it was hidden somewhere that you'll never find it. You see, your problem is that, if I have got it, I could just make one phone call and your whole world would be covered in shit.'

Caddick closed the folder and steepled her fingers. 'There are clothes in your cell. Get dressed. You're going on a trip.' She stood and walked out.

Palmer got dressed and was placed into the prison minibus which took him to the airport. A police escort pulled up outside departures and the bus pulled in behind it. One of the police officers opened the back doors and Palmer climbed out.

The police officers led him to the departure lounge and across to one of the gates where a flight to London was ready to leave. Caddick walked up behind him and nodded to the officers. One of them removed Palmer's handcuffs and they both stepped away.

Palmer rubbed his wrists. 'Are you kicking me out, Amy?'

Caddick handed Palmer his passport and a one-way ticket to London. 'Don't come back, Mr Palmer.'

Palmer smiled. 'Thanks for your hospitality. It's been a

pleasure.' He turned and handed his boarding card to the gate attendant then walked along the gangway and got on the plane.

Chapter 74

Two months later, Palmer sat at the back of the school assembly hall next to the door. He always preferred to see who came into a room before they could cause him any problems. Anna Riley was sitting next to him oblivious to anything other than what was happening on stage.

The school concert was in full swing and Zahrah Kalu was belting out a perfect version of *I Will Survive* backed by her classmates. She had settled in well at Saint Mary's Boarding School, had made new friends and was catching up on her studies. At this rate, her dream of going to university would no longer be just a dream.

Palmer was proud of her. The pride a father feels. Pride that he should have been able to have for his own son, but that had been taken away from him. He paused for a moment, lost in a memory. When he snapped back into the here and now, Victoria Thomson was sitting next to him.

'She's good.'

Palmer nodded. 'She's doing well. Thanks for arranging all of this, Vicky. I know you had to call in some favours for this.'

'That's okay, Logan. She's worth it, and you are a friend.'

Palmer looked into Thomson's eyes. 'Is it time for the payback?'

Thomson smiled. 'I've got a job for you, Logan. Nothing too strenuous to start with. I'll be outside.'

As Zahrah came to the end of her song, Thomson applauded then stood and left the building.

With the school concert ended, the pupils all left the stage and went to greet their parents. Palmer gave Zahrah a long hug. 'That was fantastic. I'm so proud of you. Your mum and dad would be too.'

Zahrah smiled. 'I wish they were here... I'm glad you're here.'

'Listen, I have to go and do some work. Help out the people who helped us. Are you okay with that?'

'Is this what you meant when you said they would want something from you?'

Palmer nodded. 'I have to go.'

'Okay. Just promise me you're coming back.'

Palmer gave her another hug. 'I promise.'

The black Range Rover pulled up in front of the school. Ruby Finn was already in the back and Thomson got into the front passenger seat. Palmer walked over and opened the back door. He looked back at Zahrah and waved then climbed in and closed the door. The Range Rover pulled away and drove down the school's gravelled access road.

Palmer watched through the rear window as Zahrah faded into the distance. He had hoped that they would let him stay with her for a little longer, but that wasn't how it worked, he knew that. He turned back around and fastened his seat belt. One more job and he would be out of the business for good. He had promised Zahrah, and he meant it.

Acknowledgments

As I always say, this book wouldn't have been published without the support of my friends and my readers. I'd like to say thank you to the following people.

Thank you to Mike Craven, Matt Hilton, Graham Smith, Ann Bloxwich, all my friends at Crime & Publishment, and Moffat Crime Writers+. Too numerous to mention here, but you know who you are, and without your unending support and freely given advice, my books wouldn't exist.

I would like to thank Amy Caddick for joining my cast of characters and reading my manuscripts to weed out any mistakes.

As always, and most importantly, I would like to thank my wife, Ruth, and my sons, Luke, and Daniel, for always supporting me and pushing me on. I love you all.

About the Author

L J Morris was born in Cold War, West Germany, but grew up in the North of England. During his childhood, books were always an important part of his life. He read everything he could get his hands on but found himself drawn towards the Thriller genre at an early age. At 16, eager to see the world he had read about, he left school and spent most of the 80s and 90s serving in the Royal Navy.

After his military service, he continued to live and work across Europe, The USA, and Southeast Asia for several more years. It was during this time that his love of storytelling resurfaced. He jotted down ideas, using the locations he found himself in as a backdrop and added details from his own experiences to make the stories feel authentic.

He now lives back in the North of England, with his wife and two sons, where he still works in the defence industry.

L J Morris is deaf and uses hearing aids. Although he is able to lip-read, the wearing of masks during Covid made that impossible and he began learning British Sign Language (BSL). He is planning to include his experiences with hearing loss in more of his work.

You can connect with me on:
- 🌐 https://ljmorrisauthor.com
- 🐦 https://twitter.com/LesJMorris
- 📘 https://www.facebook.com/LesJMorris

Subscribe to my newsletter:
- ✉ https://ljmorrisauthor.com

Also by L J Morris

Legacy of Guilt

When photographs of a Russian missile scientist, who was thought to be dead, prove he's alive, and a Soviet-era nuclear warhead goes missing in Iraq, ex-marine Logan Palmer must track them both down before the warhead's plutonium can be used to mount a devastating, terrorist attack.

The photographs are from the CCTV cameras of a hotel in Southeast Asia. The images show the scientist along with members of a private security team. A team that Palmer once led. His only option is to rejoin his old unit and uncover the plan before they work out that he isn't one of them anymore.

With time running out, Palmer and Anna Riley, his handler back in London, struggle with ghosts from their pasts as they scramble to identify the terrorists' target and stop the attack.

But, with thousands of lives at risk, Palmer doesn't realise that the only person in the world he cares about is the one that's in the most danger.

"Clear writing makes for great reading in a very believable spy thriller. Highly recommended." - *Alistair Birch*

"L J Morris uses his military background to add authenticity to his writing and the plot, which comes through. I highly recommend anything by this author." - *Tony Millington*

Desperate Ground

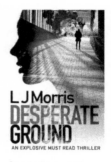

LJ Morris
DESPERATE
GROUND
AN EXPLOSIVE MUST READ THRILLER

When the secrecy of a nuclear weapon agreement is thrown into doubt, a disgraced intelligence operative is recruited to find out if the deal is still safe...

Ali Sinclair, wrongly convicted and on the run from a Mexican prison, is enlisted to infiltrate her old friend's inner circle and find the evidence.

The only people on her side are an ex-Cold War spook and the former Royal Marine that was sent to find her. Together they discover that the stakes are much higher than anyone knew, and the fate of the world is at risk...

But when you've lived in the shadows who can you trust?

"This is an assured and well-crafted debut in the mold of Tom Clancy or Frederick Forsyth. It's intelligent but also has enough pace and action to keep the pages turning long after it's time to turn off the light." – *M W Craven*

"Morris knows his 'stuff', his insider knowledge of an industry that is alien and not a little frightening to most laymen shines through, but never in a way that slows this fast-paced, rollicking action thriller." – *Matt Hilton*

Hunting Ground

Freed from prison and back in Europe, Ali Sinclair has one job... find Frank McGill.

The information he has is vital if they are to end the conspiracy that threatens to bring down the Government and push NATO to the brink of war.

With terrorist attacks increasing and a mole at the top of the establishment, Sinclair and McGill will need to use all their skills to follow the clues across the continent in a deadly treasure hunt that drags them back towards London.

But when you're being hunted by assassins and the authorities... going home isn't always the safest option.

"Ludlum, Clancy, and DeMille have competition at last" – *Nigel Adams*

"Wow! Wow! Wow! A brilliant opening sets the novel up perfectly for the action-packed read ahead." – *Crime Book Junkie*

"In short, 'Hunting Ground' has to be one of the best books I have read so far this year. Who needs James Bond when you have Ali Sinclair?" – *Ginger Book Geek*